full body shaking

LIZE DE KOCK was born in South Africa where she spent most of her early years writing nature poetry, some of which were published in local anthologies and literary magazines. Her first paid project as a conceptual writer won a competition that gained international media support for a homeless woman in Cape Town. Lize has since lived and worked in the United Arab Emirates and Europe, penning travel stories, and picking up creative awards as a copywriter, chief editor, and communications director. She is currently based in Munich. When she is not writing or travelling, she volunteers at a women's shelter. This is her first novel.

TW // Trigger warning for abuse, rape, sexual assault, pornography, racism, drugs, toxic relationships, heavy grief, dissociative disorders, anxiety disorders, personality disorders, depression, suicide ideation. Please use caution. Suitable for persons over the age of 18.

First published in 2021.
Copyright © 2021 Lize de Kock
Illustrations © 2021 Carla Kreuser

Cover, book design & illustrations by Carla Kreuser
Author photograph by Gina Gorny
Edited by Nerine Dorman

ISBN 978-3-00-068086-1 (Print)
ISBN 978-3-00-068087-8 (eBook)

Published by Lize de Kock
Perdeblom Press

A dictionary of cultural words and phrases, as used in this book, is available on my website. Also stay up to date with exclusive content by signing up for my newsletter.

WWW.LIZEDEKOCK.COM

full body shaking

A NOVEL

Lize de Kock

Perdeblom Press

For all the women.

I hope you find that safe place inside yourself.

The Music Box

February 1985, Springbok, South Africa

THE DEATH OF ME IS THE ONLY PART of my early childhood that I recall. It is forty degrees at dawn in the semi-arid, north-western part of South Africa where I spend my four short years of being alive. The town of Springbok, with its history of stone masons and copper mines, is a teaser for the temperatures of hell. It is marked by the Klipkoppie, meaning little stone mountain in the Afrikaans-Dutch language. Really, it is more of a hill.

My father is leaving. I hear him revving the engine of his rusty blue pickup downstairs in the garage. He drives off in a whiff of diesel. It is always the same. When he is not working in the photo studio on weekends, he goes to take out abalone with a friend in Port Nolloth, a nearby village on the Namaqualand diamond coast. There, people also dive for small red crayfish known as Cape Rock Lobster. Offshore diamonds, deposited into the ocean by the Orange River and spread along the South Western coastline of Africa by the cold Benguela currents and the waves, are mined here too by divers.

While my dad is away, I escape.

"Poppie!" my mom calls my name in her strict voice, commanding my presence.

The clattering of a pot or a pan signals a warning. Instead of listening, I run away from her impending temper tantrum to my secret place, a small cave beyond a woody bush in the Klipkoppie behind our house. Our town is named after the South African national buck. In summer there is nothing but stones and heat, the odd quiver tree and, today, the arrival of a few of these small buck. Their yellowy-tan skin becomes one with the colourless landscape, the blank markings across their bodies underlining, or erasing, a part of their shape.

The cave is my safe space. No one knows about it but me and Audrey, our housekeeper's daughter and my best friend. It is cool against the rock face of the cave as I slip inside behind the bushes, taking a moment for my eyes to adjust from the bright sunlight. The shade is a refuge from the dusty heat of the day.

Audrey is already here. She turns toward me to make space, but does not say anything. I squeeze past her toward the back of the cave. Here we keep a collection of stones, coloured glass and pieces of broken porcelain, which we attempt to arrange into pretty mosaics on the floor of the cave. Some of the chips are bone china with pretty flowers on them. Others have intricate blue designs or parts of pictures. We pick up these treasures around the hill and laboriously carry them back to the cave. It is one of our favourite pastimes to hunt for the pieces, in between flakes of snakeskin and tiny balls of goat droppings that look like chocolate-covered raisins.

It does not matter that Audrey does not feel like talking. I spend hours rearranging the throwaway porcelain pieces into new patterns that please my eyes. Audrey sits and watches, her breath a comfortable blanket. She plays along, arranging the pieces by colour. Besides the scuttle of a meerkat or a rock hyrax outside the cave, I hear nothing but stillness.

Eventually, our rumbling tummies break the silence. This is our call to go home. Me to the big red brick house with the tin roof and Audrey to the *buitekamer*, an outhouse in the garden where she lives with her mom. It only takes one look to agree that it is time to leave our safe place in the name of dinner.

The sharp edges of the bushes scratch my skin as I get out into the bright afternoon light. Audrey breaks off a piece of aloe along the way, squeezing out the clear gel inside the leaf to help me soothe the small wound. A tortoise disappears into its shell, attracting our attention and bringing us to sit down on the granite rocks next to it. I try to knock on the shell to see if it will come out, but it does not feel like company today.

The typical smell of rotting flesh and cat pee indicates *spin-nekopblom*, or spider flowers, close by. The stench is strong enough to make us uneasy, so we do not linger, but quickly skid back down the hill. We inevitably pass right through the host of orange summer flowers in front of us, squishing the vibrant spidery petals against the cracked clay and loose stones as we step right into it. The trashy scent of the flower sap intensifies and makes us run even faster, which leads to even more splattered leaves and the odour now sticking around for good. These flowers are fascinating and revolting at the same time. I, for one, prefer not to go anywhere near the stink.

"Sometimes beautiful things can be so disgusting." I squeal as we get to the bottom of the hill.

"Sometimes broken things can be the most beautiful of all." These are the first words Audrey speaks today. She always seems to know things that I do not. Special things, that I do not always understand. Her voice has a hum that vibrates through me, as though we are the same person.

I certainly like our collection of broken pieces of china as much as she does.

"WHY DO YOU ALWAYS HAVE TO soil your clothes, Poppie?" My mom interrupts from the kitchen window. Even from across the yard she can see how dirty my pink shorts are from sitting on the cave floor. Her blonde bob moves up and down, her red lips tight as she fixes her heavily kohled eyes on me. I feel ashamed. I already know I am a bad girl.

Audrey slices her flat hand through the air under her chin, from one side to the other, gesturing that she is getting out of here. She kicks up a cloud as she disappears around the corner to the small room behind the pepper tree at the back of the yard.

My mom continues. "How do you manage to always get that dirty? Come on; bath time."

I AM WHOLLY CLEANSED OF MY SINS and waiting anxiously for my dad when he gets back from diving in the afternoon. He drops an abundance of crayfish and abalone on the sun-burnt lawn for my mom to shell and shuck for dinner. I don't know it then, but of all the fifty-six species of shellfish in the world, South African abalone, specifically *Heliotus midae*, is supposed to be the most delicious of them all. No wonder my dad has this look on his face like he is finally happy. It is the first time in my life that I have seen him smile. I wish I were an abalone so that he would smile at me like that too, sometimes. Even just once would do. I long to be close to my dad, but my mom keeps me away from him.

"Poppie, come inside. Your father is tired." My mom interrupts me as I step outside to inspect the creatures moving and squeaking on the lawn. I smell the ocean, salty and full of slippery strings of seaweed. My dad does not look tired.

I tilt my face up to the open kitchen window, but I am drawn to my father like a magnet.

One step. Two steps. Carefully. Curiously. I make myself as invisible as possible and linger unobtrusively until they forget about me. Then I quietly sit down at the edge of the lawn, watching as my parents collect the crayfish into large stove pots and pack the abalone into plastic bags for the deep freezer.

Usually, the garden sprayer is on at this time during a sweat-infused afternoon. I like to run through it to cool down. There is nothing better than its mist when the heat is high. It would flush away the train of ants that is now running along the edge of the stone paving, and up the red brick of our house. I watch and wait as they rush by in perfect rows. Ants always have a purpose, something to do, somewhere to be.

"Hello, Ant."

I focus on a single ant and follow it until I find the right moment to carefully press my forefinger onto it. The rest of the ants make a small detour around my finger and continue along their set track. It gives me a sense of power to be able to change their course, to be able to stop an ant from following its path. I lift my finger and turn it around, inspecting the crushed ant where it now sits on the tip of my finger.

"Goodbye, Ant." I am suddenly curious to find out what it tastes like and so I put it in my mouth. Not bad. The sour tang keeps me rooted in the moment and my senses relish the distraction. This is extreme, but no one notices. I am getting hungry. It has been a long day in the cave out in the hill and I have not yet had dinner.

"Hello, Ant," I say again, picking up another. Not only is it a fun game, but it keeps me out of trouble with my dad as I sit here out of his way.

"*Koebaai*, Ant."

This next one tastes of salt and vinegar, or a very sour lemon. I am in my own world, my own little secret. Maybe I will tell Audrey about it the next time we meet.

I want to be close to my dad and I am happy when he comes back outside to plant gazanias, vygies and some of the world's smallest succulents for my mom, while she prepares the abalone for dinner. There is a scorpion in between quartz gravel and sandstone rocks in the terraced rock garden where my father is handling tiny *bababoudjies*, a type of succulent that looks like a baby's bum. My dad is not bothered, but the sight of the stinger makes me nervous. I start opening and closing the tap next to the house to rid the tension from my hands. The ants scramble and float in all directions as the splash relieves the stuffy air.

The bright green hose pipe is not connected to the tap. Rather, it lies rolled up on the strawy grass like a snake. I am watching my dad from a spot of shade next to the tap and waiting patiently for him to finish. Every now and again, I open the garden tap again to splash myself. Water gives me comfort.

"Stop playing with the water, Poppie," says my dad sternly.

I do not know how else to cool down. "Can we switch on the sprayer?"

"No, can't you see I'm busy?" This time there is more volume to his voice.

The scorpion is watching my dad from a distance. Or perhaps, keeping an eye on our cat, Shadow, who is lazing on the garden wall behind my father. She is hardly visible in the trees' shade. The sun is setting and the African daisies are slowly hiding away their petals for lack of the big fireball in the sky. They will open again when the sun comes out tomorrow.

I hold on to the tap as though I am holding the hand of a protector. I am nervous watching my dad in the garden, in between the scorpion and Shadow. He is happy with the abalone and the succulents, but he is not happy with me.

"Come on now, hold yourself in, Poppie! Wowzer! If you open that tap one more time you are going to get a hiding, chiffchaff!"

"Give your dad a break, he had a long day. All right?"

My mom peeks out from the kitchen window when I move closer. Only my mom and Audrey's mom, Lena, are allowed to touch my father. He touches them too, but he never touches me. Not even to say goodnight.

I stay in the shade close to the tap where the water is cool and soothing. I do not know what else to do. Open. Close. Open. Close. Open. The repetition makes me feel better. I also want my dad to notice me. It is sweltering and, of course, I need to be refreshed. I miss my dad. I want something to happen. Anything rather than being ignored.

"Didn't I tell you to stop doing that?" He roars. "Now come here!"

My father is furious. His face changes when he is angry. He throws down the garden spade and pulls me into the kitchen. It is dark and cool.

"I didn't do anything, *pappa*," I cry, "I was just cooling down."

He drags me a little further and takes off his leather belt. The big metal buckle jangles as he opens its clip and slides the belt from his jeans. It looks like he is going to start taking his clothes off and play with me like Lena's boyfriend, who sometimes locks Audrey and me into the *buitekamer* with him while she is on cleaning duty. The boyfriend takes off his clothes and ours and then touches us in a special way. It feels wrong, but he gives us musk candy called pink pills and tells us we are good girls.

Audrey's mom knows and she is doing nothing about it though, so maybe it is just something a woman has to learn. Audrey's stepdad is one thing, but it is the first time my own dad is taking off his belt in front of me.

My dad pushes me toward the stove. "Bend over."

His red, racing anger makes me rattle in shock as he raises his right hand with the belt.

"Pull down your pants," he says, losing control.

I am too afraid to disobey. I pull down my pants and wait. This is something new. I have no idea what to expect.

His belt slams into my naked skin and a wild gasp rises from my chest. I start to tremble. I was only looking for attention. I did not do anything wrong.

"*Pappa*, no!" I scream as he continues to beat my naked little-girl bum over and over, until I only manage to expel a faint breath, instead of explaining myself. I slowly shatter like the pretty pink teacup that I broke yesterday. *I am so sorry, Mommy, I didn't mean it. I promise I will behave better.*

My mom's frenzied voice rings out above the lashes. "Shadow was stung by a scorpion, I need to take her to the vet." Her heels click-clack on the kitchen tiles as she comes through the door. Then she wails. "Noooo, please no! Please stop that now! You're going to kill the child!"

"*Mamma*!" I feel my soul reaching for her, but I cannot voice anything further.

My father gives me a few more beatings. I lose count at the same time as I lose hope that he might ever stop. Then he drags me across the carpet in the hallway to my bedroom, closes the door with a bang and locks me inside.

I wait, alone, for what must be hours. Not even Shadow is scratching at the door. Nothing seems real. No one checks on me. It feels like I am forgotten for all eternity.

All that remains is my father's voice rattling through my being.

STOP THAT, POPPIE. *Stop opening and closing the tap. Go to your room and put on a new set of clothes. You are dirty. Go and play inside. Don't make me angry, I said I am busy. I need to do the garden now. Be a good girl, Poppie, and listen to me. Stop playing with the water. It hasn't been raining a lot this year and the old people want to drink it. Go and play nicely. Take Audrey with you to your room and get out your dolls. Be quiet. Be good girls. Skedaddle. Go away. Good girls should be seen and not heard. Don't. Don't do. Don't do that. Don't do this. Don't question me. Don't do anything. Don't be yourself. Just be who I want you to be. Leave me alone now.* Maybe if you listen and do as I say. Maybe then I will look at you approvingly for just a moment. Don't speak. Don't say what you need to say. I need you to be quiet. I am your father. You only need to listen and do. Listen and do. Is that so hard, Poppie? Is that so hard to understand? Stay out of my way. Go and play inside. Go and play inside with Audrey and close your bedroom door.

Play with your dolls for hours, so that I can sneak away to Lena's room. Then I can pretend to have been gardening when I get back into the house all sweaty and dirty as though it was all that hard work in the sand and in the sun. Take Audrey with you and keep her busy, so that she does not have to see her mother's terrible love and her mother's impossible pain. What would people say if they knew, Poppie? Can you imagine the scandal? The horror? Did you not know that Lena and I can both go to jail? Audrey is an illegitimate child. The truth would be the worst thing that could ever happen to our family. Do you understand now why you can not just keep opening the tap? Just stop. Stop playing with the water. Stop trying to be so pure and clean. Stop looking for love, Poppie. Love is doomed anyway. Stop searching for answers. Stop being yourself. Stop now and save yourself from the terror. You are just a child, Poppie. How dare you make your own decisions. Listen to me. I always know best. Trust me and I will take care of you. What do you really know anyway?

Stop opening the tap. It needs to stay tightly closed. I don't want the truth to come gushing out.

NOBODY NOTICES WHEN I DIE. The bedroom-full-of-fairy-tales where I am no longer present seems, suddenly, bigger and brighter. I am lying on the carpeted floor next to the single bed with the frilly pink quilt, four years old and all alone.

No one ever really gets to know me.

It is a relief when the voice in my head starts to fade away. Trust in me, says the snake in the Garden of Eden. Then slowly everything empties from inside me and I start to loosen myself from my body, in the same way that my mom shucks abalone, until I feel free. I lie on the floor of my bedroom and stare up at the ceiling. Everything turns bright. My whole life is a shooting star.

Koebaai, Mamma. Koebaai, Pappa.

Koebaai, Shadow.

Then I die. It is not such a big thing when it happens. It is easy once I get the hang of it. The room expands and I kind of float out of my body. That is it, my short little life. I have no further memories of my childhood. Except this ...

Someone starts singing to me as though from behind a curtain in the room. There is no one else, but I hear a lullaby. I slip out of my body and rise into the realm of something new. Looking down. I can see that the voice is coming from my own body, that pretty little girl with her angelic blonde curls, twirling around and around like the sparkly dancer inside the music box on my bedside table.

I am not strong enough to survive this, but I have another chance. I have a superpower. I can be anything I want to be, except me.

There is a doll in the mirror. She looks like me. She remembers and then I forget.

The Collector's Piece

December 2002, Stellenbosch, South Africa

THE FARM VAN ARRIVES UNANNOUNCED, pulling up past the rose garden and the avocado trees into our clay-brick driveway with a growl and a rattle. My mom opens the imposing wooden front door of our gabled Cape Dutch house in the Stellenbosch winelands and runs down the veranda steps to greet the driver with a polite handshake and a reprimand in her expression. He quickly shows her a piece of paper and a map book.

"Oh, *jinne*, yes, they did change that street name. It's because they want to take down the street names of our apartheid heroes to replace them with the struggle heroes, and now nobody knows where they're going anymore."

The guys look relieved when she changes the topic and invites them inside. She asks the five workers in overalls to pick up select pieces of furniture from all the rooms except mine and pack the clothes from her large walk-in wardrobe into boxes. Then she goes through the kitchen cupboards and points at her baking stuff and porcelain tea set.

"You can pack these too, but please be careful that they don't break," she says, as she goes to fetch a stack of newspapers from the laundry room and slams them down on the kitchen counter. "They are fine porcelain, collector's pieces from England, all right!"

My mom exhales loudly. She goes outside and sits by the swimming pool behind the house, smoking a cigarette underneath the trellised grapevine while the guys start packing. It is a novel thing, the smoking. I have never seen her smoke. It does not suit her, I think, as I watch her through the large French windows. The breeze smells of sun, grass and chlorine, tugging gently at the voile curtains. It is a pristine day in the Cape, if there ever was a perfect backdrop from which to see your mom go.

Soon gaps appear in the carefully planned interior as the guys remove my mom's favourite antique side tables, the big leather couch and the mirror above the lounge fireplace. It is not unexpected that she is moving out, but things are happening so quickly that I am not sure what to do or how to react. I go outside to talk to her. Yet we sit in silence listening to the pool filter and the birds on the thatched-roof singing into the magnificence of summer. I look up to the still blue sky until she finishes the last, long drag of her cigarette.

Then I whip up the courage to speak. My stomach feels sour. "Do you want to tell me what's happening, Mom?"

She pauses with the burning cigarette butt in her hand and looks at me with narrowed eyes.

"Mom, where are you going?" I insist.

"It's none of your business, Poppie!" She puts out her cigarette in the abalone shell.

The rising frustration makes me talk louder. "Of course it is. You're my mom."

"Poppie, I'm moving in with Doctor Labia," she says matter-of-factly, as though it is the most natural thing in the world. "Remember him? I asked him to show you your G-spot when you went for your first visit at the gynaecologist."

My mouth opens, but I cannot get the words out. I am still not able to speak about how that killed off another piece of me.

"I didn't want you going through life missing out on sexual pleasure, the way I did," she continues. "I thought it would be good for you to be more savvy from the start. Dr. Labia was the first man who could give me a real orgasm. It happened during a routine checkup when he touched me in that way … we couldn't get enough of each other. We still can't. Oh, Poppie, I want you to be able to experience this kind of happiness."

I feel a strange sensation in my body as though a chemical reaction is creating tiny bubbles in my veins. It is a strain to hold myself in.

The ache is a giant compared to the words that come out. "You had something to do with that? Mom? How could you!"

My mom gets up from the garden chair, takes a determined step toward me and slaps me across the face. My left cheek is burning.

"He is the best thing that ever happened to me, Poppie," my mom says. "Don't you dare disrespect him."

I feel the bubbles in my veins starting to push up in a rage, but I keep my expression as neutral as the cream wrought iron garden furniture. "Will you at least tell me where you're going to live now?"

Her monotone answer seems to come from somewhere far away from me, far away from here, beyond the wine valley and the fruit farms full of grapes and plums and strawberries, and further across the postcard-pretty Great Drakenstein mountain range and the twin peaks of the Stellenbosh mountains, out past the very tip of South Africa, where the Atlantic and Indian oceans meet. Her voice comes from beyond the sea breeze, from that place where the world ends. "He has a farmhouse in the Franschhoek wine valley. It's only half an hour's drive."

"Aha," I say quietly, "and who's going to cook Dad's dinner?"

She animates herself again and swishes her blonde bob determinedly. "It's your own fault, Poppie. I would have stayed with him if you were a bit more supportive, but you're always in your own world. You probably don't even know that your dad is still seeing Audrey's mom after all these years. I kicked Lena out of the pool house, but your dad still went after her. They would not give it up."

"That's not true!" I can not be sure that it is my own voice speaking. It is as though I am standing next to myself watching the scene of a mom and daughter at a swimming pool in an upper-class neighbourhood of South Africa. The bubbles pop in my veins and my heart starts reeling.

Before I can respond, my mom stomps off, heels clicking on the quarry stone patio. Then she pauses and turns around.

"Wake up, Poppie! Apartheid is over. Cross-racial relationships are no longer illegal. It's easier now than it's ever been. In fact, I just walked in on the two of them a few days ago, naked in my marriage bed with the family quilt carelessly scattered on the carpet. I will, not, do this anymore, Poppie."

My ears close up the way they do when driving through a tunnel. "Where's Audrey?"

She continues to strut into the house, her syrupy perfume trailing her steps as I scream after her. "Mom, where's Audrey?"

I follow her as she rushes through the house on her red heels one more time before getting into the front of the van with the driver. The engine noise reverberates. She ignores me until the van starts moving.

"*Koebaai*, Poppie," she says out of the window. "You know, I'm not that complicated. All I want is the odd bunch of flowers and someone who says that they love me."

"*Mamma*," I beg, "where's Audrey?" I feel a wet splat on the crown of my head and look up to the roof to where the doves are cooing. "That's right, just leave me behind with the bird poop," I mutter to myself.

When the truck drives off, she waves at me as gracefully as royalty.

Her silence rings out for a long time. Then her words. It is your fault, she says. It is my fault.

I take the few steps over to the veranda, past the jasmine and tea roses and suppress the impulse to reach over and pick one of the fragrant blooms. I want to run after *Mamma* with my whole heart, but I push the large front door closed, making sure to turn the oversized copper knob until it clicks. There is a niggling echo in the silvered mirror of the porch stand that keeps saying, "Oh, yes, it is Poppie, it's your fault. All of this is your fault. You should have picked her flowers a long time ago. Too late now."

IN A PARALLEL UNIVERSE, I could be enjoying my life like a normal student, perhaps drinking pretty cocktails in a nightclub somewhere with friends. Or eating popcorn, watching movies and giggling about boyfriends, while sipping on strawberry slush. Instead, I have now got the task of telling my father what my mom could not when he gets home later.

Time drags on as I lie down on my blush-pink cast iron bed, keeping the window shutters closed. The wooden ceiling looks extra high today. I feel the house vibrating in resistance to all that is happening. It wakes me up from my almost-nap. My bed is moving from side to side, the frilly pink bedside lamp next to me rattles and my college history book slides down from the bedside table that my dad made for me in his garage. We study foreign history for now, while the new government rewrites the narrative of South Africa. All the stories about my country that I used to learn at school have already been destroyed. Everything I believe and think I know is gone, erased, untrue.

I no longer know who I am. I have never known who I was and I do not know who I want to be.

The bookshelf shakes and my porcelain doll slides and cracks her head on the floor. I try to get up, but slip on the small Persian carpet when I put on my sandals as though I am about to be taken on a magic carpet ride. I make sure to land like a superhero, leaning down with one hand and holding my head high. It does not seem as odd as it should be, after the revelations of the day. In fact, I might even like to be whisked away from here to a place where the world is completely different.

Anything other than this.

The Earth moves on its own axis around the sun—and, sometimes, from under my feet. Everything I have known so far in my life is a lie. Not only the rules of society, but also the illusion of the stable family that I supposedly grew up in. It is all a big lie. From history books to street names and wedding rings. Everything is different to what I think I have known. Even family is no solid ground. I need to keep moving. I need to go.

As the Earth moves, I will keep moving until I can find a place to be beautiful.

"POPPIE, ARE YOU OKAY?" My dad shouts as he gets home and the front door opens with a metallic squeak of its hinges.

"Yes! Hello, Dad!" I move through the house toward his voice.

"Wowzer, did the earthquake also move out some of our furniture?" he asks with a dazed expression as we meet in the living room. "What happened here?"

I am stunned. "There was an earthquake? Well, that explains it. I thought I was dreaming."

"Yeah," my dad confirms. "Just a small one, two point two on the Richter Scale. I could feel it on the steering wheel of the car as they announced it on the radio. Poppie, where is our furniture, what is going on?"

"Dad, sit down." I point him toward the nearest chair, my favourite taupe velvet wingback, hoping that I can rearrange the words so to hurt less.

He runs his fingers through his thick head of short grey curls as he sinks into the corner seat and places his hand on his belly, which slightly hangs over his belt. There are gaps in the wall behind him, where the paintings of flowery desert landscapes used to hang.

I say it as it is. "Mom left. This time for good. She came with a van of farm workers and took some stuff. She said it's my fault. I'm sorry."

My dad covers his mouth with his hand and holds his breath. I see his shoulders drop. His face turns down in phases, as the realisation hits home. Then he looks at me with an unspoken question.

"Just like that, hey. Chiffchaff. I can't believe she brought the farm workers into our house, wowzer." His laugh has the sound of sawing metal. "I hope they didn't steal anything. I'm going to have to get a security system installed. Now that they know what we have, they could be back any day to steal the rest of our stuff!"

When his laughing fit is over, he gets up and heads directly for the phone book, opens it and starts writing down numbers. In his paranoia, he calls a security company in Cape Town. I hear something about an urgent appointment for burglar bars to be installed, "… right away, on all windows and security gates to be set up where necessary. Right-oh, see you tomorrow. Cheerio."

I am not sure how that is a good idea. "Dad, we have an old house with tall windows. Security bars would totally ruin the ambience."

"Poppie, you have no idea what's going on out there. Why don't you organise us some dinner. Stick to what you're good at!" He snorts as he turns his face away from me.

I hardly notice the dismissal, relieved to be able to focus on something else as I head for the kitchen. "What do you want to eat?"

"Just not salad, Poppie." He shouts after me. "I'm not a goat."

When I look back the pity in his face makes me scatter; an insect half-heartedly getting out of his way.

AFTER SCANNING THE FRIDGE, I decide to make his favourite pasta. I should know by now that it will not make him love me, but I can always try harder, turn myself into a better cook. After all, I can be anyone I want to be …

First things first. I turn up the oven. Then, a quick visit to the herb garden on the opposite side of the pool patio. The smell of fresh thyme lingers on my hands as I pick a few sprigs for our meal, lifting my mood. Shadow's food bowl is sitting forgotten outside the door. I take it inside and give it a rinse, wondering if my mom will come back for it or buy a new one.

When I stand on tiptoes like a ballerina, I can pick the thickest recipe book from the top of the kitchen shelf. I open it to the page with the folded corner and make sure that I have all the ingredients. It is a simple recipe, but it has all the right elements for a feast.

BUTTERNUT, MUSHROOM AND BACON PASTA

500g cubed butternut
Olive oil for drizzling
4t thyme
2 cloves garlic
200g smoked streaky bacon
240g brown mushrooms
400g penne
250ml cream
Salt and pepper
Freshly grated parmesan

Pottering around the kitchen calms me, as though preparing food is a type of meditation. The repetitive task of peeling and chopping a butternut puts me into a trance-like state. By the time I spread the colourful cubes onto a baking tray and drizzle it with olive oil and fresh thyme, I feel a sense of release. I know that, at least this one thing, is going to turn out well for me. While the pumpkin roasts, I fill a pot with water, salt and a dollop of butter and bring it to the boil. I slice onions, mushrooms and bacon with a blunt knife, which makes for chunkier pieces. The pan clunks as I slam it onto the stove to give the onions and bacon a good simmer before adding the mushrooms. A smile involuntarily turns up the corners of my mouth. I hum inwardly, allowing myself a moment of pleasure as the mushrooms melt into the buttery infusion. When the water comes to the boil, I drop in the penne and do a little happy dance. Then I fold the deliciously sticky, roasted pumpkin cubes in with the rest of the ingredients. It all comes together into a beautifully creamy, salty, sweet, and pungently earthy sauce.

"Dad, dinner's ready!" I beam as I lick off the tasting spoon and quickly set the table for two. I put the parmesan and the pepper mill on the table, for garnish.

When I hear him coming toward the kitchen, I quickly drain the pasta, mix it with the sauce and dish out two bowls of food. "Would you like to have some bread with that?"

He sits down at the round yellow-wood kitchen table. "No, thanks, Poppie, I'm not that hungry after everything that happened today."

The reminder steals the joy from my face, but not from my heart. My dad would never say it, but the food looks amazing. Besides, I was able to forget all about my problems while making it. Good food is always good, no matter what happens.

We eat in silence.

I try my luck. "Dad, are you still in contact with Audrey's mom?"

"Of course not." He rejects the conversation, but something in his manner comes alive in a way I have not noticed before.

"MORNING, MORNING." My dad is delighted when Jake, the owner of the security company, arrives at our house in person and a whole fifteen minutes early. He is pumped up and ready to install security doors around the house with his guys.

"Everywhere?" Jake says it more as though it is a pact between my dad and himself, rather than a question. His straight, charcoal-coloured fringe falls across his cheekbones as he concentrates on my dad, while showing off a sideways smile.

"A decision is a decision." While burglar bars will not fix the problem of his marriage, my dad looks chuffed as though it gives him hope.

The large shuttered windows are being spared, at least for now. I can feel Jake's focus shifting to me and decide not to move from the chair where I am reading my book. It is a curious feeling, to be noticed. I feel an inner trembling that I do not understand. Every now and again, our eyes meet, turning me into a little kitten lapping up attention. I become aware of the tight shape of his bottom under his jeans and his calculated way of moving as he sets up the security installations with his team.

"I'm Jake." He introduces himself, moving near to me as soon as they have finished their job.

I get up from my reading chair, but I am too shy to look him in the eye. He is so close I can feel the heat coming from his body. The skin on his arms is the colour of vanilla icing sugar. He probably does not like to get too much sun.

"Poppie," I say, conscious of my flushing cheeks. My head is a light bulb.

He hands me a note with his phone number and name. The palms of our hands touch gently as he passes his details. Static. Crackling and tickling. I close my hand too quickly and take a step backward.

My heart is beating so loudly that I am hardly able to hear his next words. "Poppie, if you're ever in Cape Town, give me a call. We can go for a drink somewhere."

"Yup," I say and I know I will.

I see him as though magnified, taking in his long eyelashes as he winks at me in slow motion. "Would you call your dad for me,

Poppie?" The way he says my name sounds fabulous. "I need to finish up my business here and get back to the city."

I want to live in Cape Town too and hang out with Jake at bars. It is about time for me to move out, anyway, as soon as I get my college results.

"DAD," I START HESITANTLY once the guys are gone. "I want to move to Cape Town and get a job as soon as I've got my diploma."

"Poppie, look," my dad says, "it's safer for you to stay here with me and find a job close to home. With a college History certificate, you can't really do big things. Just apply at the library. You don't have to move away for work. We're a family, you and I."

I smile sweetly. If I stay with him, I will never be free. "Ha ah, Dad, I can't stay with you forever. I need to find my own life. Maybe I can become a tour guide in the city, or something like that."

"Do you know what's going on out there, Poppie? Have you seen what they're doing? You can count yourself lucky to have a safe home," he says, as though I have not the faintest idea of life beyond his reign.

"You need to let me live my own life, Dad." The thought of leaving without his permission becomes scarier than asking him to let me go. "I want to go out there and see the world—and not just Cape Town. I want to travel the whole world."

My blood slowly drains as he refuses. "Wowzer, you clearly don't understand how dangerous things have become. Who knows, there might even be civil war soon."

I feel tied down by invisible chains, but I shake my head and hold on to the yellow-wood chair in front of me to steady myself. "You should see how much the people of my generation are coming together. Cape Town is cosmopolitan. I want to be part of it."

"You are not moving to Cape Town. It is out of the question." His words fall like night on our conversation.

The calling in my soul does not stop though. I cannot give in this time. "Dad, you need to let me go."

He does not budge. "I said no: you're staying here. I will take care of you."

That familiar expression of disappointment and suppressed rage moves across his face.

I do not know where I find the courage to speak, but the words come out nevertheless. "I no longer have to listen to you, Dad. I'm an adult."

It is as though I am no longer myself, but another person altogether—one who can stand up for myself.

My father's grey-blue gaze scatters across the room. He stops at the copper bucket on the sideboard as though he wants to throw it at me and, for a moment, I am not sure if he would do it. I feel like I have nothing to lose.

"Either you let me go," I say slowly, as I let the feistier version of me take over, "or I am simply leaving without your permission. I would prefer if we part on good terms."

He can no longer control his anger at my disobedience. Or perhaps it is too much to handle two women leaving him within the span of a few days. He grabs the tall candlestick on the dining table and throws it at me. I duck and it misses me by a few inches and crashes into the glass cabinet behind me, making a traumatic sound. Not only does the glass door shatter, but the impact brings the rest of the porcelain cups sliding and crashing onto the floor, one after the other, like dominos. Perhaps it is for the best that my mom took the valuable pieces with her. Who knows what my father will do with the rest.

We both stand in silence, looking at the damage, then at each other. I can see that he knows I am right, even though he is red with rage.

"You're just like your mother." He says it as though it is a curse, as though I am letting him down as a father and as a man, as though this is something unforgivable. I feel a trickle running down my left leg into my leather sandal as I start peeing tiny drops.

The early evening crickets fill the silence with a raised pitch.

Gasping for control at the situation, my dad finally concedes, "Right-o, Poppie, if that's what you want, then go to Cape Town. I only have one condition. You need to leave right now. Pack your things and go."

I stand, mesmerised, unable to grasp which reaction would be the safest.

"Poppie, I spoke. Pack. Your. Things. You've got five minutes."

I scramble into my bedroom, scrape some clothing into my rucksack and, before I can think about what else I may need, he is standing at my door with crazy eyes. "Time's up, Poppie. Skedaddle."

My vision crisscrosses from his outline in my door frame to my dressing table and over to my backpack.

"Poppie, I said go!" He takes me by the arm as I grab at a few photographs and stuff my lollipop pink, polka dot bikini into the side pocket of my bag.

My feet barely touch the ground as my dad pulls me all the way to the front door, tightening his grip as he pushes me outside. I fight to gain my balance and stop just short of falling down the stairs into the rose bush. The smell of jasmine jolts into the disorder as though it is a promise.

I cannot wait to go, but I see a rare trace of longing cross my dad's face when he pauses midway before closing the door. "Don't ever get married, Poppie, okay?"

I hesitate. I think about Jake and get that floaty feeling. I cannot wait to see him, to finally be accepted in the world.

"Look what happened to me, Poppie," my father says, presenting himself as evidence against love. "Trust me, it's best to stay alone."

"Right," I deny myself to keep the peace as I wave goodbye, "*Koebaai*, Dad."

I see something much alike tears in his eyes and wonder if he is better off alone.

As the door of my family home slams shut, I stay standing in front of it, a statue held intact by the rattling of the antique hinges.

It is still light by the time I make it to the Eerste River in the centre of town. I am surprised until I notice the full moon. It looks much closer than usual. The sky is deep blue and the Evening Star has appeared on the horizon above the oak trees and the Simon's Mountain. I find a payphone in the university area and take some coins out of my small leather purse. Deep in my dress pocket, I find the piece of paper with Jake's handwriting. I unfold and unfold the note until his full phone number is revealed.

For the first time in my life, I am truly excited about something. I hold the note. It is my ticket to everything I wanted: to get as far as possible away from everything I have ever known, including myself. I believe there is a world full of love, somewhere out there. A place to be happy. A place to be beautiful.

I am giddy as I turn the dial of the payphone, doing a tiny jump as I hear the first ring. He answers right away.

"Jake Adam, hello?"

"Adam, as in 'When God made Adam'?" I blurt out before thinking.

He only speaks when he is sure that I will not continue. "Who is this then? Eve?"

I laugh. "No, it's Poppie, Poppie Poggenpoel."

"Poppie," he says my name as though he is conjuring up my image and relishing it. "You called!"

I see my phone time running out and quickly slither another coin from my purse.

"Jake, can you pick me up? I'm at the university, close to the sports stadium. I'll wait for you at the tiny wooden bridge at the Eerste River, okay?"

He does not ask any questions. "Okay, Poppie. If you're sure. I can be there in about forty-five minutes."

My heart gushes. He wants me to be sure. "Yes-yes, Jake, I'm sure."

He mimics my double excitement. "Cool-cool, I'll be right there."

I feel as though I have just run a marathon as I put down the phone and sit on the sidewalk to catch my breath. Then I waltz down to the river. I feel dreamy. Stellenbosch is a bit of a ghost town during the summer holidays when the university shuts down, but on this starry summer's evening, it feels good to have it all just for me.

As I sit by the river, a group of hyped joggers pass and then there is nothing but me and the rhythmic water. Suddenly, I have the urge to get out of my sweaty clothing and soak away my past life before stepping into my new beginning with Jake.

I move a little away from the bridge toward a spot that is secluded by trees and a few ferns and bushes. I strip down and bundle my dirty dress into the one empty side pocket of my backpack. In the other pocket is my bikini, but I want to be a rebel and immerse myself butt-naked into the river. I want to feel the stones press into my skin. I want the sensation of life flowing through and into and over every single part of me.

There are a few street lights burning in the distance, some faraway voices echoing. I hurl my sweaty sandals as far upstream as I can and tiptoe into the river. The water is pristine and cool, quite the opposite of me. I find a smooth stone and sit on it, letting the water flow over my lap and between my legs. I splash my breasts, my face, and my hair, before leaning back into the river. I allow the moment to be, as though I am watching myself from a distance. I am finally free here. I can do what I want.

The force of the water pushes onto my head and over my face. I let go of my confusion and the nervous shaking in my chest. Gravity presses me onto the smooth river stones. I stay very still. A fallen star. A reborn doll. A woman looking for a chance at life.

Headlights startle me.

How long have I been here?

Wait. Could that be my dad?

I get up from the water, knowing full well that whoever it is can see every part of me. The evening breeze makes me shiver and tiny goosebumps appear on my skin. I zip over to my backpack as fast as I can and pull out my bikini and a flowery pink dress to pull over it. Water trickles down my back. I did not pack a towel.

I hear the car door open and the muted base reveals itself as house music. Jake's voice is flat and yet my heart gallops when he speaks. "Poppie? Is that you?"

When I come out from behind the trees, barefoot and dripping wet, he neither looks surprised nor pleased to see me. I feel acorn husks crushing beneath the soles of my feet and squirm as I walk toward the car. "You don't have shoes?"

"I, er ..." I am too shy to tell Jake that I threw my shoes away, so I pull a pair of flip-flops from my bag and slip them on.

He opens the passenger car door and gestures for me to get

in. There is a towel on the leather seat. "I wasn't sure if … I saw … I happened to have one in the boot. You can dry yourself or you can sit on it. I just can't have you dripping in my car."

"It's all cool, I'm drying quickly in this heat. It's just my hair." I reach for the towel, but he takes it from my hand and places it neatly back onto the seat.

"Oh, we can take the roof down for that. Air drying. Get in!"

He puts my bag in the boot, then he takes the driver's seat and slowly brings the convertible's rooftop down.

"Top down, Poppie. As you like it, it seems. Where to, *madame*?"

I sigh deeply, taking in the fresh air of the future. "Anywhere but here. Let's go to Cape Town. Show me where you live. Show me everything."

The V8 growls as we take off into the night, speeding through the quiet streets of Stellenbosch and on to the highway and into the city. I sink into the deep, low seat, letting it hold me tight. When I see Table Mountain, lit up by floodlights in all its glory, I do a spontaneous, exuberant dance right there in the car seat. My hair flutters wildly in the open air and I do not care that it is all in knots as we start our approach to the city, past Cape Town Harbour. The lamps along the last part of the highway resemble fountains, cascading light onto the tar. I look up and let the glow fall over me too, the same way as the river water earlier. I let it light my face to see whatever may come.

"Good night, baby," says Jake as he pulls the car into his double garage in Bantry Bay and closes the electric door behind us. I almost respond before I realise that he means the car. He frowns when I start to giggle. It was not a joke.

Jake's house is modern and spacious. The sparsely furnished interior includes beige leather couches, and spotless tiling and marble surfaces that sparkle in the bright ceiling lights. Jake puts on soft music and turns to me with raised eyebrows. "Drink?"

He hardly waits for me to nod before getting two round crystal classes from his cabinet and pouring us a gin and tonic with ice. He even has sliced lemon garnishes ready in his bar fridge. I take a seat on one of the high chairs at the counter and fiddle with the framed photographs of Jake posing with famous South African models.

"Here's to you, Poppie!" Jake looks me right in the eye when our glasses touch with a ching. He takes a deep sip, exhales and puts his glass down. "When is your dad expecting you home?"

I fight the panic, wondering what Jake would think of me knowing that I got kicked out of home. "He isn't," is all I can manage. I am relieved that he does not go on to ask a million questions, but simply tops up my drink.

It is a combination of being exhausted and drinking too much alcohol that makes me pass into a dreamless sleep on the pretty couch, but not before falling into his arms in a hopeless giggle. I am too shy to kiss him, so he just lets me lie down and puts a fluffy blanket over me.

I SMELL THE GARDEN ROSE before I open my eyes. There is a note.

Good morning, Pop, make yourself at home. There's food in the fridge. Have a swim. Whatever. Had to go to work. Will be back in the evening. Jake x

No one ever gave me a pet name before. I like it. Pop. Finally, someone thinks I am special. Finally, a life away from my parents.

I pick up the single rose next to the note and twirl around as I hug it close. It is the colour of peaches and cream. I find a glass behind the counter of Jake's small house bar and fill it with water. It is perfect, I think, as I slip the bloom into the glass and place it on the coffee table next to the couch. I think how the rose is just about to open and will add a splash of colour to the otherwise monochrome room.

Jake arrives home with sushi at lunch time.

"I couldn't wait. I wanted to tell you that I called your dad and he thanked me for taking you off his hands."

"I see. Like a doll." I try to imagine the conversation between Jake and my dad, giving me away like that. "That's what my name means. Poppie is Afrikaans-Dutch for little doll."

He unpacks the pretty snacks onto two big plates and passes me some sticks. "He gave me your mom's new address to pass on to you. In case. You know. You want to contact her."

I am more fascinated with the food and the sticks. "Never mind my mom. What shall I do with these?"

Jake looks kindly amused. "Never used chopsticks before?"

I shake my head.

"Sushi?" He laughs.

More shaking.

He moves around the kitchen counter and hugs me from behind.

"Look. You rest the sticks in the soft bit of your hand between your thumb and your index finger. Then you use the stick as a lever to pick up the sushi."

His hand guides mine as he lets me hold the chopsticks. I can not remember when last I tried something for the first time. I feel clumsy.

"Or," Jake says, grinning, "you can just use your hands."

"No, I want to try." I want nothing more than to look cool in front of Jake. No way am I going to give up on chopsticks if this is his thing.

Jake passes me pink slithers of something that smells like preserves, as well as a green paste.

"It's ginger and avocado. You take a tiny bit of the ginger and a dollop of the avocado and you put it on top of the sushi roll. Then, you put the whole thing in your mouth."

"The whole thing?" My face must be in a knot because Jake starts chuckling.

It does not sound ladylike at all, but enticing. Jake's eyes look like spinning marbles.

I open my mouth wide and stuff it with the new adventure that is a salmon and tuna sushi roll with a lot of avocado on top. As soon as I bite into it, a burn kicks into my nose and throat, spreading into my body until I feel numb. I want to be brave, so I do not spit it out. Instead, I keep chewing through the tears and the irritation in my nasal passages.

When I come to my senses, Jake is clapping. "Congratulations, Poppie!"

"What was that?" I cry.

"Not avocado. Clearly. It's wasabi, a Japanese thing. You're supposed to only have a little bit." He takes more than a little pleasure in making fun of me.

Once the first shock subsides, I start to find the taste of the seaweed and wasabi addictive. My favourite rolls are a combination of soft shell crab and prawn, laced with a delicate type of mayonnaise. For me, it is love at first sight. Now that I taste sushi, I do not know how I have lived without it. As for Jake, I want to be with him all the time. I want to jump in with my whole heart. Wasabi and all.

"Just don't eat too much rice, doll," says Jake. "It will make you fat."

SOON ENOUGH JAKE SLAMS a business card down in front of me.

Donald De Beer, Restaurant Manager, Reds on Camps Bay.

"Let's get you a *joppie*," he says.

It is not difficult. Through Donald, I now get to greet patrons at this fancy Camps Bay establishment called Reds. I flirt a little and make sure that everyone is having a good time. A *joppie* for Poppie. It is exhausting work being a hostess, running around after people's demands all night, trying to find solutions with important bookings and extra guests and table settings until the early hours of the morning. I hardly have time to retreat into the kitchen and grab a bite. The waiters have one up on me, being able to snack on calamari tempura and chocolate mousse in between serving tables. I am glad I do not have to run around with their heavy ice buckets though, or the gigantic plates of lobster thermidor. I do not think I would be able to carry those heavy dishes. I am not going to the gym, after all. It is just that I get really hungry. Despite being slender, I have a majestic appetite and I suffer when there is no time to snack. When the kitchen is cleaned up and the food packed away, putting something, anything, into my body is better than nothing.

"Give me a gin. I'm hungry," I say as I drape myself over a bar stool and slip off my stilettos.

Soon after having a few drinks with the staff, I find myself sitting on Camps Bay's sweeping blue flag beach in front of the surf club, watching the fire dancers who come here to practise and hang out every week. It is entrancing, especially through gin-tinted eyes. I am sitting with the bottle in my lap, taking swigs, while my colleagues pass around a joint. I am too scared to try smoking weed, I have never done drugs before. Around us, candles in brown paper bags make a beautiful soft light. This is how it should be. I am sitting here with Afrikaans people, English people, Xhosa people, Sotho people, and Indian people. One of my colleagues is British, another Polish. Some are rich, some are poor, but we are all people who talk and laugh together. It is healing to focus on the bond between us as humans, rather than the cultural divides we have lived with for too long in this country. We are all more the same than we are different.

Jake joins us later on the beach and does not take his eyes off me. The night takes on a mystical edge that makes me feel excessively happy. He is more handsome tonight than I remember, this time in a sort of blurry way. I shake out some moves for him on the sand and he cannot resist pulling me close.

His whisper tickles my ear. "You dance like seaweed."

The waves crush into my drunken ears as he slides his tongue over my mouth with the skill of a surfer.

My lips tingle. "You kiss like a tidal wave."

We laugh. We stay up till sunrise and then end up in his bed. The good thing about not having to prioritise marriage is that I do not have to worry about waiting for my wedding night. I do not have to protect my virginity or care about staying pure. I am free to make my own decisions and take things at my own pace—admittedly, in this case, things are being sped up a little by an overdose of alcohol.

It is my first time having sex, yet I do not remember anything, but glimpses—which is fine, since I am not a virgin anyway. The honour of deflowering me went to that rascal, Jan Bos, for breaking my hymen with his finger as a teenager. I wish I could forget that experience and remember sex with Jake. I have to wait until the second night to be conscious—and the third. It is not a life-changing experience. I cannot say that I like it or hate it. I do not think it is worth the hype.

Yet I am happy when I am close to Jake and he cannot get

enough of me. On our fourth morning together, he brings me coffee and kisses in his king-size bed, as well as a tomato cocktail with vodka. He pulls the light, breezy curtains and slides open the blinds and then the glass door to reveal the small wooden deck leading off his bedroom, with a ten meter, single-lane infinity pool. Beyond, lies the still beauty of Bantry Bay, windless and glittering in shades of sapphire and emerald. We spend all day moving between the pool and the bed, naked—and with that view of the ocean, there is nowhere else I would rather be.

I am shy when Jake unties my polka dot bikini top in the pool. I have never been naked outside in broad daylight.

"Don't worry, no one can see us here." Jake coaxes me into giving the sun a naughty glimpse of my nipples.

"Stay just like that, Poppie," he says as I stretch out fully naked on his deck chair. "I'm going to get us another cocktail."

"I've had enough, thanks." I am already feeling dizzy and dehydrated after starting the day with cocktails. I cannot drink anymore.

"But you haven't been drinking—you need to catch up!" he insists.

"I can't!" I squeak.

"This time I'm shaking up a personalised cocktail for you," he says. "I will call it: The Poppie. You've got to try it." He ignores my wishes and goes to his bar.

I cannot even see another drink, but I do not want to be a spoilsport. If he can do it, so can I. We are a team, Jake and I.

"The Poppie!" Jake introduces the cocktail as he hands it over, clearly chuffed with himself. "A new cocktail served in a tall glass filled with hazelnut liquor, lime, crushed ice, pear juice and cherries."

The waft of more alcohol is repulsive.

"Come on, try it," says Jake when he sees me putting the glass down on the side of the pool.

"Jake, I'm taking a little break." I tilt my head teasingly and try to act sweet.

He moves toward me, takes my hand to lift me from the deck chair and pulls me into the pool with him. The water is refreshing and we both laugh and kiss and kiss and laugh. Soon, he grabs my cloudy cocktail from the side of the pool, takes a big sip and presses his lips against mine. The hazelnut-pear liquid slips into my mouth and I swallow.

"It's good." I giggle. "But I really can't drink anymore today."

"Don't be such a pussy," he belts and takes another big sip to feed me. I swallow and giggle again, pretending it is a joke.

I do not want him to get angry, so I try to be tougher and take it.

Soon, I cannot move anymore and seek shelter in the coolness of his air-conditioned bedroom. Jake joins me there, tracing my body with his fingers as the room starts to spin.

"Don't worry, I've got you," he says as he holds me close.

THAT IS TWO MONTHS AGO ALREADY. Since then, Jake has been picking me up for a date every Friday night after my shift. It means so much to me that I now have a real boyfriend who takes me out on weekends. I finally feel loved. It is a floaty feeling, as though I am consistently hovering slightly outside of my body.

Only tonight, Jake is ghosting me. I have not heard anything from him and he does not pick up when I call. I am so hungry that I feel an intense and sudden anger. Tonight, again, it is too late to eat. I pour myself a gin and tonic, two, three, alone at the bar, while Donald closes up the back office.

Jake finally calls back and I rush outside right away, expecting him to be there, smiling, in his V8. I do not see his car.

"Hi, Jake, where are you?" I pick up the call as I look around the parking lot. A row of palm trees shine underneath the streetlights. In the distance, I hear the hush of the ocean. For a moment the cool, salty air is almost refreshing.

"Hey, doll," says Jake in a lazy voice. He must be doped. "Where are you? I looked for you at home. I'm just dropping you a call to say I'm going to be late, but I'm on my way."

I do not like his accusing tone. "Jake, I'm at work. You know, I'm working tonight." This feels wrong, so I make myself continue. "Well, you could have let me know in advance, Jake. I've been getting a bit worried."

"Yeah … my bad," he responds flatly.

There is something about the sound of his voice and the flirtatious giggling in the background. I am convinced it is because he is with someone else that he cannot pick me up in time. He is acting strange, out of character. I just do not trust him. I want him to be the right one so much that I keep lying to myself. He is not a good guy, but I feel trapped, unable to leave him or get away. I hear another giggle in the background. I know how easy it is to cheat. I have seen my dad do it all those years with Lena.

"Who's that?" I dare.

"Ah, no one." For the first time, I detect a thrill in his voice.

Is it the risk of getting caught that gets his blood pumping, or is he too much of a coward to break up with me before moving on?

"Right! Come on, Jake, don't lie to me!" I feel the alcohol-fuelled anger rising.

"Just chill, Poppie. I'll be there soon." There is no sign of a good excuse, or an apology.

"Don't you dare tell me to chill." I lose control of my anger.

It is as though my heart is leaping out of my body and exploding like a grenade.

I throw my cell phone out into the dark parking lot at the back of the restaurant. I hear it breaking into pieces. I do not bother to pick it up. I just walk straight into the restaurant manager's office.

The sign on the door says: DONALD DE BEER. He is making lines of cocaine on his desk for some of the waitresses, who are still hanging around.

Don looks up at me in surprise. I do not usually stay long after my shift. He seems pleased to see me and offers me the rolled R50 note.

"Wanna have a line, Poppie?"

Cocaine is big in the restaurant industry. "It keeps us on our feet," says Don.

I watch him roll the paper money into thin straws and carefully sniff the line of cocaine into his right nostril, while holding the left one closed with his other hand. He is always doing coke and he is fine. It cannot be that bad.

I take the rolled note, bend down over the desk and inhale the fine line of powder. The chemical smell irritates my nose. Almost immediately, I start to feel as though I am elevated above the world, above myself, above my problems, above the betrayal I feel. I now live to the limit—and outside of the lines. It is as though the world is suddenly in order, it is a simple mind shift that makes all the difference. I have never quite felt this fine.

When Jake arrives, I am calm and collected. I put my head on his skinny shoulders as he takes me in his arms and holds me tight. I look up at his shabby charcoal mop, his piercing green eyes, and his luscious, heart-shaped lips. I cannot be angry with him for long. Besides, I am not feeling anything right now. The drugs have lifted me above my emotions. We go to a bar to meet his friends and drink a few shots of tequila. Jake spends the night talking about doing a triathlon with a pretty personal trainer and I am not convinced that he wants to participate. He is a great swimmer, but I am not so sure about cycling. He does not even own a bike. I am sure his interest is rather the girl than the event. I know him well enough. I can read his face. I should be jealous, but I do not feel anything. Instead I perch myself on to the counter and make sure to draw the attention back to me by standing up to dance. Then I black out.

There are times like these, when I do not remember how I got home. I mostly wake up in bed next to Jake (admittedly, with my pretty sandals still on) and find the city car I am using neatly parked in the garage next to Jake's baby. This time I am in the convertible next to Jake when I regain consciousness.

"You need something to eat," he says, as he sweeps his flat, inky fringe out of his face and revs his ego around the corner.

We stop at a service station with a twenty-four hour fast food outlet. As usual, it is packed with the beautiful Cape Town party people grabbing a greasy snack to blot out the alcohol before hitting the highway to the suburbs. Driving drunk is high risk. Nevertheless, I myself can not even count how often I drive Jake's smaller city car back up from the beachside restaurant where I work in Camps Bay aiming for the white line so I can be sure to stay on the road. It is an all-or-nothing kind of attitude. Table Mountain watches over me, its majesty all lit up in floodlights as it is tonight. In contrast, the adjacent Devil's Peak is hidden behind its characteristic wisp of fog, that covers up the outline of the mountain top in the same way that the point of this evening is concealed in my mind.

"Is she going to be here too?" I complain, trying to clear up the facts. "I don't feel like an after party."

"Who?" asks Jake, slightly annoyed.

"That personal trainer chick from the bar, didn't she ask you to meet here?"

Jake huffs. "So what, Poppie?"

He turns his back and keeps walking as I speak. "So, I don't feel like watching you flirt with other girls anymore tonight."

I wobble a little, in my heart and on my stilettos, as I walk behind Jake. I am so used to walking in stilettos now that it is like second nature. It is just that, I am not even able to keep my inner balance right now. My jaw feels tight.

Jake puts his hand in the small of my back. It is my favourite place to be touched. It holds me steady and it makes me feel like he is proud to present me at his side. I too feel proud to be held like that, framed by his strong arms. I push my chest forward and relax my shoulders. I am always taller than my boyfriends and I like to wear high heels. I need a man who is confident enough to be seen with me. Like Jake. Though tonight, he is edging on the rather aggressive side.

"I'm getting you a burger and chips." It is a warning. He would never allow me to eat a burger when he is sober. My figure is too much of a priority for him.

Jake does not look at me directly. He is distracted by the who's who posing like rock stars behind me at the plastic tables laden with takeaway pizza in the corner—sunglasses and swooping fringes blocking out the unflattering light.

"You're showing me off like a fancy car, Jake, when you prefer to drive the new one you're looking out for already. You want me to stay with you and yet you can not focus ... how am I supposed to feel?"

"Come on now, calm down." He pinches me with a force that hurts.

Jake grabs a spot at a table of young girls as soon as our burgers are ready. I flop down onto the chair next to him, listlessly chewing on a few fries, while listening to them chatter. The smell of deep-fried onions and barbecue sauce makes me feel nauseous. I can see the look in his eyes and I know what is coming next. Watching me eat turns him off. He looks back to smile at the girls before we reach the exit.

"Come on, I need to get something from the vault," he says as he pulls me in the opposite direction of the car.

We walk around to the back of the gas station, where Jake owns one of the many high-security vaults around town. Here, people keep their valuable art and jewellery, gold coins and guns. Since there has been an ever-increasing amount of burglaries in Cape Town over recent years, Jake is doing well. He has someone managing the business for him now. The only reason why he pops in here at night is to get his cocaine. Same as everyone else around me at the restaurant, he is taking drugs regularly. What is different with him is that he says cruel things to me when he is high. I know better than to try and stop him. He is the kind of guy who does what he wants, when he wants. He will not listen to me.

I do not know why I get in the car with him again, but I guess I believe in seeing the best of people and try to make the best of the worst situations. Yet there are things that can not be ignored.

"So, Poppie," he says as we are speeding home, "you make me buy you all that dinner and then you don't eat a thing. You just want, want, want. More and more. And more."

"Jake, I've never asked you for a thing." I frantically try to explain. "Perhaps if you stop flirting around with other women, you would finally deserve to be happy with someone like me."

He puts his foot on the gas. "You argue like a girl."

I choke back a sarcastic laugh. "I am a girl."

He turns his head to roll his eyes at me. "Poppie, you know, nothing I do is ever good enough for you. You are always complaining."

I squirm to hold on to my self-worth. "You collect women, Jake. We are not playthings that exist solely for your entertainment. A woman wants to be special."

"I'm so sick of this, Poppie," he says, as though he is spitting at me. "I'm so sick of you. Look at you. You're drunk. You're disgusting. Just get out of the car."

Is it society or human nature that makes men want to control women? To contain us like the set of Russian dolls that my parents brought back from their last holiday together; breaking us down layer by layer until there is just a tiny hollow, painted shell left over? Is it because we are so hard to grasp; to pin down? Because we rip out the hearts of the men who are supposed to love us? Or has it got to do with a possessive nature?

I look at him with a glassy expression as the car tires scream to a sudden stop.

He is right. I am drunk. There is no point in arguing further. I feel myself cracking. Never mind teacups, it is the whole set of my life dropping into pieces this time. Slowly, I get out of the car and stumble halfway up the street.

Then I stop.

All the weight of the pain of my seemingly perfect little life pushes on to me as I start to come down from the drugs. There are no longer enough chemicals in my body to protect me from my own feelings, from the reality of my empty existence. I feel the heavy blow of hopelessness, not knowing where to look for answers or who I can go to for a few scraps of love. Certainly not Jake.

A weird noise leaves my body as I throw myself onto the tar road in the middle of the night. It startles me as if it is not my own voice reverberating through the quiet of the street. I shiver. I sound like a witch from hell. I wish intensely that a car would come around the corner and drive over me. If only to save me from the heartbreak inside.

Jake looks at me with pity and disgust as he idles by and spits at me out of the window. "Don't look at me, you've only got yourself to blame."

His scathing becomes so much more intense when we are drinking.

Only the ridiculous howl of the wind adds to the drama. Then he drives off. He drives away. He is leaving. He is leaving me here. The thought of him leaving feels like a scientific impossibility, as though it is against nature. He is a part of me. I need this part. How can he abandon me now? It can not be real.

It can not be over. He would never end this. Yet, he is really going. He is just leaving me here. The voice in my head rattles through the howling of the South Easter, Cape Town's infamous gale force wind.

No, no, noooo, he is not going to leave you here.

Yes, yes, yessss, he is.

Please, no, please do not leave me.

Never, never leave me.

Come back ... back ... back...

He is gone ... gone ... gone ...

Don't go. No, don't go.

It is over. He is gone.

It is done.

He keeps driving further away until I can no longer see his car. The universe must end, but somehow it goes on. Jake is no longer holding me up. I am falling. I am alone.

I cannot live like this on my own. I can not, Jake.

Jake?

The tar is still warm from the sun, even though it must be late. Or maybe I am going cold. I let my full weight sink into the earth as I shudder. The road is uneven and my shoulder slips into a small pothole. I can smell the dust tinged with rubber. Then the wind blasts a gust of sand into my face. I do not want to move. I wallow in the discomfort of my unnatural position and lean further in to the sharp little stones piercing the skin on my back. Sometimes, pain can be pleasure and pleasure can be pain.

Nothing happens for a while. I lie very still. Time passes slowly when you are waiting to die. Yet the only thing dying right now is the wind. It is a sudden change that leaves the night very still. Everything is silent at this time. Even my heart is quiet now. High above me, I see a shooting star against the blackout sky, but I have nothing left to wish for. I keep believing what my mom says, that having sex can be so empowering. Well, look at me now. I just want to go to sleep with the wind, forever.

It becomes boring on the tar, with no late-night party people speeding around the corner in this Cape Town quarter as they usually do. Bad timing. I can hear only the ticking of the faux gold watch on my wrist.

Waiting for death. I guess it is different from trying to kill myself. I wish to die, but I am not quite willing to do it. I put myself here, in the street, knowing fully that if a car would speed around the corner—as they usually do at this time of night—it would all be over and I would be relieved from the pain. Yet I am not brave enough to take my own life. I simply lie here and wait. A coward.

I feel an intense obsession to get rid of myself. In a huff of adrenaline, I decide to head toward the trashcans. My pink ruffled top gets stuck to the rough parts of the tar as I try to get up. I do not hesitate to rip the chiffon to pieces. This look is not getting me anywhere tonight. Perhaps I should have worn a mini skirt, instead of jeans.

I get into a dumpster outside an apartment building and decide to wait for the removal truck to take me where I belong. There are a few refuse bags inside and enough space for me to curl into the fetal position on top. I let the lid drop down. It is darker than night. My body slowly weighs down the bags. I hear glass clinging, tins and plastic squishing. Something oozes out loudly.

The smell I cannot quite figure out, but it is as rotten as my core.

Again, I simply lie here and wait. A few creatures move around beneath me, crawling through the trash. Is that a cockroach running all the way down my arm? I despise crawling insects, yet I can not collect myself enough to move. I want to get rid of me, but I wait. I wait for others to take the decision for me. I can not end this on my own. The alcohol and adrenaline are rushing through my veins, all shaken up with cocaine.

I wait and wait and wait, but the waiting is way too uneventful.

The next best thing is to flip the lid back open and fumble in my bag for something that can hurt me. Perhaps I have been too passive.

Lighter, no. Jake has my lighter. Car keys, yes. I kind of fall out of the dumpster. It is not a long walk up the mountain to Jake's place. The door remote will still work, his parking spot would most likely be empty.

I SLIP INTO THE CAR AND DRIVE, without heeding any traffic regulations, not stopping at any red lights, my wheels spinning as I speed around every corner. I drive all the way to the farm address on the piece of paper that I left in the cubby hole. It is an hour out of town. I put the pedal to the metal as I get to the dust road that leads up to the thatched-roof farmhouse in Franschhoek that my mom now shares with Dr. Labia.

When I stop outside their place, I do not know what to do.

I was hoping for a fatal accident along the way. Sometimes, the angels take care of me a bit too well.

"Agh," my mom sighs with annoyance once I tell her that Jake left me. "What's that smell? Did you fart, Poppie, or did the cat drag something in?"

I flop down onto the natural leather couch in the middle of the living room. "Mom, he just left me."

She walks to the furthest corner of the room and sits down in a patterned easy chair next to a fireplace lined with copper pots. "Who?"

"Jake, Mom." I look at her across the clay vase on the wooden coffee table, which is full of creamy, star-shaped farm flowers called chinkerinchees. "I have ... had ... a boyfriend."

"Oh," she chirps, "does he at least have a nice car?"

"Mom ..." I moan. "Can you just not be the material girl for once?"

She gets up and plumps up the quilted cushion on her chair. "Well-well, Poppie, so what did you do this time?"

As she walks toward me, I hear the heavy footsteps of someone coming through the back door of the house.

"You know, you should stop being so conservative," she says. "Just loosen up and have a little fun. Men want to have fun, Poppie. Otherwise, he will find someone else."

I kick at the edge of the Moroccan carpet in front of me and get up to face her. "But what about me? I'm not having any fun at all."

She walks past me. "It's late, Poppie. Get yourself cleaned up and go to bed. We'll talk in the morning. Wait. What is that? A worm in your hair?"

"Well, hello, Poppie," Dr. Labia suddenly pitches in as he walks in, pinching my bum as a sort of greeting. "How nice of you to pay us a first visit!"

Only God knows why I am still alive.

SHADOW CUDDLES UP WITH ME as I cry myself to sleep in one of the many rooms in the spacious farmhouse where my mom now lives with her lover. The room is sparsely furnished. Rustic antique pieces are set off by colourful abstract paintings with splashes of bright yellow, fresh green and blossomy pink. A brass bucket full of arum lilies sits proudly on top of the heavy, solid wood chest of drawers. Arum lilies, with their subtle, sweet fragrance, always give me a sense of peace. They are wildflowers that grow here, free, without having to try hard or do anything at all to be able to bloom. There is a lesson in that. One day, I will find a place where I can simply be myself, where I can be beautiful. I fall asleep with Shadow on my chest, her purring like the song of an angel.

When I wake at dawn I decide to drive back to town right away and go to work—with enough make-up I could get through the breakfast shift swollen red eyes and all—if only to avoid the inevitable "talk" on how I am becoming a man repellent.

I leave before anyone gets up.

I look better than I thought when I hesitatingly check myself out in my wardrobe mirror when I get home. Who is this new person in my reflection? It is as though I am playing a marvellous dress-up game where I am the doll. I can wear anything to work I want as long as it is blue. I choose tight cigarette pants and a halter neck top, all zhuzhed up with silver hoop earrings. I masterfully hide my real face under a layer of foundation, shimmery pink rouge and lots of pastel violet eyeshadow. A generous swish of eyeliner and my brown-black mascara cover the evidence of the night before. With a final touch of juicy baby-pink lipgloss, no one would ever guess that anything is wrong.

As long as I keep looking amazing, no one will ever know that I am not.

My eyes linger on one of my dad's photographs of the Namaqualand flower time, placed in a thin golden frame on the side table in my foyer. Back there, in the Garden of the Gods, the wildflowers are always facing the sun. Today, the photo looks like a sea of colours across the arid earth, or magnificent make-up all over the face of an ugly woman.

I walk out into the bright morning light, turn my face towards the sky and go to work. Chest forward, chin up. I take a deep breath of ocean air before I step into the resort. So much effort goes into pretending what I do not genuinely feel, but I am used to it by now. I can make it through with a smile.

"You're so beautiful." Donald de Beer soon makes it his business to help me get over my break-up.

He is a big, blonde man with a perfectly symmetrical face. Besides his cocaine habit, he is a fairly stable influence. He always has everything under control—though, admittedly, with help from the lines with the girls in the back office.

Don and I stay behind in the restaurant to drink whiskey and talk after everyone else has cleaned up and left. It is nice not to have to be alone, to have the feeling that somebody cares. It is a plaster for the ache in my heart.

"No." I say it even before he offers me a line. I can say I tried it once and it did not fix any problems. It only makes things worse. "Do you really need to stay awake or are you addicted?"

He looks like a little boy when he smiles, as though he needs a hug. "It's probably just because it's around all the time, you know. I have to organise it for the restaurant guests. They give me big tips, so it keeps me financially sound. Jake keeps coke in his vault, so I can buy it from him anytime. He's safe. It's easy. That's all."

My eyes well up and I want to apologise.

"Never apologise for your heart," he says. "Pain is pain. It's toxic to keep tears inside your body."

We look at each other for a long time. "I don't think I'm beautiful. Right now, I hate myself. I can't believe I dated a drug dealer. That's a lot more toxic than tears."

"Check how men look at you, Poppie. You're this tall and regal, totally hot babe."

His words make me get up to leave. I do not want to lose myself in his flattery.

Don takes slow steps toward me. "Your eyes are so unusual … green with brown dots, like chocolate sprinkles … which makes me remember that … I haven't had any chocolate sprinkles for ages …"

I am surprised that I do not want to hide my strange eyes from Don. Instead, I let him in deeper. No man has ever paid me a compliment that made me feel seen until now. Usually men look at my outline, not at my eyes, especially not the details. I feel comfortable with the intimacy it brings. He plants a kiss on my lips and weaves his fingers through mine.

I feel the coldness of his wide wedding ring. "Look," I let go, "I know how it is. Even if you leave your wife for me, it will still be too complicated. I don't need another divorce in my life. It was tough enough with my parents."

"I love you, Poppie," is his only answer.

It takes all my willpower not to laugh, but I still have tears in my eyes and that would only make me look hysterical. Men have a thousand charming ways to reel in a woman. For me, these words have lost their meaning. How do I live with an open heart, yet protect myself from getting hurt and losing my life energy?

It is not fair to put a woman in this situation. Clearly I cannot

continue to work here anymore, at least not for much longer ...
but what is next?

"PLEASE ... DON'T COME ... ANY CLOSER," I tell Don the next
night, "ever."

I know that I have to express my sensuality in order to stay
sane, but I do not want to be promiscuous and I do not want to
sleep with Don.

The same evening, a poster placed inside the window of a
car catches my eye as I leave the restaurant, perhaps because I
am looking for it or at least looking for something, anything,
to distract me: *The beauty of a dancer vibrates in every part of her
body–call today for belly dance lessons with Lola.*

I want to feel beauty through and through me. I want to feel
beauty in my body, instead of alcohol and drugs and loveless sex.
I want to connect with the smallest bit of beauty I can find within
myself. I want to vibrate with beauty. I want to dance and celebrate
my body. I know nothing about belly dancing, but I contact Lola
the very next morning and end up being her first student in Cape
Town. She is a large, nature-loving, colourful woman, who wears
bright feathers in her long curly hair and paints mandalas and
reads tarot cards. Her studio is full of amethyst and self-made
costumes, beaded with crystals and seashells.

Belly dancing soon helps me find more balance in my emotional
life. The movement is natural, feminine and wholly satisfying.
It embraces my loose sexual energy and expresses it in the form
of beauty, joy and female power. The shimmies and undulations
mimic the natural movements of the body during sex and child-
birth. It is not an intentionally provocative dance, but one that
celebrates what my body naturally wants to do. It makes me feel

really good and strengthens my self confidence. An unashamed celebration of what is.

Lola says that belly dancing has many special properties. "It's a way to connect with your own inner self and learn to love your every curve—that can give you courage. Dance can help you turn your life around. You are the keeper of your own body and mind. If you don't collect that power and put it in motion, someone else will."

I do not want my life to be small anymore. I want to say yes to the world and breathe in the lovely energy that is all around me every day. I decide to dye my hair the deep colour of chocolate. I am done with the busty blonde.

"Hello?" I pick up when my new yellow cellphone rings.

"Poppie, it's me, Jake. I want you to come home." He pauses expectantly, but I have not been waiting for his call. Not this time. "I will never do it again, Poppie. I ..."

The neat electronic beep sounds over his voice as I put down the phone and check in at a backpackers lodge in the centre of town. I am not up for a sequel to our story.

The Marionette

October 2005, Cape Town, South Africa

CHANGE OF HAIR. CHANGE OF MIND. I notice that I do not turn as many heads with my new non-blonde hairdo, but that people take me a bit more seriously as a brunette at the Camps Bay beach restaurant. This is where the models and film directors of the Cape Town studios like to hang out. Respect is something I have rarely had the chance to experience in my life and it surprises me that a little bit of henna hair dye can make such a difference to who I am. It feels good.

Since a few nights ago, I have been having some interesting

conversations with a South African Indian filmmaker called Rajit. He is back every night now for a chit-chat against the backdrop of the majestic Atlantic Ocean. He books a table for one next to the floor-to-ceiling window and has a three-course meal and a whole bottle of award-winning Pinotage, all on his own. It looks as if he has all the time in the world, as he sits there with his hair slicked back, watching the sun set in rose hues over the turquoise ocean until I agree to go on a date with him two weeks later.

"I will come back every day for the rest of my life," he accents the last four words by patting his luxury watch, "until you say yes."

Not that it would have taken that much dedication to convince me, but it sounds good. This kind of chivalry is different to what I know. There is space here for the man to genuinely woo me, just like in the movies.

RAJ PICKS ME UP FROM THE HOSTEL in his fancy British car and takes me out to a city restaurant that looks like a showroom because I am "the kind of girl that should be in the spotlight". He knows that I prefer wines from the Nuy Valley and we finally have the chance to share my favourite Pinotage, a fine complement to our generous rib-eye steaks.

"Cheers, Poppie! To your cinematic beauty!" He giggles without holding back any of his joy. "Stick with me, I'll make you a star. Did I tell you that I'm a travel documentary filmmaker?"

I take a sip of the peppery wine and savour the spiced berry flavours. I do not feel invisible with Raj. "You make me feel like a star. Does that mean we can travel the world?"

He puts down his glass and focuses his eyes on mine. "Where would you like to travel to?"

The question makes me fiddle with the tablecloth. "I don't know. I have never thought of that. Everywhere, I guess."

Raj laughs a lot. I like that. "Poppie, the world is very big. There are close to two hundred countries out there. If you visit one each year, you won't be able to see it all in a lifetime."

I take a moment to process the information and continue rubbing the corner of the tablecloth between my thumb and index finger. "Then anywhere. Anywhere away from here."

He looks pleased. "You could apply the same skills you use to entertain guests as a hostess in the restaurant, to entertain an audience as a presenter in front of the video camera."

It is not as ridiculous as it sounds and I suddenly see my whole future in front of me. I sit up a little straighter, stretching into the thought as the smoky aftertaste of the wine lingers on my tongue. "It could be fun."

After dinner, he takes me for a drive all along Sea Point beach road, where dozens of palm trees are lit up along the promenade and the beautiful people are drinking cocktails at sidewalk cafés. As we continue, I slide down my chair to get a better view of the Southern Cross, clearly visible in the quiet sky.

"Look," says Raj, pointing at some girls in high heels, posing on the sidewalk along Green Point main road.

I am confused. "What are they doing here?"

"Poppie, they're prostitutes." Raj laughs.

"Really?" I realise how naïve I must sound. "Ah, of course."

I try not to look too curious as we pass a few more ladies of the night along the road. It is hard for me to fathom the attraction. Then again, I am sure Raj is not that kind of man. He is old-fashioned and, after all, he has got me.

"It was an exquisite evening," Raj laughs and shakes his head as he double parks in the busy street in front of my hostel. "I shall wait here until you get inside safely."

His face softens as he leans over to brush my lips lightly with his own. Almost a kiss.

"Your eyes are such a blissful shade of green." His beard softly tickles my face. "Goodnight, I hope you fall into a blissful slumber." As soon as I open the car door, we are hit by a thick waft of marijuana in the air. I start walking away quickly, but Raj calls me to turn back. "Poppie, can we do this again tomorrow?"

I flush with anticipation. "Yes, of course. You can pick me up same time, same place."

SIX WEEKS AND MANY FOODIE DATES LATER he says, "I love you, Poppie. Come on, come with me to Asia. I'll make you famous."

"Give me some time to think about it." There is no good reason for me to say no, but something in me hesitates although we have had a grand time together over the last few months.

"Take your time," he says, "but don't take forever. I have to go and it will be weird being away from you. Come along if you can."

I know Raj is devoted to me, but I cannot help feeling as if there is something missing in our relationship. How charming that someone is so struck with me. It is the closest thing I have known to being loved. Never mind flowers, he buys me bags of basmati rice and fragrant whole spices from the Bo-Kaap. Star anise, cinnamon and nutmeg.

These thoughts are running through my mind as I walk into the restaurant parking lot after a day shift. I am just about to meet him and Lola at the hostel for a dance and curry evening. The owners let Raj cook in the kitchen and share food with the guests. Lola teaches belly dancing and does psychic readings. We have fun. We meet interesting people. What more could a girl like me ask for? I can hardly wait.

It is quiet in the parking lot outside the restaurant. There is a stupid smile on my face as I suddenly feel a knock from behind. I am pushed further out of the way and stumble into a king protea bush. The tips of the large pink crown-like flowers scratch my skin. How rude, I think, as I see someone running into the distance, entering an empty rugby field. As soon as I get back up, I feel a second blow, this time to the side of my head. Hard metal. The pain starts to pulse just above my ear. I look back. It is another person running with a small pistol swinging along with his flailing arms as he tries to catch up with the previous man who knocked into me.

It takes a while for my conscious mind to be in the moment, as though the events are not happening in order and are, therefore, not possible to fully comprehend. Time suspends in the ocean air and I feel taller, rising slightly out of my body in anticipation of final death. The proteas look fine, not a petal out of place, their herbaceous smell dampening my fear. It is easier to focus on the pretty pink flowers. This species of fynbos generally flourishes in places where other plants would die. Not only are they hard, but they are also hardy. I have seen proteas survive extreme heat, wildfires, floods, frost, storms, droughts and, now, also gun runners. No wonder it is the national flower of South Africa. What a contrast to myself, fading away here in fear.

I am still stuck in a fynbos freeze-frame when I hear a sound. For a split second I doubt myself, but I know instinctively that it is a gun shot. It is unmistakable, unbelievable, unreal. Yet. Very. Very. Real.

The air drains from my lungs and then I breathe in again. I am forced back into the reality of the moment and do a quick check to see whether I have been hit. I shake out my arms and legs. Nothing. I am alive and alone, in the middle of a gun fight. The sound of the revolver has a muffled echo. My sense of time becomes elastic, as if it is a piece of chewing gum. I cannot figure out how far they are. Having run that fast, they could be very far away by now. Or not.

The silence rings in my head. For a moment, even the breeze stands still.

A couple of seconds pass until I hear a painful moan of the air deflating from a human being's lungs. It is not profound. In fact, it is only a hushed cry. Yet the last hum of life loudly travels across the silent, indigo evening. Human being to human being, I am witness to this last breath of another. Then I hear the amplified thud. It is a body dropping dead; the unmistakable sound of a no-longer living being drawn down into the Earth's gravity. Nothing is more certain than death.

I should know. I have known it, once.

I get into my car as quickly as I can and lock all the doors. I have been given yet another chance to steer this body of mine further along. I want to make the most of it. The killer knows that I know. I am the only person here right now in this parking lot, the only loose end. I breathe through the fear and drive home as quickly as I can. As I look into the rearview mirror I notice the blood streaming from my gun-smacked temple. I look much worse than I feel. The image of myself reflected back is the stuff of nightmares.

As soon as I am safe in my room, I call Raj.

"I'll come with you to Thailand," I say decisively.

There is a long silence on the other side of the phone. "Hey, did something happen? I'm just on my way over. You can take your time."

"I don't need any more time," I say, slightly short of breath. "I've just been inside a real-life murder scene and I want to get out of here. When can we leave?"

As if I would need another reason to leave, the owners at

the hostel freak out when they see me like that in the kitchen. Our curry evenings get cancelled, just like that. Same thing at work. The restaurant manager Don does not want me to work with the bruise on my head. He is afraid that I would "scare the customers". I quit my hostess job on the spot. It is long overdue anyway. I need a break away from Don and the growing crime in the city—and besides, my relationship with Raj deserves a chance.

At least, we both think so.

Our families, not.

His mom calls me "that woman" when she screams at Raj on the phone. It is loud enough for me to hear when I am in the same room. She refuses to meet me and never mentions my name. The Indian community in South Africa is conservative and likes to keep their race pure. They do not encourage mixed marriages.

Neither do people from my Afrikaans-Dutch heritage.

Not that I have that much contact with my parents, but my mom refuses to take any of my calls as long as I am with him. It makes me feel guilty and yet I cannot change my heart.

My dad is, surprisingly enough, a little more supportive of our choices.

"Listen," my dad says in a voice message to Raj before we get on the plane to Bangkok, "just don't get married! Or make her pregnant! Good that you're getting out of the city, I told her it's not safe."

"Yep, Dad," I say into the air, secretly rolling my eyes at the airport ceiling. Pregnancy is not much of a risk anyway. Our relationship is not very physical. We only kiss and cuddle. It is nurturing. Raj and I will do what we want, no matter what anyone thinks. We follow our own story and go.

I have always wanted to leave—to see what options I have other than the pain that is my own life, what other identities I can clutch on to, rather than being who I am. My chocolate-coloured hair seems to work well as a cover for being a target, hiding my naturally blonde hair and attracting the good guy–Raj–as opposed to the usual *think-Jake* type bad boys who think that blondes are nothing more than toys. Changing my hair helps me to change my life–but does it change who I am? Soon, my blonde roots will probably start growing out. Good thing I have packed another box of henna.

THAT IS HOW I HAVE COME TO BE LYING IN A HAMMOCK on a Thai beach called Karon, listening to the corals tinkling in the waves. They sound like soft giggles suppressed by the whispers of the ocean. Raj is reading books on Thai food, with his back resting against a palm tree. It is only the two of us, creating our own reality away from everything.

I sit up and play with my toes in the sand. It is as fine as powdered sugar. Or MSG, as the favourite ingredient is called around here.

He looks up at me and smiles. "You're so beautiful, puppet."

I am not able to believe it, so I change the topic. There is something on my mind and I speak it as I do with Raj. With us, there are no secrets. "This couple we met yesterday, from the street food restaurant where you want to film, it's Nalan and Montri. Right?"

He nods.

"I wonder why they say so many bad things about Western people when I'm around. I mean, it's interesting. Western people often think other cultures are immoral, but, here, Montri says, 'Western people come here, pollute our beaches, take drugs and make whores of our women'. Why would he say that in front of me?"

"Have you looked in the mirror lately?" Raj giggles with the rolling tinkle of seashells in the evening tide. "We've been here six months now. Not just that but, many Indian women have very light skin … and besides, you hang out with me. They're just completing the picture in the way that makes most sense to them. Don't worry about it. It doesn't matter."

I let the thought sink in and take a look at my arm. My skin has become pretty tanned. Long days on the beach, or frolicking in the ocean. I did not think that life here would go so far as to shift the perception of my identity or my ethnic origins.

More than that, it upsets me how polarising culture can be. How do people allow themselves to judge others by the tone of their skin rather than the colour of their heart? By their choice of shoes, rather than their capacity for kindness? By their accent, rather than the way they choose to live their lives?

"Even your hair looks Indian, puppet. Don't be so serious. Just go with it." He continues laughing.

"Almost forgot about that," I say. "Which reminds me, I should get a mirror before we do the food show. I will need one to fix my hair and my make-up."

He wobbles from all the laughing as he gets up slowly and takes a few steps toward me. Raj likes to make light of my vanity. It surprises me that he adores me without make-up. I have to admit, a part of me despises not having a mirror in the house, despite only living in bikinis and sarongs. Seeing myself in the mirror reminds me of who I am. Without a mirror, I tend to forget myself.

"You're perfect just the way you are, my little puppet." He starts planting little kisses all over my face, "but we may, indeed, need to," kiss, "powder," kiss, "your," kiss, "face," kiss, "for the camera."

When he is done laughing, he shuffles along. "Hey, I'm going to get us some videos from the shop down the road."

I wave him off and stay on the beach until it is almost nightfall. When I am alone I can go swimming and stay under the water for longer without having to explain myself or getting Raj worried. I could just stay in the water all day.

Palm leaves and orchid prayers and wreaths line the beach, left for those who died in the tsunami. That, and some water damage to the parking lot, are the only visible signs of what happened. Most of the hotels and resorts have been rebuilt and several large open markets, street food stands, and makeshift stores line the beach road.

I walk back along a neon-lit area full of nightclubs and a few frisky go-go bars. Cute little dancers are shaking their hair and doing shimmies on bar counters. The smell of chemicals and alcohol pierces through the salty air. An excessively dolled up dancer in a pink tutu makes eye contact with me. It feels like an implied transaction. I look away quickly, but she runs after me calling her price. I do not feel like fighting with a prostitute and walk faster, but her last words make me stop and turn. She looks a bit like a boy.

"With Raj."

"How do you know his name? Have you been watching us?" The whole gang starts laughing, hiding their mouths behind their hands as they look at me in amusement. It is off-season and all, but business must be really bad if they have nothing better to do.

"We're not here for souvenirs," I say. "Stop hassling us." I move on and decide not to let the incident spoil my lovely, hazy day. After hours of swimming in the balmy water, I can still feel the tide calling the rhythm of my body. My hair is tangled with sand. My skin is baked hard by the sun; a dried-out seashell, flaky and peeling off. This is the happiest my life has ever been—and I will not let sex workers taint my perfect reverie.

For the first time in Phuket, it feels like coming home when

I make my way up to our house on Fantasy Hill. It sits on the highest ground in the area, which is why people gathered here during the tsunami. Montri says that the tsunami happened slowly in Karon beach. The sea pulled back so far that people walked all the way out to pick up seashells, without anticipating any trouble. Then the tide came back in slowly, unlike other areas which were surprised by a big wave. People had time to head up the hill, right here between the beaches of Kata and Karon where Raj and I are renting a little house.

Our immediate living area is filled with pink and purple orchids and seashells that I collect on the beach. Thai silk scatter cushions liven up the worn-out couches. Colours, flowers and treasures make up for the nasty kitchen at the back. It is basic, but equipped with everything we need to cook up our own delicious Thai food. Everything, as long as it is plastic. Beyond the open-plan counter, everything is full of old plastic. I refuse to go into this kitchen, but Raj is more than enthusiastic. He is becoming quite an expert in cooking Thai food. I am simply the tough critic, reviewing and advising on each attempt. Just enough feedback to make sure he keeps improving.

As I have a bath, I fully observe how much the daily sunshine has changed the colour of my skin. It is not that I have not noticed my suntan, but I now understand that I might not look Caucasian anymore. It is a pleasant feeling, as if I am someone else or escaping from myself. I like the thought of being able to transform. I play with the candle wax on the side of the bath, making a tiny figurine out of it while it is still warm.

I am so tired that I do not even hear Raj coming in very late. The bedroom has a big bed so we can each have our own space when we sleep. There is no avoiding the pools of sweat, but we do not make it worse by getting too close all the time.

OUTSIDE OUR BEDROOM WINDOW there is a big mango tree. It has small fruit that are sweet and delicious. Except that they fall, doof! Doof, doof, doof on the roof.

Yet it is the tropical sunlight falling across my face that wakes me up from a deep sleep. I smell the strong, gritty coffee before Raj appears with a cup. "My sleeping puppet, I got some great movies for us."

"Good morning to you!" I sit up. "What about our own film? Shall we start to plan a shoot date?"

"I've already arranged that with Nalan," he calls as he disappears back to the kitchen. "We'll go down to Patak Road tomorrow morning early when they start preparing things."

I hear him chopping away and get up to see what he is up to for breakfast. "You could have told me. Why didn't you? I thought we shared everything, not just food at Nalan's and Montri's."

The bowl of ripe mangoes casts an orange sheen on the kitchen counter. Shadows can have some colourful nuances, it seems.

Raj pushes a plate of cut fruit over to me. Pink dragon fruit, orange papaya and yellow banana. "What else is there that I don't know, Rajie?"

Without responding he turns away to get bean sprouts, banana flower and shallots from the fridge, putting it next to the shrimp on the back counter. He checks on the soaked rice noodles and smiles as he starts to drain the water. "I'm making pad thai."

"That's all you have to say to that?" I let it slide without further questions. There is no reason for me to pry. The smell of roasting peanuts fills the air and I try to refocus. "I will rehearse some lines."

Acting is something I have always done, in a way. To get away from myself. To please others. To forget. I put on a better morning mood with a little improvisation. "How about: 'It's 4:30 am and I'm in Phuket with Nalan and Montri cooking fried noodles with beef and basil, as well as a red fish curry and no less than eight more dishes. We still need to finish a green chicken curry and a yellow beef curry to be ready in time for breakfast. Yes, that's right. It takes only one and a half hours to prepare ten different Thai dishes. Not only do people here eat the same kind of food for breakfast, lunch and dinner, but, in Thailand, they love eating so much that they make sure to spend more time actually doing that than working in the kitchen.' And so on. What do you think?"

Raj swoops around like a balloon, as he tries to hold in his laughter. He puts his arm around me and holds me tight.

I continue without allowing him to interrupt me. "Then I'll ask Nalan to comment about how no Thai dish should take longer than twelve or fifteen minutes to prepare, since Thai people prefer eating to cooking."

He laughs with his whole heart. "That's fine, puppet. You can be spontaneous. I'm sure we'll get some good snippets. Just keep it natural. You can also mention the chilli and spices which help to preserve the meat out there in the sun all day."

I know that I can only relax once I have planned properly. "Well, at least a rough script. I also need to decide what to wear."

While he finishes up the pad thai, I quickly model a few simple shirts and dresses. This is something I have grown a habit of doing–showing off new clothes to my friends and family. People have commented that I should pursue a career in modelling. I am tall enough, but I never had the confidence. Yet being with Raj gives me a lot of validation. If someone loves me, then I cannot be too bad.

"No patterns," he says firmly when I put on my favourite dress. Raj bought it for me. He enjoys dressing me in bubble skirts or wide-legged pants and cotton poplin tops. Out of all the things he found for me though, this is the piece I really like: a wraparound Thai silk dress with a colourful floral print. I understand better now why women dress for men. It feels so good to have him look at me with appreciation. We go through a few more outfits and settle on a linen shirt with an Asian collar and short sleeves.

Now that my wardrobe is sorted, I sit with Raj to try this morning's egg-fried noodle concoction. It is hot and sweet and sour and umami in equal measures. "You're getting really good!"

I bring another greedy spoonful of perfection to my mouth. "Write this one down on that notepad next to you. It is my favourite pad thai so far."

He refills my coffee and picks up a pen from the kitchen counter.

Pad Thai for Poppie, he writes.

> *Fresh shrimp to taste*
> *Handful of soaked rice noodles*
> *2 eggs*
> *Some julienne veggies*
> *Bit of bean sprouts*
> *As many chillis as you can take*
> *4 shallots*
> *Banana flower – optional*
> *Touch of fish sauce*
> *Teaspoon of tamarind paste*
> *Little palm sugar*
> *Roasted peanuts*
> *1 fresh lime*
> *Oil for frying*
> *Green leaves to serve on the side (any herbs, spinach or lettuce)*

> *Fry the shrimp and veggies in hot oil, then add the noodles into the wok. Add the tamarind, fish sauce, eggs, sprouts, shallots, red chilli and palm sugar. Toss together and stir until it is all cooked. Serve*

*with roasted peanuts, a slice of banana flower, a wedge of lime and
lots of fresh green leaves for Poppie.*

With love from Raj, he signs the recipe.

He even draws a picture of pad thai on a plate before passing
the notepad to me. My heart pumps like a sea anemone. I cannot
imagine a better kind of love letter than a personalised recipe.
Sharing a love for food is something so intimate.

Raj goes off to exchange one of the videos as I drift along in
this feeling. I am walking on air for the rest of the day, as though
a love bubble has wrapped itself around me, making a sphere that
goes all the way around the bottom of my bare feet.

This is me, floating along in love.

ON THE DAY OF THE SHOOT, WE JUMP IN A TUK-TUK with Raj's
camera equipment. The vehicle is a motorised type of rickshaw,
with rims, a chrome interior and blue lights. Our driver plays pop
music along the way and tells us that his is the most high-tech
tuk-tuk in the area. We get the special treatment as there are no
more tourists around after the tsunami.

Nalan arrives wearing a traditional print and Raj explains
that a heavy pattern will not look good on film. At first, she is
offended and the discussion wastes a bit of time. Raj has enough
experience with this kind of thing to stay calm. Good thing he
asked me to bring a few extra tops. I soon have her eyes glinting
for a simple wraparound.

Raj places his camera on a tripod in the kitchen while I arrange
the scene, clean up some excessive plastic and try to stay out of
the way of the actual cooking that is racing against the clock.
The regulars actually do pitch up at 5 am to pick up their food.

I wait for the right moment to get into position.

"And … action!" says Raj.

The moment absorbs me into a strange kind of adrenaline and I feel as though I am slipping away behind an invisible screen where I can no longer see or hear anything that happens. In my ears, everything is muted. It is an exhilarating feeling where time is no longer linear and I am no longer me. I feel dizzy and distant from myself during the filming, yet I am vaguely aware that I am going through the motions. Some very able part of me automatically takes over and gets the job done. This part of me knows what to do in front of the camera, while the rest of me sort of hovers on the side.

I only fully resurface to the real world when I hear Raj say, "That's a wrap. Great job, everyone!"

Back at home, I feel nauseous and rattled. I have to look at the film to see what happened during the shoot. I do not remember a thing, as though it was not really me presenting Nalan's kitchen to the camera. "It looks good, but I have no idea where I get all those great lines from. They seem to flow effortlessly from this person who is supposed to be me. Perhaps it is something like a show blackout, if that even exists."

Raj looks at me and simply laughs it off.

WHEN WE TRY TO SHOOT A FEW SCENES on the beach over the next days, I get stage fright as soon as Raj points the camera at me. I am nervous and blocked. "Are you here with me, Poppie? What's up? You were such a natural the other day."

Around us, frangipani flowers sweeten the air and, every now and again, gracious little butterflies with scanty lace-like wings pass along the tree-lined beach. "I don't even know how I did it. I'm too nervous!"

He is patient with me. We go back home and eat homemade tom yum soup and watch movies all night. Early the next morning, he returns our set of movies and comes back with the next batch a few hours later. He is definitely addicted to films.

I NEED A FEW DAYS TO GET INTO THE RIGHT MINDSET for our beach location shoot, but I have a good feeling when I am ready.

"Action!" Raj says and it is as though I am hypnotised. I am in tune with the part of me that knows what to do in front of the camera. A blank space empties my mind of everything else around me. I zone in completely on the task at hand, as though this is the only thing I ever want to do. I am made for the camera. My whole body tingles. I feel my lips vibrate as I speak even though I have no idea what I am saying.

When I get stuck, Raj gives me cues on what to say. All I have to do is follow his direction. It is a bit like a dance where he is steering and I simply follow his lead. He has a way of effortlessly getting me to do exactly what he wants.

When we are done I feel faint and have to sit down on the beach for a moment. Raj passes me a fresh coconut that he buys from a local vendor. I dig my feet into the fine beach sand and inhale the coconut water through a yellow plastic straw. It takes a while until I reconnect with being present in the moment, on the beach, in my body.

He watches his take while I finish my drink. "You are enchanting and playful and find exactly the right words to entertain the audience. You're a natural, Poppie. Yesterday was just a bad take. You'll catch on. Don't worry."

WE DECIDE TO DRESS UP AND CELEBRATE the end of our filming with a real pizza and a glass of wine. Our own little wrap party for two. It is not quite Nuy wine, of course—but still a welcome change from our indulgence into Asian-only flavours and delicacies.

On our way to pick up the takeaway from the only Italian restaurant in Karon, Raj stops in his tracks and points. "Poppie! Look!"

I gaze up. It is as though his finger has waved a magic wand and hundreds of tiny stars are twinkling in the twilight around the tropical bushes that line our way.

First amazement, then disbelief, fills me. "Are they fairies?" I ask as I notice that the stars are fluttering.

"Fireflies—but, if you ever needed proof of the existence of fairies, then this is as close as you'll get," says Raj, as we walk closer.

"They do exist."

I stop and stare in wonder. Close up, they are as twinkly and sparkly and beautiful as they are from far away. It is what I always thought fairies would look like. Delicate wings, with a scintillating colour—in this case, an almost electrical shade of green.

"Perhaps this is where fairy tales come from." I think of my lost childhood friend, Audrey, and imagine her shining amongst the flutter of wings.

I hear her voice in the back of my mind. "Be careful," she says. It is almost as if I could turn around and see her. "Any role you play takes you away from yourself. That can even be good for a while, but you have to be able to come back to what is true about yourself." It sounds like a riddle. Audrey always knew more about life than me.

When we pick up our pizza, it is already cold. Not that it matters. We are fed to the brim with enchantment.

At home, I pour each of us a glass of Sangiovese Bianco, an

Italian white wine that we found at the supermarket. It is so pale that it looks almost powdery in the glass. It smells of violets and vanilla. We make a silent toast and sip on the refreshing, fruity wine before getting into bed with his laptop and the rest of our movies.

"WHY DON'T YOU JOIN ME AT THE VIDEO STORE?" Raj is as convincing as can be the next morning. "They are so nice over there. I would like you to meet them."

"Why not?" I pull on a loose cotton dress, the colour of pineapple.

On the way, we stop at Nalan and Montri's shop to have fried noodles with beef and basil for breakfast. I add lots of chilli and sweet vinegar. It is one of my favourite Thai meals. Everything is served with a big plate of fresh leaves—herbs and tiny eggplant and whatever fresh greens are available. It helps to neutralise the abundance of chilli.

Later, we stroll along to the video shop hand in hand. We stop here and there to look at silk shops, or buy freshly-squeezed jackfruit juice garnished with orchids, from the street food stands. It is the best feeling to just be happy with someone who loves me the way I am.

"Here it is." Raj pulls me down an alley in between the tourist stores.

He says "Hi" to an elderly man sitting around on the steps. The man gets up and looks at me questioningly.

"It's cool, she's with me," says Raj, "she's fine."

The man nods and starts walking further down the alley. Raj follows and pulls me along. When I resist, he gently continues to pull me along.

"Raj, what's this?" I ask.

"Aw, Poppie, just relax," he tries to coax me. "We're going to the video place."

The tiny street looks dirty and it feels dodgy. "Here? Why not in a normal shop?"

Raj laughs from his belly and looks at me like I am overreacting. "Just come along, Poppie, you'll see."

The guy walking in front of us stops and turns around. He looks annoyed that we are so slow. Mainly he looks annoyed with me.

Raj takes my hand. "Poppie, I really want you to come along. We're almost there."

I reluctantly take a few more steps and then the guy heads into a door on the right. There is no store sign on the building. It looks like a normal house. I look at Raj with big eyes. He smiles and holds my hand a little tighter. We go through the door and follow the man up a narrow flight of stairs into a small room. I am startled as the man closes the door behind us. Raj gives me a comforting smile.

I slowly become aware of a tiny room. There is not a lot of light, so it takes a moment for my eyes to adjust. On the walls are shelves with all kinds of bootleg Hollywood movies and porn DVDs. They go all round.

The man who brought us up here is looking toward a frail teenage-looking boy sitting on a crate on the floor. He gets up and talks with the older man in Thai. They seem to be arguing about me. The older man looks me up and down, measuring up the pros and cons of my every curve. The young man looks at Raj accusingly.

"Oh, no, don't worry;" Raj says as he reaches out to the young boy and holds his arm with an intense tenderness that makes me feel violently jealous. "She's here with me, she's cool."

The boy visibly relaxes into his touch. Raj giggles and beckons me to come closer.

I look away and then turn around toward the blockbuster DVDs behind me. It is not that I am interested in these films, but I need a moment to think. Something in this room is grabbing at my throat and tightening my chest. I want to get out as fast as possible. There is too much familiarity in the way that Raj and that boy are touching each other. It is always my first reaction to escape when I do not like what I see. I want to run away and never return. I want to walk into the ocean and drown myself.

However, I do not want to make a scene. I take a deep breath. Then I take one of the DVDs down from the shelf and pretend to be reading the back cover, something about a thirsty sailor. All the while I am thinking that I might be here in the same room with Raj's lover. At least that is what it looks like to me. If I have to gauge by how tenderly he is touching that boy, I am quite sure that I am right. The sense that Raj is not faithful and that he has intimate needs that I will never be able to meet as a woman, shatters my love bubble. If I think that what we have is something honest and safe, I am so wrong.

I want to leave, but Raj has the key to our apartment and my return flight ticket. I have no access to money and am, therefore, fully reliant on him to take care of me until we get back to Cape Town. I have to pretend that nothing is wrong, at least for now. I focus on my breathing. I can pretend. I can do this. I can do this well. I pretend to look at a few more DVDs before I turn back around. Raj is now gently stroking the boy's arm.

When I see how the Thai boy in the video shop looks at Raj, the strange feeling hovering over me suddenly slips down my spine—a barely-there crawly touch of a spider spinning a trap. Raj starts tittering like a little girl. We stay for ages and I can barely focus on the films we want to buy while trying to figure out the vibe in the room.

When Raj tries to pull me close with himself and the young boy, I jerk myself free and head for the door. It is locked. When I turn around, the older Thai man is holding up his mobile phone, showing me pornographic photos of the boy, mere inches from my face. There are photos of him with men, with women, with men and women. I smack at the phone, but he does not budge. He is stronger than he looks.

Then I recognise someone in the next photo. "Wait. Go back. That's Don? My old boss at the restaurant ..."

The Thai man holds up the photo of Don once more and I look past him towards Raj.

"Don't look so serious, puppet. That's an old photo. Don is no longer involved." He laughs. "I had to take all his stuff down. A rich housewife in Camps Bay is now renting him exclusively. He is getting paid, a lot, for that."

"Raj," I plead across the room. "I want to go. Please, let me go."

Raj laughs and winks at me teasingly. "Come on, Poppie. I thought we could make a video of you and the boy. I filmed a lot of Don's waitresses. It's good fun and good money."

"You must be joking, right?" I look at Raj and soon my resolve softens. I do feel the stirrings of love for him.

He takes two steps back and slides a shelf of DVDs out of the way. There is a door behind it. The Thai man nods and gets his keys out to unlock and open the door. It leads to a small room. From where I stand, I can see a neatly-made bed and a tripod, already set up with camera equipment. Raj keeps his eyes on me, trying to pull my strings.

My heart wants to make him happy, but I am unable to move.

I try to think about it, to convince myself, but my mind is a sea sponge.

All eyes are fixated on me now. "Raj, I need air, please let me out."

He nods to the Thai man, who then unlocks the door we first came through and walks me out through the alleys and onto the main street. I no longer notice the day's bustle. Unsure what to do, I wait a while. Raj does not follow. I hang around in the area, pretending to look at stores and hoping to catch him when he gets out, but he does not appear.

So much for love.

WEEKS GO BY BEFORE WE TALK ABOUT IT.

"… but I swear I've only ever been with guys since we're together, Poppie," says Raj. "I would never cheat on you with another woman. It's a side business, there's good money in porn. I wouldn't mind if you want to play with some of the guys, or girls for that matter. You would look great in a porn video, Poppie. We can make loads of cash."

On Christmas Eve, he pulls out a broken seashell from his pocket and plays with it nervously. It is shaped like a smooth ring, neatly polished by the ocean. Raj takes my left hand and tries it on to my finger. "We can get married, Poppie. Let's get married. We can have kids, buy a house. We can do anything we want. I will be loyal to you as my woman. Just let me have this bit of fun …"

The seashell gets stuck on the tip of my pinkie finger. It has an irregular shape which prevents it from going any further. My throat feels thick and I struggle to swallow my green papaya salad.

"It doesn't fit, Raj. I'm sorry." I pull the shell from my finger. I will not be kept. Not like this. On Kata Beach, across the road from the restaurant, people are lighting lanterns and sending them off into the sky, where they float peacefully across the ocean.

I watch the emotion on Raj's face as he fights with himself. He does love me, but he cannot have an exclusive relationship. He loves porn and money more. I should have known. Our relationship is hardly sexual. We are more like best friends. I am not into porn or looking for a variety of lovers, or the excitement of trying out sex with different cultures. I just want one love. I am happy with my Raj. Why does he need more than me?

"Actually I thought …" Raj continues, "I thought that we could get married and still have playthings on the side. I thought that maybe you would like the boy too."

"What?" I vent. "You mean, you thought you could be my pimp? Pawn me off to Thai boys for some extra cash?"

"Yes. I mean, no," he stutters. "No, I just thought that maybe we could have some fun together. You are an open, sensitive person and so is he. I love you, Poppie. I don't want to lie to you, so I thought then I might as well include you. He is a very popular porn artist and we were going to shoot a video together. I wanted you to meet him first, that's all."

"I'm sorry, Raj. This will never work," I say, "Let me go back home to Cape Town."

"Many women have a price, Poppie. Certainly many of Don's waitresses do. You obviously don't even know what extra services they offer the restaurant patrons for tips. You're so different from the others. You're special."

On the day we leave Karon to go to the airport, he takes his time to go and say goodbye to the video boy. As I do not want to end the trip with bad memories, I push it away. I bury it under the tropical beach sand to deal with maybe never. I take a walk along the ocean, a last moment to take wonder in a few seashells. I hold a big cowry to my ear and listen to its hollow sound. That is me. I am not that much different to a seashell. My body and mind feels increasingly separate and there is a growing vacuum inside me.

I dip my feet in the translucent sea, wave goodbye to the rustic wooden fishing boats which are anchored in the bay and take the time to breathe in deeply and smell the frangipani scent wafting on the ocean air. I inhale until it fills all the spaces in my soul.

Tropical flowers give their fragrance freely. No matter if you are good or bad. Most people choose to give only when others deserve it, or suffer for their reward. Or when they have worked for it and earned it. Or when they can get something in return. Flowers are not like that. They create happiness for others as if it were their own. Without being judgemental of character. Without expecting anything. Without strain or stress or fear or any sense of loss. It is the simple act of being–beautiful. Sharing their true nature perfumes the air with joy. No matter what happens around them. No matter if you are sick or sad. I breathe in the fragrance until it becomes a part of me. Until it cleanses me.

I wish I could love Raj like a tropical flower, but I can not. I do love him. I just do not want him to touch me anymore. He is no longer a safe place to be beautiful. I wish I were a mermaid–that my drowned spirit would reveal its deepest power to me. Instead, I feel as shut as a sick clam.

I snooze with my head on Rajit's shoulder all the way back to Cape Town in the plane. He did not only break my heart. He also gave me an important gift. He helped me to see that I can be beautiful on camera. For a moment, I wonder if I can try to make a transition into porn, but I keep hitting a personal boundary that I am only just getting to know. As long as I keep snoozing, I am fine. Snoozing is the only safe place. Not sleep. I do not want to fall asleep. That is where nightmares hide.

"It's not your fault that you're hollow, Poppie." The voice comes out of nowhere.

I straighten up with a jolt and look around. I could swear that was Audrey's voice, but there is only a plane full of strangers. There is a glint in the plane window though as I lay back down on Raj's comfortable shoulder. I keep my eyes open and I am sure that I see her reflection reaching for me.

"It's not your fault, but you have to try and find as many pieces of yourself as you can. The more whole you are, the less bad things will happen."

I HAVE NOT LOOKED AT MYSELF IN THE MIRROR properly for months. I look different. It is a kind of feeling of displacement that strings me out. There is a power in endings. My henna is growing out, my ends need a trim. My body tells me when it is time to change. My limbs are moving in a different way, or not at all. My gestures are transformed. I am no longer who I used to be. The more I look, the more I know. It is time for another new beginning.

This time I choose highlights and fashionable, rock-chic layers in my hair. A new look for a new life chapter, whatever that may be. Wherever it will take me.

The Trophy

September 1994, Springbok, South Africa

I ALREADY KNOW. THE WAY MEN LOOK AT ME only means trouble. I notice with big eyes how the contours of my body blow up in the mirror at my ballet class, as though my lean child's figure is slowly filling out with hot air. Today, a busty blonde airhead smiles back from my reflection, dressed in a pink leotard. She knows too—and she likes it.

It is almost time for my thirteenth birthday and I have been attending Miss Blom's ballet classes twice a week since I was eight. By far the tallest in the group, I am also the first to develop my female curves. It is embarrassing when the girls point and whisper my way.

I look away from the mirror, shaking with horror, as I move my right hand into second position. It is dreadful getting breasts because it puts my body so much in focus, that I feel the person I am disappear behind it. Hopefully, they will deflate as soon as the heat of the day dissipates. Then I can feel like myself again. If bodies grow, then maybe they can shrink too. I try to hide my curves by changing my posture ever so slightly.

"Don't slouch, Poppie," commands Miss Blom in a warm, breathy voice, as she sweeps up behind me while I am doing pliés at the barre. She is a physically strong yet filigree woman, with the ability to glide across the school hall as quietly as a cat. I never know that she is standing behind me until she starts to speak. With one hand she holds my lower back and gently pulls up my shoulders with the other.

"Chest forward," she says, as I straighten up. "That's your power right there. Don't hide your power."

I wonder how my chest can be my power when it makes me feel so insecure. I am more afraid of this so-called power than anything, so I do not dare to ask.

Miss Blom pushes down on my shoulders. "Now relax here, just release all the tension. Always keep your head as high as possible, don't lose the length. That's right—soft arms, soft shoulders. That's your grace."

I feel clumsy, not graceful at all. Why she is always picking on me?

"Lovelies, time's up!" These are the sweetest words.

Finally.

I feel as though I am made of wax. Even with the windows open, I am melting.

"That's it for today, girls," says Miss Blom, while moving into a fast yet elegant curtsy. "Now remember to keep your chins up! See you next time."

Miss Blom's surname means "flower" in Afrikaans-Dutch language. It suits her, because when she smiles at the end of class, her heart opens up like a Namaqualand daisy turning its petals to the sun. We return the curtsy, one foot in front of the other, a short bend at the knees—and send flamboyant air kisses toward Miss Blom, who loves receiving them.

"Thank you, thank you, thank you, girls." She beams.

I immediately take the pins out of my hair and shake it free as I walk to the girls' locker room. My fast-forward movement creates a stir in the dry air and the sweat instantly evaporates from my scalp as my hair loosens. In the changing room, two girls behind me whisper and giggle in their voile tutus, glancing my way. They are small, cute, and popular. I do not waste time getting out of my leotard, but just throw on a yellow crop top and denim shorts so I can finish and go.

When the scene repeats itself outside, I have a déjà-vu. The two girls from class pass me on their way down the steps where I am waiting under the shade of the tin roof for my mom to pick me up. This time they are talking loud enough for me to hear.

"Ah, the dirty blonde again," says the one.

"Probably bleached. I've heard she's done it with almost everyone," says the other with a smirk.

Leather pendants and beaded bracelets chime as they move along in their matching tie-dye shirts and lace-up shoes. No wonder they take so long to get ready.

The words prick at my heart, yet I do not understand exactly what they mean. Their giggles follow me, as though I am being attacked by a hive of bees. I flare with pain inside, but do not show it. I have already learned how to push away uncomfortable feelings and pretend that nothing bad is happening.

Their attention turns from me toward the school driveway, where a boy is cycling past the bottom of the stairs. He hums and throws back his messy head of copper curls as he glances up the stairs toward me. The guy circles around and passes by again, doing wheelies. When he comes back the third time, he winks at me and starts head banging. The humming becomes louder until I can hear him singing the chorus from a rock song about a certain "she" who has got "that look".

The girls from ballet roll their eyes at me. I cringe and wish myself away. Now they will hate me even more. They point and giggle in jealous amusement, making a fool of me. I do not even know the guy's name. When I continue to ignore him, he moves toward a corner of the parking lot where the girls are hanging around to see what happens. They seem up to giving him more attention than me. I am relieved that the focus is off me finally. Soon, the three of them disappear around the bend in a burst of laughter, but not without looking back one last time to stick out their tongues and make rude faces at me.

Today, the air is not moving. Not even when I turn my head. I look away from their haughty laughter, out across the rock garden that displays a kaleidoscope of rare local succulent flowers and, beyond that, the Namaqualand High sports fields. The stony hill in the background where I live looks like a paper cutout in the visible heat. My mom says Springbok is one of the hottest towns in South Africa. She cannot stand the warm weather, but she has no problem leaving me here to sweat.

Where is she? Why does she have to be late again today?

Thirty minutes later, my mom pulls up in a flash of silver on tar. Besides the sound of her spinning tires, the grounds are now desolate, if not for a few sonbesies, an extremely well-camouflaged type of cicada, chirping loudly in the summer mirage.

How could she do this to me on the hottest day of the year?

"Jump in, Poppie," says my mom as I open the door to her full-blast-air-conditioned and cream leather island of fun. "We're going shopping."

Two guards with guns are stationed at the school gates. They nod and raise the boom to let us out. Everyone thinks there is going to be war. That is why I am not allowed to walk home anymore. It is because we have brown girls in our school—this week for the first time. During break time, they get stared at as they sit under the pepper tree, away from us. I want to talk to them, but I do not dare to break the invisible divide. At least not for now.

My mom looks at me conspiringly. "How are things going with the new kids in school, Poppie? They're already starting to cause trouble, right? Tell me, hmm …?"

I sigh. "Mom, what's the big deal? They have the same skin colour as Audrey. I wish Audrey could come to school with me too."

"We've spoken about this, Poppie," my mom says sternly. "Audrey belongs in a different school. Anyway, Audrey and her mom might be moving out soon. I want to do something different with that part of the garden."

We pass the Klipkerk, the stone church where I go with my parents on a Sunday. I throw my eyes up at the façade, carefully constructed by stone masons in the 1920s. "Mom, Audrey and I grew up together. Audrey and her mom have lived with us since I was born. They're part of the family. They've only ever been good to us."

"Now, that's taking it too far." My mom shakes her head and starts to look for a parking space. Her blonde shoulder-length bob swings from side to side. "They're not our people. You need to stick with your own kind. You hear me?"

I do not respond.

My mom slows the car right down and turns to look at me. "Poppie. You. Need to stay away. From those people."

I look her straight in the eye. She just does not understand that my love for Audrey stretches across the political divide. "What people, Mom? Aren't we all just people?"

She turns her attention back to the steering wheel. "Don't try to act all smart now. You know exactly what I mean."

"Ha ah," I insist. "I don't understand. Why?"

Clouds of heat and dust collect as we swerve around a pothole. "They are not one of us."

"Why?" I look away toward the quiver trees that dot the road. "Audrey is my friend!"

"Stop asking so many questions now, Poppie. Listen to me and stay away from them. Full stop."

My mom lies in the sun all day covered in tanning oil and then tells me that I should not have friends with brown skin. How am I supposed to understand?

I turn up the radio as we make a U-turn to park along the other side of the road. They are talking about Nelson Mandela's inauguration as the President of South Africa. Everyone seems to think that the regime change is a big thing, but from my perspective, nothing is different, except for my mom's sudden fear of "those people". She listens with her mouth open until the news report is over, then she takes a moment to touch up her lipstick in the rearview mirror.

"What?" she says, as she studies my face. "It's about time we get you some makeup too! You're starting to look a little pale."

I quietly follow my mom through the only big supermarket in town. She bats her long lashes and smiles at the schoolboys who look right past her toward me. For a moment, she slows down her pace, as though she took a punch. "He's handsome, Poppie, but he's looking at you? I'm used to guys looking at me."

I slouch in an attempt to draw less attention. My stomach feels empty although I am not hungry. I have let her down. She looks even more beautiful today in one of my dresses. She is tiny enough to fit into anything from my wardrobe.

"That's it; I'm going on a diet," she says, distraught. My mom is always on a diet, somewhere between binging and starving—never, ever allowing herself to weigh more than fifty-four kilograms.

I rub my eyes and feel my mood shift away from the discomfort of the moment. I linger at the magazine stand as my mom marches further through the supermarket. It would be easy to find her again. I just have to listen for the confident clicking of her heels.

There is nothing quite like disappearing into a magazine, with its visual stories of exotic locations and glamour. It is the best solution for slipping away out of the present and into the fantasy of an idyllic life.

One photograph in the back of a woman's glossy grabs me: a tower of lights reaches high above an artistically sculpted old city and points upwards toward the stars. In the foreground a couple dances in front of a river, the red dress of the lady making ripples as it turns. The story celebrates how the end of apartheid allows for sanctions against South Africa to be lifted. The world is, once again, open to South African tourists. It shows possible itineraries for all-inclusive European tours. The title of my favourite photo says: *Enchantment evermore at the Eiffel Tower in Paris.*

Paris. It must be somewhere on the other side of the world. I wish I could be as full of light as this Eiffel Tower. In this picture, everything is in harmony: not only the light and architecture, but also the colours of dusk and the reflections on the river below. Nobody I know has ever been to Paris, or anywhere abroad. Most people have not even been to Cape Town. I hope I will not grow up to be like most people.

"Poppie, what are you doing? Come and help me with the groceries!" my mom interrupts.

I switch back from my daydream and help my mom push the supermarket trolley full of packed plastic bags. As soon as we have put the groceries in the car (she is stocking up on tinned food and breakfast cereal for the apparently impending war), my mom looks at me pensively.

Suddenly, she shrieks excitedly and pushes the trolley aside. "Come on, we are going back. I want to get you something."

"But, Mom," I complain, "I want to go home." If this is going to take much longer I will miss seeing Audrey at our secret meeting place behind the house.

My mom locks the car and turns around, back toward the shopping area. I shuffle along behind her. As we pass the entrance, the police pull a familiar-looking man to the side. The man is excessively nervous and moves away fast, arms and legs flailing aggressively, as though he is a red roman, one of those fiery, rat-like, ten-legged local creatures that race after human shadows. He is giving the policemen the same kind of creeps, judging by the looks on their faces as they start beating at him wildly.

"Mom!" I point in their direction. "Look, we have to help that guy. Isn't it Audrey's mom's boyfriend that they're hitting?"

"That's none of our business, Poppie." She drags on my arm and walks very fast. Clearly there will be no further discussion about this.

It is no surprise that we end up in a fashion chain store. Clothes shopping is my mom's favourite pastime. This may turn into a long afternoon. I am surprised when she does not stop to look at the new collection, or the latest offers. She does not even demand that I try on some of the latest trends for teenagers and model them around the store.

Instead, she keeps going, past the shoes and socks to the

underwear section. It happens too quickly for me to register how she eyes my small breasts, admiring them as though they are pert rosebuds ready to bloom—and finds the right size in a silky fabric decorated with a silver charm.

She hands me the bra. "I thought you were just getting fat, but maybe it's time to try this."

I am not ready. I think about those magazines full of naked girls next to the lavatory in our house and about the floozy I see when I look in the mirror. The tears come gushing as though I have two open taps on my face.

"You're a teenager now." She ignores my distress. "Who do you think you are to walk around like that without a bra?"

She treats it like some sort of ceremony, touching the immaculate selection of silk lingerie as though they are something magical, her manicured fingers running slowly over the trimmings. She has perfectly sculpted, tanned arms that end with a golden ring on every finger. The best one is the giant diamond that she got when she married my dad. The light pirouettes through it and reflects all the colours of a rainbow. It sparkles even here, in the fluorescent light of the store. If I could just vanish into that light.

"Poppie!" My mom's voice brings me back into the moment. "Stop crying now. A woman's body is the most beautiful thing on Earth."

I am not impressed. I pout and refuse to take anything in lace or silk.

"So what will you take then ... Choose something. Don't be like that!"

Pop music blares over the loudspeakers in the shop. It is a rock song about the girl who has that "look"—the one the wheelie guy sings when he head-bangs past me on his bicycle. Why is it important what a woman looks like? What is the right look?

I do not want to be confined to the outline of my body. I

do not want to celebrate my breasts, and I do not want to look attractive. Therefore, I decide on the ugliest thing I can find. A sports bra. If I am forced to choose something, I will rather take something practical, rather than something pretty. It helps to take the emotion out of the moment.

My mother is horrified and is no doubt deeply disappointed that this is not such a "special" experience as she hoped it would be. The rest of our day will be spent with us both quietly sulking.

"Your luscious lips will stay in that pout forever if you don't relax, Poppie … Trust me; you don't want to be spending lots of extra money on anti-ageing creams later in your life just because you were a grumpy teenager." She pays with my dad's credit card and we get to head home at last.

I really want to see Audrey.

"On that note, we should think about getting you some cosmetics next time. You could do with a little colour in your face." I keep quiet as my mom reiterates her statement by revving the luxury sedan all the way up the rocky hill to our house in Berg Street.

I cannot find the words to speak, to say that I am not ready. My body has yet to show the slightest sign of monthly bleeding, yet I am already fully equipped with sanitary items. Now I also have a bra and by the sounds of it I will soon have cosmetics too. In the face of her excitement, I refuse to show my despair at the thought of becoming a woman. From what I have seen so far, there is nothing to look forward to.

WHEN WE GET HOME, MY DAD IS BACK IN HIS STUDY, preparing camera equipment for our flower-watching trip. Spring is the only two weeks in the year when he takes the time to drive us out into the countryside for a picnic, instead of working on weekends.

"Where are my spare rolls of film?" he belts out as he hears us coming in.

In the background, he is violently opening and closing drawers and banging things on his study desk. I make sure to stay out of his way. If I stay scarce and refrain from speaking when he is on edge, I can usually stay out of danger. I do not know what is right and wrong around him, so it is easier to disappear. Almost anything can set him off. The last thing I want is for him to cancel the trip.

I sneak out of the kitchen door at the back of the house and meet Audrey at our small cave in the stony hill behind our house. The aloe bush almost covers the whole entrance of the cave, but we are both skinny enough to slip in behind it without getting hurt.

Audrey is delighted. "I heard your parents' car pull into the garage and I knew you would be coming to see me here!"

She has a small bruise on her forehead. On closer inspection, it is bulging and blue and swollen, but that is not so easy to see against her seal-coloured skin. Audrey's mom always tells us that the skins of the Cape fur seals in Port Nolloth are rare and valuable. I like how they shine.

"Eish," says Audrey and then, "Oh, that ..." She notices me leaning forward to get a closer look at her. "My mom's boyfriend tried to get it on with me again."

"No!" Perhaps he deserves getting beaten up by the police at the supermarket after all. He is more than scary looking, he is actually dangerous.

"Not a red roman then," I think out loud, "but a tarantula."

Audrey gets it, but she pretends to yawn and makes a bored face. "I'm scared of him, but I don't want to think about it anymore now. Come on; tell me about your day."

Her golden eyes are full of expectation. She goes to a different school than me and she does not like it there. She has been waiting around for my stories all afternoon while fighting off the boyfriend, it seems. Audrey and I have been through trouble with her mom's boyfriends. It connects us, knowing each other's pain. No one else can understand what we have been through.

I tell her about the mean girls at the ballet class and the guy showing off on his bike. She listens intensely.

"Yoh," Audrey says as she sees my tears, "you are so innocent and still people hate you. Ai, I just don't get it."

Audrey is my friend. She is the only one who gets how sensitive I am. She puts her arm around my shoulder and we sit in silence for a while until I am cried out.

"Poppie, your dad was screaming at my mom today." Audrey speaks slowly as soon as I stop shaking. "He said that we have to leave here forever and slammed our door so hard, Poppie. Yoh, it vibrated in the frame for quite a long time afterwards."

"I'm sure he is just angry that my mom said you have to move out," I say. "You know how he is, he overreacts. Hopefully everyone will calm down soon."

Audrey's eyes widen and then she winces. "My mom, she was crying a lot. I have never seen her crying like that before. She cried on my shoulder. Poppie, she said to me that she loves your dad."

The light starts changing to a dim orange colour outside the cave. Inside me something changes too, the twilight of a realisation that things are not as they seem to be.

I shift my weight. "Oh, please! What about my mom? Come on, Audrey, we have to go back before it gets dark."

We both nod and start getting up to leave. I take her hand to help her up and we both smile broadly.

"Audrey, I think my dad only loves abalone." I make light of it as we wiggle ourselves out behind the aloe bush. "All he ever talks about is his next diving trip."

We burst into a mad giggle and rush back to the house together, skidding on the stones and succulents here and there as we race. The sun is already down, but it is still fairly light outside. The sky is turning indigo and the Evening Star is out. It is a soothing time of day, when it is getting cooler and the light is softer, but the night has not yet fallen. We get to the bottom of the hill at almost the same time.

"I win!" Audrey says proudly.

"You've always been faster than me!" I do not mind giving her the credit.

We are both heaving, all red-cheeked, at the last heat of the day.

"Oh, now I've got the headbanger guy's rock song stuck in my head, Audrey," I shake my head. "It's so annoying!"

Audrey giggles. "Having a song stuck in your head is better than having no song at all."

We jump over the wall at the back of the house and Audrey and I go our separate ways. Her face glistens with tiny pearls of sweat that catch the last light of day as she waves goodbye. Audrey goes to her mom's room at the back of the garden and I continue further through the yard and sneak quietly back into the house.

BACK IN OUR BITTERSWEET-ORANGE-LAMINATE KITCHEN, I quickly make myself useful and help my mom to prepare chicken mayo sandwiches with wholewheat bread for my dad, and cheese and tomato sandwiches with normal toasted bread for us. We wrap this in foil and pack it into the fridge, ready for our road trip tomorrow.

"Mom, can Audrey join us for the flower-watching?" I ask when we are done and try to anticipate some of her usual excuses. "It's the weekend, she doesn't have to do any homework."

"No." My mom makes a whacking movement with her hand, as though I am a fly getting in the way of her preparing our evening meal.

"Why not?" I stare at the faded orange kitchen cupboards and wonder why someone would choose that colour for anything, really.

My mom stops what she's doing on the plastic kitchen counter and looks straight at me. "Because I said so."

"But, Mom," I keep trying, bobbling my knees in frustration and anticipation of that small chance that she might change her mind at the last minute. "Audrey is like my sister. Why can she never join us when we go out?"

My mom lifts her left eyebrow. "Poppie, listen to me. Audrey is not your sister. She's not. End of discussion."

I barely pick at my food during our wordless family dinner. The clinkering of knives and forks dominates as I quietly mash up my gem squash and move a few pieces of flaked fish and potato around on my plate, revealing the flowers below.

Then I try to excuse myself.

"You're not getting up from the table until you finish your food," says my dad as I start pushing back my chair.

I know it is his last word. I do not want to risk any trouble, so I force as much as I can down my throat and hide the rest of it by turning over my half-eaten gem squash. Then I leave the table quickly before either of my parents can notice that I am cheating.

From my bedroom, I hear my mom and dad fighting. They are not talking about the obvious issue but about Lena's boyfriend being arrested. The tone of the conversation turns down to an aggressive hush when they get to the topic of war.

"He may be hurting Audrey, but could he start a war, Shadow?" I ask my cat as she jumps onto my bed with a purr. Shadow ignores me flat. She paws away at my feet until she finds the perfect spot to fall asleep, draped over me like a heavy blanket. Her deep breathing is comforting and lulls me into dreamland where all is calm.

THE NEXT MORNING I WAKE TO THE SOUND of what I imagine to be bullets, at my bedroom door. For a few moments, I am not sure what is going on or where I am.

"Poppie, it's time to wake up!" My dad's voice resonates with the kind of military tone that I know from the TV series that he likes to watch.

My dad is banging hard on my bedroom door, bringing me back from a dream. Shadow is doing an annoyed cat stretch.

I, too, uncurl from my fright. "Yep, Dad, I'm awake. You can stop breaking down the door now!"

I get ready as fast as I can and boil the kettle to make chicory coffee with milk and sugar. My dad does not thank me when I present him with a stirred cup. We sit together at the kitchen table without talking. I watch him run his knuckles over his short beard while he pages through the newspaper with his thumb and forefinger. Then he gets up to pack the car.

It is a fresh, cool morning and we head out with the windows open. The crisp dawn makes the heat of the day so much more bearable. We drive past a police roadblock as we go out of town. The officer gives us a jolly smile and waves us through. We continue on to wide patches of African daisies, a lone kameeldoring tree and splashes of colour as far as the eye can see. A wind pump stands ready to churn water from the dry earth, but there is no wind today.

Spring is almost over now. It is my most-loved time of year, when the flat, half-desert landscape of the barren Northern Cape transforms into fields of bright orange gousblom, slimy yellow pietsnot, red, pink and purple gazania flowers, as well as thousands of other native plants and colours, all bursting out of the cracked clay after the winter rain.

A few springbuck are grazing on the flowers, not very far from the road. "Look, Poppie," says my mom excitedly. Their tails look like small paintbrushes, adding to the smorgasbord of the landscape.

Around the next bend, we happen upon my favourite sight: carpets of glittering silver flowers. They are dewy Namaqualand daisies, sparkling in the bright sunlight. In the distance, a bontebok towers above it all. The bontebok is a much bigger, more majestic buck, with sharp spiralling horns. It is uncommon to see these deer around here, but it can happen. This special moment calls for silence and awe. We stop, take the camping chairs out of the boot and sit down to have our triangle sandwiches and instant coffee with condensed milk. Apart from the odd "ah" or "wow", we do not talk. My dad is in a good mood; staying quiet keeps the peace. Afterwards, he walks away with his camera.

My mom and I collect moss, quartz gravel, twigs and wildflowers and map a small area between the rocks where we build a garden for the fairies, with quartz pathways, soft moss carpets and a flower bed. My imagination takes over and I pretend that Audrey is a fairy. I use her beloved satin-like white and purple ray florets to decorate the dream garden. They are bigger than daisies and make perfect seats or beds for the fairies to rest on in between dancing on the moss. My fairies always want to dance.

I find two *langoorleeubekkies*, nemesia flowers that look like fantastical lions with long, pearly manes, purple eye patches and big yellow jaws. These I place at each side of the garden's entrance for protection.

My mom hands me stones and flowers, but does not interfere. It is unlike her not to tell me what to do, but she simply sits next to me and lets me landscape the miniature garden my way. Occasionally, she sighs.

"Poppie, listen, when we get back Audrey won't be there anymore," my mom says while I am making a sparkling garden path out of washed quartz gravel, adding a cluster of pink flowers called *bokhorinkies*.

Though I hear her clearly, I do not understand these words. Either that or my mom misspoke. I focus on the petals of the pink *bokhorinkies* and how they twirl together into green tips, like magic horns.

"What do you mean she won't be there?"

"Well, they won't be living with us anymore," she says nonchalantly as she shifts her weight away from me.

I try to find some comfort in fiddling with the soft tendrils of a white-and-yellow succulent flower next to me, as though it is the frilled edge of a cosy blanket. "What you do mean, Mom? Where will they go?"

My mom starts getting up. "You ask too many questions, Poppie. Everything's going to be fine. Don't worry. This is best for both of you."

"Mom, I love Audrey." I jump up to follow her, dusting off my mustard yellow corduroy jeans. The truth hits me like a slap and I feel my heart muscle beating back in my chest. "She is like my sister. Why are they leaving? Where will they go?"

My mom closes her face, as though a shadow passes over it, yet there is not a cloud in the sky. "This can't be, Poppie. Audrey is not your sister. She has to go away, you're both getting older now and it's only going to cause trouble. Her mom understands that it's better this way."

"It's better? To take Audrey away from me?" I gasp.

She puts her index finger on her lips. "Shh. Poppie, stop. One day, you will understand. Just trust me right now that it's better this way."

I feel like running or screaming, as my heart makes a somersault and it feels as though my insides bounce right out of me and high up into the sky, but know I can not make a scene. It would make everything worse if my dad gets upset. Maybe someone will get hurt, or he could smash the windscreen like last time. It is always my fault. I have to make sure that I am a good girl. It is like a game, playing the pretty little good girl. This is the only way to survive.

By the time my dad gets back from his photography session, I am still physically building fairy gardens, but I am no longer present. My body is sitting with the quartz and moss and flowers, but my heart is broken and my soul has shifted out of place and away from the pain, as though I am drifting somewhere above my body. As though I am only half-alive. I sleep all the way back in the car, waking occasionally to watch the full moon rising.

When we get back from our day trip, I run to the *buitekamer* at the back of the garden. I run as fast as I can. The door is open. I go inside. The space feels emptier than anything I have known. Audrey and her mom are gone and they have left behind nothing. The bed is gone. The poster of *Psalm 13* on the wall is gone. The love is gone. It is dark and cold. God has forsaken us.

Moon, moon, can you hear my heart? Can you hear Audrey? Can you save us? If God can do anything, will he help us? Will he deliver us from evil?

IT DOES NOT FEEL AS THOUGH LIFE CAN GO ON, but it does. The days are a blur. I cry myself to sleep and wake up to the burning sunrise. For a few seconds, I forget and I think Audrey is still here—then I remember and it feels as though a part of me is missing. Audrey is my friend; the only one who understands me. I do not have a friend anymore.

My mom says no, Audrey cannot come back to live with us. I do not understand why my mom would not help Audrey. My bedroom is big enough. We can both stay here. Audrey would be safe with me. No one hears me. No one wants to listen.

At class, I tell Miss Blom about the dancers' fairy garden. Her voice echoes into the hollow places inside me. "When the fairies dance, all is in order with the world."

I would like to believe her, but that cannot be true. I do a few extra twirls across the large wooden floor as the ballet girls rush out of the school hall, so I can find a few moments alone with Miss Blom.

"Fairies don't exist, do they?" I say it as soon as I get the chance. If fairies were real, they would bring Audrey back by the power of their wands.

Miss Blom narrows her eyes and dips her chin, while keeping her neck elongated. There is pride and elegance in her stance, her neat bun completing the line of her profile. "Poppie, I'm almost forty and I still believe in fairies. Don't ever stop believing."

Something inside me stirs at the chance of hope. I cannot deny her optimism. For a moment, I hesitate, swinging from one foot to the other. Then I catch her smile. I am convinced. I want to believe and so I nod. "Yep, Miss Blom."

She looks at me with astonished curiosity. "You have a glint of magic in your eyes, Poppie. They are unusually green today. I haven't noticed that before."

Miss Blom's comment makes me panic and I look everywhere, but at her. I have speckled green-brown eyes. Sometimes, they are more brown than green. Sometimes, the other way around. My eyes change depending on my mood. It is not that strange.

Is it?

"Well," says my mom when I ask her later. "Your eyes were blue when you were born. It's no big deal. If your eye colour changes again, then don't worry about it."

Stranger things happen when I cannot sleep. I need the bathroom, urgently. On my way across the hallway, my eyes only find trouble. I notice that the night light is on in my parents' bedroom. My dad is holding a pair of scissors like a weapon, pointing at my mom. I hover to watch him cutting up her credit cards. He throws the pieces at her and grabs her by the neck. My breath gets stuck in my throat. He presses her up against the wall until she is blue in the face. Then he lets go. I can not move, but at least I am breathing again. My mom regains herself and gets into bed without making a fuss.

I wait until their light is out before I go to the bathroom and vomit. Nothing comes out. My insides are already empty.

BACK AT SCHOOL, I BARELY NOTICE how everything around me changes. Soon, I have other things to worry about. During the weekly bomb drill, someone catches the elastic at the back of my bra and pulls it. When I notice that I am trapped in his grasp, I stop. Jan Bos lets go. I pause and the strap slaps back onto my skin. It burns.

"Ha, look, Poppie is wearing a bra," he announces to his friends. I turn around to see him standing with his legs apart and his pelvis forward. He is rocking on his feet so that his copper curls make a kink in the air. Now the boys are laughing at me too. Jan has a way of sweeping the others up.

"Go, Bos!" they cheer him on. Bos is not only his name, but also local slang for "wild".

The boys calm down when the police officers walk past us with their sniffer dogs. Jan runs his hand across his head and sniggers at me. We walk outside to join the rest of the school on the sports grounds while the police do a routine bomb search in the building. The teachers take it all so seriously, but it is kind of fun. We do not have to sit in class for a while. Instead, we get to stand outside under the blazing fire in sky. I turn my face upwards towards the sun, hardly noticing the sweat dripping down my back and my legs and evaporating again into the dry air before it even hits my school socks.

I do not mention the bomb drills to my mom, but I do want to talk to her about the guys at school. She is busy revamping the room at the back of the garden into a study though and I do not find a moment. When the study is ready, she starts helping an older girl with homework after school. It is my mom's first paid gig. She needs shopping money now that she has lost her cards. There is no alternative: a life without shopping would be her own personal hell.

The student's mom comes over after the lesson and I hear my mom talking to her. "My daughter is a brilliant ballet dancer. She is so smart and talented … an overall dream child."

She goes on and on, showing me off like a trophy. "Just look at her!"

Though I am not in the room with them, there is a photograph of me strategically placed on the display cabinet in the lounge, where they are having tea out of pink porcelain cups. It is a close-up of me with a harlequin flower in the middle of a field of daisies, my blonde curls like a wildflower wreath.

"My daughter also makes these oat cookies," my mom continues to brag. "Aren't they delicious? I am so lucky with Poppie."

Truth is; I am not that great. I am another idealised accessory to her glamorous life, the same as a pretty handbag. My mom likes showing off. She has to be the centre of attention and so she uses an exaggerated image of me as a way to flatter herself.

The story quickly spreads about my mom's classes. The girl's mom knows another mom who knows Jan's mom. It is a small town. That is how loudmouthed Jan Bos pitches up a few days later for extra classes with my mom. She spends more time with him in the study than she needs to, but he does not seem to mind. He comes to the house after his lessons to visit. He could have asked me out, instead of going through my mom.

"Jislaaik," he exclaims. "I've learned more about biology in one afternoon with your mom than in my entire school career."

I wonder what exactly she is teaching him.

My mom prepares instant coffee and a plate with crunchy cookies and syrupy koeksisters. She sets it on the ebony kitchen table next to a large vase filled with clear glass marbles and a bouquet of elegant crimson-velvet tea roses and alyssum that I picked myself. Our garden fights against all the elements for those flowers: harsh sun, hardly any water—and yet, the deeply fragrant petals keep blooming, filling the whole house with the rich scent of sweet neroli and fresh honey, season after season.

"Well-well, you two. I hope that the sparks will fly in here …" she says with a wink and closes the door before I can protest.

From behind the door, she adds another word of encouragement. "If only my mom would have given me this kind of freedom with guys …" She leaves us to our own devices in the hope that romance will bloom.

Jan is three years older than me. I am not sure what he has been doing with my mom but I am not ready for what comes next. Jan takes my hand and pulls me toward him. I have been raised to be polite and obey orders, especially coming from a man. When he moves in to kiss me, his stubble pierces my delicate skin. I try to pull back, but he holds me closer, pressing his body against mine. I cannot be rude, so I smile and do nothing. It feels surreal.

He takes my hand and places it on his crotch. I do not want to but I do not object. Rather, I leave my body so that I do not have to be fully present. I understand by now that this is an expectation of a woman, not a choice.

I am not ready.

He slides his hands over my soft sunflower-printed dress, feeling my breasts and my bum; then slowly dipping his fingers under my skirt. I do not like the way he touches me—but, I do not want to be impolite so I pretend to enjoy it.

He plays with my panties and the tender lips of my vagina. I try to step back gently, but he pulls me close again with a flick of his wrist. I feel uncomfortable as he guides my hands back to his blue shorts. I can feel his penis growing hard. Jan pulls the elastic of his underwear and slips my hand inside. When I try to resist, his grip grows stronger. I am not ready for anything physical with Jan Bos. People are supposed to get married before they have sex for the first time. That is what the honeymoon is meant for, but I am still too young for that.

Shadow jumps on to the windowsill and announces herself with a purr. She watches us with an irritated swish of her tail.

Jan Bos's penis is hairy. He lets his pants slip down to the floor and folds his right hand over mine. I let him guide my hand up and down as I feel his hairy penis expanding. He pushes his middle finger in and out of my vagina, following the same rhythm. The rough bits around his fingernail scratch and tear at the soft places inside me. I want him to stop, but he forces me near and then excitedly inserts two fingers, pushing deeper and harder into my burning, sore vagina. I want to cry, but I am afraid. His muscles are tense and he does not want to let me go, so I take a deep breath and bear it. I look down toward his penis as he grips my hand real tight. It is swollen and bulging with blue veins.

When it becomes unbearable, I let the floozy in me take over. She is at least a little more enthusiastic about the whole thing.

I feel as though I am no longer in the moment, but watching myself from a distance, watching the floozy in me fulfilling his expectations. Jan Bos slides my hand up and down his thick, ugly penis, going faster and faster until he ejaculates and a disgusting white slimy fluid spills onto both his hand and mine, tainting us.

I am relieved when it is over and he pulls his fingers from my body. I am free again, but the sensation of a prickly creature inside me remains. We wash our hands in the kitchen basin next to Shadow and have a few cookies in silence. I am so embarrassed that I cannot look at him.

Jan starts visiting me often. He brings me flowers. Lilies, roses, carnations … I do not like carnations—and he is shorter than me.

I prefer daisies, simple bright daisies from the garden. These I can pick myself as they flourish in Springbok at this time of year. It brings me joy to pick daisies, whereas accepting Jan's offerings makes me suffer.

But I do not know how to say no.

My mom is delighted to have a gold medal-winning sportsman show interest in me. He is a long-distance athlete and competing on a national level. She approves of Jan's bouquets. "You're old enough now to have a boyfriend. It's time!"

"Mom, I didn't choose him," I try to explain, "I don't even like …"

"That's all right, Poppie," she interrupts, "because he chose you. The man is the one who chooses. You simply have to go with his decision and make sure that you always look nice. Don't worry, we can go shopping."

That is what all women I know do. They go shopping. They do their hair. They make themselves pretty for men. Why does it feel like a trap? Why am I the only one who does not catch on to the excitement? Why do I resent my inner vixen?

Some of my classmates come over to our house while my

parents are out. We sit around on the wrought-iron garden set and talk about secret things they have tried with guys around the sports grounds at twilight. Kissing behind the stadium, or fondling behind the trees. They want details from me too, but I do not manage the swooning and the cooing. I do not like kissing Jan Bos. The thought of the prickly creature gives me chills, but I do not see a way for myself to get out of it. I am just a woman and then there is all the social pressure. Either I have to get used to it, or I have to get away.

Instead of joining the conversation, I look away and light a cigarette from the small chocolate box where I hide them from my parents. They will not be home until late. The cigarettes are merely a prop that I prepared to impress the girls. They all want to try, looking at me in awe as they cough and giggle. I pretend to smoke, using the abalone shell on our stone terrace as an ashtray—too bad for soiling the mother-of-pearl—while we drink from water bottles laced with cane spirit. I will brush my teeth and go to bed before my parents get home and no one will know about our girls' night.

At school, Jan Bos starts calling me "Shaggy Plum" after the most well-known whorehouse in town. He laughs with his friends. They are a few years older than me.

A big guy with pimples call out to me. "Jan says you're just a 4. With me I bet you could get up to like a 7."

I pretend not to notice, but the nasty feeling burrows itself even deeper into me. I do not understand. Why is he degrading me when I am doing everything he asks for? Do I not make him happy? Am I not trying hard enough?

ONE DAY, HE BREAKS MY HYMEN WITH HIS FINGER. Just like that. In the kitchen. While my mom is watching American soap operas in the TV room with Shadow. It bleeds. I understand that something important happened. It tugs at my soul. I feel restless and angry. It is my body and I do not want Jan to break anything. Especially not him.

Jan tells all his friends at school. Both the girls and boys gossip when I pass by. He shows me off, claiming me as his and getting respect from his buddies. I am a catch. Once caught, the trophy is hung and the hunt is over. I am marked forever as Jan Bos' thing. He loses interest as soon as the glory starts fading. He has gone as far as he can push it without marrying me. More than shame, I am relieved when he stops harassing me.

My mom is disappointed when Jan stops coming around to the house. "He was so nice … You really should have a boyfriend, Poppie!"

She buys me a "nice" blue dress to wear when her new male student is around, "so he can look at you." When she brings him over to the house after class, she says, "Why don't you go and put on your new bikini, Poppie? It's a perfect day for cooling off in the pool."

Surrender is like a bad dream. A spiritual poison slowly collecting in the soul until it becomes so unbearable that the mind has to hallucinate to survive. Some things are so painful that the only option other than death is a complete escape into fantasy.

In ballet class, Miss Blom says, "Girls, you can be anything you want to be if you set your mind to it. You can create your own world."

I conjure up images of myself as an extravagant showgirl in Paris, shining among colourful lights. I am coveted and adored on a wide and well-known stage, away from greedy hands, my true beauty safely tucked away under feathers, sequins, and glitter.

"But be careful what you wish for," adds Miss Blom. Her dream came true, she says, but not in exactly the way that she wanted. "If you wish from the heart and detach yourself from the exact outcome, then your wish will come true."

The Mannequin

April 2007, Paris, France

I AM A WOMAN IN THE RIGHT PLACE AT THE RIGHT TIME. At first, it is only the odd modelling job, here and there. The castings keep going well and now I am suddenly in demand. I am taking to my new life as a high fashion runway model like a mollusk to water. It is incredible how fast things move when I am in my element. The Cape Town modelling agency believes in me enough to send me to Paris for the shows. Not only that, but I also get to be here at a famous Parisian nightclub with my new friend,

Amy, having a drink to end the day within the opulent ambience of heavy wood and soft light.

I look down at my dirty Martini and stir at it pensively. The empty crystal ashtray glistens moodily against the polished bar table.

"It feels like a dream come true," I tell Amy, as she crosses her long legs and props herself up on the bar stool. "My ex set me up for that swimsuit audition in Cape Town where I first met you and now I'm here in Paris for castings with you too, despite having no experience at all as a model."

She swoons and whisks a perfect wisp of light blonde hair from her forehead. "You're a natural, Poppie. You're gonna do well. I'm sure you'll get your gig here on the Paris catwalk. Last year, I did four shows, but my dream is to do a showstopper—I want to walk the finale in a big glamorous gown for one of my favourite designers."

I mirror Amy in raising my glass.

She makes a toast. "To you, Poppie! And to your natural flair for the catwalk!"

"And to your showstopper, Amy! Thank you," I say, "I guess I should also thank my mom for making me walk up and down the changing room aisle as a teenager during all of her shopping sprees. I was always the best-dressed girl in school. No wonder everyone hated me."

I wink. Amy giggles.

"Now you're twenty-something and they hate you because you're a model. There's always a reason."

"Yeah, you're probably right. Short women hate tall women. Brunettes hate blondes. Why don't we just all learn to love ourselves for what we have, instead of what we don't?"

"It's all about looks, my dear." She laughs. "We've simply got too much to lose to each other. That swimsuit shoot was the bitchiest I've ever been on though," Amy says as she points at me with a Kir Royale. "Competing for money and attention gets even more personal when it's about showing your body. Do you remember how cold the water was in Camps Bay? We stayed in the icy ocean so long in those skimpy bikinis, that we both had a cold afterwards. No wonder everyone was in a bad mood."

"The good thing about it is that we met." I smile and wink at Amy. "Now we can laugh about our perfectly-painted toes turning into ice blocks."

"Now, yes." She raises her glass and giggles wildly, turning several heads in our direction.

Amy is the only model I know who makes a point to listen and cares to laugh at my jokes. Even if they are not that funny. She keeps laughing, finding the humour in everything and making the time we spend together so much fun. It is my first sign of female friendship since I was a child. Not that it goes deep or anything, but still.

There is someone else in the club tonight who seems to be keen on spending time with me though. I have been noticing and deliberately ignoring his interest via the corner of my eye. Nevertheless, a big guy with voluminous short blonde hair walks up to our table and introduces himself, laughing confidently.

"I'm Heath," he says, "looking straight into my eyes, "and you're beautiful!"

He gently takes me by the fingers and plants a wet kiss on the back of my left hand.

Heath is tall and round like a bouncer, yet his body is soft, rather than muscular. Not really my type. I know in the first few seconds that he is not for me. Relatively charming, but I am already bored with the conversation when he pulls up a seat. He misses a step before he sits down and tries to flatten his hair. He must be either clumsy, or drunk, or both.

"Heath, I'm here with my friend Amy tonight. Girls' night. Okay?" I tell him.

He looks disappointed. "Can I at least have your number?"

"No." I turn to Amy without looking back and hear him walk away with heavy steps.

"Go on, Poppie, just give him your number. You're not being wooed in a city like Paris every day," Amy says, "and, besides, he's already coming back."

"No, I don't want to." I refuse, despite the smooth electro beats setting the perfect scene.

Amy gives me a look. "Well, you're never going to meet anyone ever again if you're like that."

The charming man with the big, most possibly drunken, smile walks up to me again and begs for my number on his knees. He takes my hand and kisses my fingers. For a moment, it looks like he is going to propose.

"Well well, you can have my number." I give in, if only to please Amy. "But then I'm going home. I'm tired."

He hands me a fountain pen and a small artisan notebook. I write down my number and say goodnight.

"I'm going to call you," Heath says, "tomorrow."

"I might be busy." I gather my things to go. Then I leave much too fast.

Amy calls my name as I reach the bottom of the stairs. Oops, I think, as I turn to see her waif-like figure coming down the steps with a handsome man on her arm—as I forgot to pay. She is perfectly blonde and gorgeous. He is tall and sporty. The two of them are quite a sight. A showstopper, especially within these surroundings. She did not yet get to do her dream finale on the catwalk, but take a look at her now.

I wait for them to join me on my way out. "Amy, I'll settle my part of the bill with you later."

"Heath is paying, he insisted." She lifts her eyebrows and pushes her soft pink lips into a smile.

I am flabbergasted. "Oh. Why?"

"Poppie, this is Giuseppe." She changes the subject to introduce her catch of the night. It is pretty quick, considering I only left the table minutes ago—but that is Amy. She does not waste time when it comes to collecting tall, handsome lovers.

"*Ciao*," says Giuseppe with a naughty smile.

"*Ciao*, Giuseppe." I respond with the usual European double-cheek kisses.

We all walk together to the hotel in Madeleine where Amy and I are staying for the duration of Fashion Week. It is in a central part of the old town, close to the Champs-Élysées.

Giuseppe sings Italian arias all the way through the quiet Parisian streets as we make our way slowly in the chilly early morning hours. Every now and again, he grabs Amy's hand and they dance a little and then kiss a little in some corner or another. It is incredible how the attention from this man makes her shine. The scene is so charming that I am happy to be able to take it all in, as though I am watching a live romance show. I do feel a bit like a third wheel though and leave them to practice their French kisses in private as soon as we reach the hotel.

This is Paris. The city of lights. Light is love. Love is beautiful. Beauty is a light in the heart. In the heart of my dreams … well, maybe Heath will be waiting for me there in dreamland. I am not quite convinced about him, but it is nice that someone is thinking about me anyway. In the meantime, I will be going to bed alone, thank you very much.

AMY AND I START THE NEXT DAY AT 5 AM. The early call time is just one of the downsides of this job. We are both getting ready for a casting with one of the lesser-known couturiers at the Spring/Summer shows. It would be an honour to walk at any of the shows, for that matter. Never mind the big names.

We arrange for an early breakfast package at the hotel where we giggle like teenagers over a quick chocolate croissant and coffee. She is gushing about her night with Giuseppe and I tell her that Heath sent me a *Good morning, princess* message as I woke up in my king-size hotel bed. Amy sneaks out an extra croissant for Giuseppe, who is tucked away in her room.

Besides having to get up before sunrise, we do not prepare for castings. Or even shows for that matter. Amy and I are lucky to be born with the right measurements for being catwalk models. We sometimes watch what we eat so that we can make sure to have a flat stomach–but mostly, we just pitch up on the day. Preferably not drunk. It is nice to have a friend in this kind of world where everyone is judged only on superficial things. I am happy that we can be here together. In this industry, no one cares what we have to say or who we are as people–that is not part of the job.

Couture for the world's major catwalks is painstakingly hand-crafted to a certain specified set of body measurements. These criteria set for waistlines and hips are not meant to drive women to eating disorders. I hate how people criticise the modelling industry. My natural measurements are thirty-two, twenty-five, thirty-seven and I easily maintain it by living an active lifestyle. I may not like working out, but I love to dance, it especially keeps my core muscles strong. Which is enough for now. I am still young. I started a bit too late as a model though and probably only have a short window to make the most of it. It is worth a try.

Of course, I have seen some people trying to kill themselves to fit the size requirements–but that is like trying to be an airline pilot when you simply do not have the right physical profile. Either you are a ramp model or not. The body shape for the couture catwalk is one that have been proven over time to be the most flattering shape for showing off clothing. Designers arrive from all over the world with their collection already done. They do their last auditions while simply finishing off the finer details. After months and months of hand-stitching and beading, the models are human hangers that fit the clothing and bring the design to life on the catwalk (not the other way around).

Heath arranges his entire schedule around my day and picks me up for lunch in between castings. He makes a theatrical, if somewhat clumsy, curtsy. "So, what do you want to eat, princess?"

I play along. "Well, dear sir, actually I'd love one of those warm goats' cheese salads, it's typical French. *Chèvre chaud*, I think it's called."

"Just you wait," he says, "I'll show you something even better."

Heath hitches a taxi and we get out in a tiny street close to the Notre Dame. The restaurant is simple, all dark wood and neatly-ironed tablecloths. I let him order for me.

"A glass of Champagne for the lady." He nods, more in my direction than toward the waitress.

I like that, knowing that he knows what I want. Not too much, not too little. I still have to work today. Which makes me wonder out loud. "What do you do here in Paris, Heath?"

He straightens up. "I'm in Exotic Credit Trading."

It sounds fancy. "Exotic ... what does that mean?"

"It means that I make a lot of money, Poppie. I can buy you anything you want. Why don't you stay in France longer so we can spend a few days in Champagne together? We can stay in Epernay and visit all the famous Champagne houses. What do you say?"

"That sounds like a grand offer, but let's get to know each other first. Take it slow. I don't want to rush anything."

My salad arrives masterfully plated. A circle of Tête de Moine cheese like the ruffles of a wide chiffon skirt, interspersed by endive tips packed in the shape of a star. A scatter of raisins and a few drops of dressing rounds it all off. It is so impressive that it is almost too pretty to eat. Almost too perfect.

I SOON START TO FEEL AS THOUGH I AM GLIDING in Heath's presence, as though my feet are travelling above the ground, instead of on it. He just knows how to create these exceptional experiences for me. It is the things he does for me, rather than who he is, that makes me fall for him. I am hardly able to lose the stuck smile when a casting director asks for a pissed off, or more serious, attitude during my next call.

Mostly, the floaty feeling serves me well during the castings though. Sometimes, I wait in a queue with many other girls. It is easier to pass the time when I am feeling so high. This weight-lessness is simply magical.

Other times, I am in and out of the casting room in just a few seconds. Every casting is different.

"No, not her," someone says while ironing crystals onto pieces of bright orange lace. Then I do not even have to walk any further into the room. The decision has been made at first glance. I just say thank you and leave.

Finally, I enter a classic loft-style apartment with wooden floors and big windows looking out onto a small courtyard. It is my last casting for the day. Everyone is quiet, except for the odd nervous laugh.

In front of me, an older woman with smartly-styled short hair and chunky jewellery is holding a notebook. She looks up at me.

"There, take off your jeans. I need to see your legs." The voice comes from the back of the room.

I turn to look across the floor. A man appears from behind the room divider and takes a few steps toward me, tilting his head slightly forward in order to look over the top of his thick, square-framed glasses. "I want the energy to be clean, simple; easy. Powerful."

I slip out of my faded jeans. It is not the first time I have had to undress so quickly at a casting and I can manage this without much effort. No one takes a second glance at my little pink slip. I am just a hanger to them anyway.

I take a deep breath. Head up. Mouth closed. Straight knees. Feet forward. Then I take long, swooping steps across the wide floor. Step, slide, turn—and back.

"Yes, yes, yes, you can do the second number." He starts to move back to whatever he was doing before.

For a moment, I am not sure if he wants me to have another go or what exactly he means.

He notices the confusion and looks at me forgivingly for my seeming stupidity. Then he stops briefly to get the attention of the woman who I will soon find out is his casting director.

"Can you get her down?" He waves at her, then quickly disappears again—and just like that I have a gig on the Paris catwalk. I am in and out of the room in no more than fifteen minutes.

I fall into Heath's embrace afterwards and cannot wait to tell Amy at breakfast.

"Last night Heath said that he thinks I'm 'The One'. We haven't even slept together. It's all so chivalrous and old-fashioned. We just hold hands and let the tension build between us. It's kind of sweet—and also wonderful."

Her delighted "Ooooh!" comes a little too loud for the rest of the guests in the elaborately-wallpapered breakfast room and we try to keep it down. "Who would have thought that we would both fall in love on the same modelling trip, Poppie!"

I realise that Heath may be quickly becoming more important to me than Fashion Week, but I do have further news to add to my daily check-in with Amy. "By the way, I got a gig at the Vionne show. I'm doing the second number; day after tomorrow."

"Whaaat? And you only tell me now? That's wonderful, Poppie," she swoons and flings her arms around me, "Awwww! Congratulations! Vionne … that's a great up-and-coming label. French, too! Oh, I do love their stuff."

I lean back to face her. "To be honest, I had to look at their website afterwards. It is not one of the big names and I have no idea, being such a newbie to it all. I am excited to be wearing classic couture! It is all whimsical designs, like stepping into a fairy tale."

Amy shrieks and hugs me again. "Poppie, I just knew it! I knew it that you're gonna get a gig! That's amaaazing!"

The elderly couple next to us give us another annoyed look.

"Thanks, Amy," I say sincerely. "You're my biggest fan."

Heath calls me just as our taxi leaves the hotel. "Meet me at six today at the Notre Dame. I want to take you on a grand night out. There's this little restaurant next to the Eiffel Tower and, on the way, I want to show you something. It's a surprise. I will be waiting for you as long as it takes."

"Right, see you there …" I say, caught up in the mystery, romance and intrigue of it all.

"What did he say?" Amy asks excitedly as soon as I put down the phone. She is glowing even more as I tell her about our agreed time and place. "That is soooo romaaaantic!"

"Will you see Giuseppe again?"

"Yes, I'm going to call him as soon as I'm done with my final casting this afternoon."

Later, I get a text message from Heath saying that he has to go on a last minute business trip for a few days and will not get to see me again before I have to leave Paris. I am disappointed. It all became somewhat magical really quickly and I am swept away with the enchantment of it all. The lights, the beauty; the *joie de vivre*.

I spend the evening walking down the Seine, watching as the Eiffel Tower lights up in all its sparkle. The city lights reflect in the flow of the water as I pass Pont Neuf, the oldest and most scenic bridge in the city. This is the dream. Exactly as my school ballet teacher, Miss Blom, always said; my dreams are now coming true but it does not feel the way I always imagined. There is a lot more sadness than I could have ever dreamed too. I feel as if I am a character in a movie, as though I am looking at myself from a distance. Melancholy me. Somehow perfectly out of place on this magnificent, still evening. I let the sights of Paris fill my soul. Yet the sensation of absence remains. I have not heard anything further from Heath and I wonder if I will, ever, see him again.

THE NEXT DAY I AM SITTING in a very large room with golden-textured wallpaper and thick carpets with heavy wool details. I am excited and chilling at the same time. Paris is more than I expected. One does not get to see a lot of couture collections in South Africa—fashion shows are more for entertainment there than anything else. People have the choice between going to the movies, or a fashion show. In Paris, it is all very serious. It is overwhelming how beautiful it all is and how many people are involved. The details, the time. The buildings look like dollhouses. Being here feels more like playing than doing a job.

A serious kind of playing, I wink at myself in the mirror. I love the elaborate mirrors inside these rooms.

The dedicated make-up artist from Japan is sticking rhinestone crystals on my face, while a hair stylist from London weaves many colourful little plaits into my hair. It is a kind of glamorous 70's hippie look, with jewels and flowers in the colours of the collection. The hair stylist sets the plaits into a low sort of roll and pulls out a few tendrils of hair "to create that romantic, carefree and feminine feel". In the corner of the room, one of the model's baby is happily gurgling.

I could stay forever in this moment, sitting here and getting my hair and make-up done. It is such a lovely feeling to be pampered, to be touched as though I matter. As though I am valuable and important. When I look in the mirror, I see a mysterious and glamorous woman. Deep smoky eyes, with thick eyeliner and a rhinestone teardrop catching the light between her brows. Matt rouge and lipstick. No gloss or sparkle, except for the rhinestone. It takes me a few moments to believe that this woman is me. My hair is looking so beautiful I could just cry. Not now though; there are only a few moments to go before the show.

My opalesque-cream-turquoise lace gown requires a rhinestone tattoo to be done on my skin last minute. I can feel the tension. It has to be perfect. I focus on my breathing. No one says a word. The couturier himself, Monsieur Vionne, carefully sticks the delicate crystals down my spine with a steady hand.

His assistant brings my shoes. They are too big. I feel clumsy. The dress is comfortable. But. The earrings are too heavy. And then I have to go.

I have learned how to do this, no matter what. I take long steps in the uncomfortable, unstable shoes, filled with the rush of being on the ramp. It is even better than cocaine; it is the best drug on earth. I know by now that I do not need any chemicals to get high. The blinding lights, the glamour and the energy in the room ... all eyes on me wearing this gown. Everyone is making their first comments; taking their first photos ever of this moment in time. Step, slide—wait for the camera man, turn. I feel powerful as I glide across the gilded mirrored room, with tiny little seaweed-lace tendrils hanging from my arms. I am a professional mermaid.

Who needs reality anyway? Sometimes, I feel as though I am not even quite myself on the ramp. Sometimes, I can not even remember every little detail. I feel this incredible high and then I slip into the motions. I prefer being here, far away from real life.

I live in between reality and dreams.

I live in the seams. Tucked into the edge of things. In between worlds. In between words. In between flutes of Champagne. In between lights and guest lists and uncomfortable sandals. In between seasons and in between time. In between sips of wine. In between steps and gowns and scenes; it is the pauses that are most divine. I turn to pause for the camera and the audience one more time, before disappearing backstage.

After the show, Monsieur Vionne takes the time to acknowledge me. "*Voilà, très, très bon*, Poppie!"

When he says my name it sounds more like "Puppy" than "Poppie" which is kind of cute. Vionne gives me little cheek kisses and then stands back to peek at me over the top rim of his square-framed glasses.

"Poppie, you want these?" He holds out two tickets for the last catwalk show of the week. "None of my team wants to go. Everyone's tired, or on their way out of town already."

I take the tickets before anyone else can claim them. "It would be my honour. *Merci*, Monsieur Vionne!"

He nods and then disappears just as fast as he came.

I INVITE AMY TO ATTEND WITH ME, as neither of us had a chance to see any of the shows. She also did not get any gigs this year, but, then again, it is about what is in vogue. Last year, she walked four ramp shows and this year they are looking for a different kind of look. In this industry, one certainly cannot take things like that personally.

We make the most of the chance to dress up and enjoy a night out. The venue is hidden across a quaint courtyard behind some opulent buildings. It feels as though we are discovering a secret and magical lair. The lights are dim. The guest list is limited. The show is an intriguing display of headpieces casting curious shadows on the wall. It is clear that the shadows are the main focus, rather than the real models on the ramp. The whole thing is quite theatrical. I love fashion shows for their pure extravagance.

We only have standing tickets and, by the time the show is over, I regret my choice of heels for the evening. We still have a long after-party ahead of us. Giuseppe is already waiting for us at the party venue and I have a feeling Amy is going to have a hard time saying goodbye to him when we leave for Cape Town tomorrow.

"*Mi amore*," he greets her and she blossoms.

We point out our names on the guest list and step inside with the fashionistas. I am grateful for my youth and my ability to blend in without being a threat to the who's who. Giuseppe's natural Italian style is spot on and he is charming enough to present us with two glasses of Champagne without even asking.

I make a toast to Paris.

"To beautiful moments," Amy says.

"... in Paris." Giuseppe adds.

After the first sip, Amy's face drops.

"Amy, are you okay?" I ask. Giuseppe looks confused and follows her gaze.

"That's, that's, oh no that's not possible. It's him. Yes, it is. He's here, but with someone else and he's kissing her. Poppie, it's Heath. He's here with another woman. Isn't he supposed to be away on a business trip?"

I feel something drain from the top of my head to the tip of my toes. My knees buckle and I almost collapse. Giuseppe holds me up until I regain my balance.

"Don't look, Poppie," says Amy. "He's acting like an asshole with that model."

"I need another glass of Champagne." I quickly throw back the rest of mine.

"I'll get a bottle," says Giuseppe and leaves us alone for a few moments.

"You were right, Poppie, not to want to give him your number. What an asshole," Amy says, steadying me with her arm.

I am staggered. "Well, the thing is, now I kind of, I kind of fell for him. Almost literally."

She gives me a big hug (which holds me up, as my knees are still feeling wobbly) after which I proceed to down Giuseppe's bottle of Champagne.

Amy and Giuseppe manage to change the topic, but I am going all queasy inside. Something about begging for my number and then ditching me for another woman makes me feel angry and desperate to get him back. How can he be with another model if he can have me?

"I have to go and find him," I say as they start looking deeply into each other's eyes. They vaguely notice as I head off on my Champagne-driven mission.

I walk straight up to Heath, surrounded by a crowd of women.

"Oh, there you are darling," he says in his usual nonchalant tone as he holds out his arms to me.

"I thought you were meant to be on a business trip," I snipe as he showers me with kisses all over the side of my face.

As I turn my head, I see one of the young make-up artists I met over the last few days looking at me in absolute horror. I separate myself slightly from Heath's embrace as she comes right up to me. "Poppie," she says, "this guy, he's been buying me and my friends champagne all night."

"Oh ..."

She throws in another lashing of attitude. "I hope he's not your boyfriend."

"Well, he is," I say. Then I turn to Heath and kiss him. I claim him. In kisses. In French. Kisses. Since we are, after all, in Paris.

"Get this girl a bottle of champagne," he says.

Eventually, the crowd of women dissipates. I do not let him out of my sight for the rest of the night. Later on, Amy finds me with Heath and tries to persuade me out of it. No chance. I have my heart set on having him and I am not going to give up my guy to some model, or make-up artist, or whatever.

"Heath, why are you always paying for everyone?" I ask when we leave.

"Because I can," he says.

I take him with me to my hotel, but I am so drunk on Champagne that I pass out right away.

The next time I open my eyes, he is already awake. We are in our underwear and cuddle for a while. It is nice to wake up and be close to him like that. He starts to fiddle with my underwear and we kiss a little, trying not to share too much morning breath.

As soon as we are both naked, a fat flicked-tail creature emerges from under his eyelids and pins me firmly to the bed. The sharp sensation that twists into every part of my body makes me feel desolate. A snigger rattles in my ears as the creature starts to feed on my sudden fear. I am unable to move as Heath rolls over toward me in what seems like slow motion, then quickly jumps on top of me. My chest hurts under his body weight and it pushes out my breath.

At first, I hope that Heath is only playing; that the creature is only a bad morning dream. Yet the sniggering becomes louder and then there are flashes where Heath becomes the devilish creature and others where the creature is pointing and laughing at me. I attempt to push the weight off me, but the creature is already tying up my hands, while Heath penetrates me without a condom. The whole scene is a terrible farce that could not possibly be the reality of my life. A life where I have no power. It cannot be that there is no chance for me to consent, or even think about if I want this, or if I am ready. The violence of it tears me up inside. I try to move away, but invisible cords hold me in place with an unworldly strength. A numb feeling is the only thing protecting me.

"Oh, no, no, no, no," I say as he continues to get more and more excited.

Heath continues to force himself into me, neither caring about consent, my comfort, nor my pleasure. He needs this aggressive act. His creature needs my writhing and my fear. "What is wrong, Poppie? This feels so good!"

By now tears are streaming from muffled grief. "Oh, no, oh, no, oh, no … Why are you doing this? You were meant to take me for a *grande* dinner at the Eiffel Tower."

My begging gets him there faster. Only then does he speak. "We can't go there, Poppie, because that's where I asked my wife to marry me."

The words knock me out, like a poison exploding in my head. I am naive to think that most people around the world are looking for love, or even for an exclusive partner. Never mind an exclusive marriage.

When he is done, he gets up and leaves the hotel room with a tiny flicked tail carelessly hanging out of his ear. No goodbye. Just like that.

The best way to describe what I feel is that it is like dying. My life as it is is over. Nothing would ever be the same. I cannot be the same. Something snaps inside my soul.

I feel Audrey stroking my hair while I cry and cry. "You did nothing wrong, Poppie. It's not your fault."

My heart is beating so fast. It is not adrenalin, the same way I feel it before a show. It is mad panic. "How will I ever trust anyone again? Even when someone pursues me and wants to spend all his time with me, it still doesn't mean that it's real. Look what happened to me. How can I ever look anyone in the eye again? I'm dirty. No one will ever love me. Love is a lie." Love is lying here, discarded like last season's fashion.

Audrey sighs. "Rapists are cowards, Poppie. I wish we both knew that before it was too late." Her breath is a temporary balm. "And you're not ruined. So many young women sleep around. Unconscious. Uncommitted. Under the influence. It makes you no less for being raped. No one has the right to judge you. Especially not for something that you could not control."

I CAN NO LONGER GET OUT OF BED IN THE MORNING. I go through the motions of my day-to-day without really being present, as though I am constantly being suffocated by life.

I forget appointments. I am late to castings.

One day, my agent simply says, "You had a lucky shot in Paris, Poppie, but since then you've lost your energy. Even your eyes changed. It's as though your light has gone out. Maybe you're just, basically, too old. By the way, the casting you missed was for a private airline brand shoot. Good money. You screwed up massively."

Maybe. Maybe not. I no longer fit. I want to rise above the judgement and criticism of society that wear me out. Go somewhere I can be beautiful for who I am, instead of who I pretend to be in front of the camera. I will not give up on my search.

I look up the airline and make an appointment for a different kind of casting. I want to fly away to a place where I can simply be, the real thing.

It is time to continue my journey.

The Lucky Charm

November 1995, Stellenbosch, South Africa

I AM RELIEVED WHEN MY DAD MOVES his photographic studio far away from the hot, dry town of Springbok and that guy, Jan Bos, who keeps harassing and humiliating me. We now get to live all the way in the Western Cape Winelands. Our gabled Cape-Dutch house in the quaint town of Stellenbosch has a jasmine trellis intertwined with passion fruit. It frames the edge of a large vegetable garden with a strawberry patch and a lemon tree. The scents infuse my life with a kind of spell that makes me feel supernatural.

"Oh, hell, Poppie, I wonder what's wrong with you." My mom peeks out from under her straw hat while tending to a patch of carrots, vine tomatoes and squash flowers. Besides gardening, she has nothing better to do than worry about the fact that I am having an irregular period. "We need to get you some help. I hope you're not pregnant!"

I have fantasies about running away from home. I am already seventeen. The only remains of my childhood is that numb look in my eyes, now framed by ripe pimples and the first signs of hair on my upper lip. I shake the scorched curls that reach to my waist. My hair covers up a lot of flaws, especially when I let a few strands linger on my face. "Ha ah, Mom, I don't even have a boyfriend."

She wipes her brow with the back of her jewelled wrist. Her bangles glisten in the sunlight. "Why? Why don't you have a boyfriend? It's so nice!"

"Mo-om," I protest.

Shadow twirls herself around my ankle, giving me a little squeeze. She follows me into the herb garden where I pick a bunch of lemon verbena for making tea. The scent of basil and lemon zest cheers me up, but not enough. Shadow keeps running herself against my legs and almost gets caught under my feet as I escape back into the cool kitchen. It smells of Lena's freshly baked bread.

I TRY TO MAKE FRIENDS AT SCHOOL, but they never invite me to parties. I hear the girls talking about meeting the first team rugby guys after school for sneaky swigs of local sweet wine over ice-cream—and stolen kisses under the oak trees next to the Eerste River.

The guys do not invite me either. I am too tall for most of them, but I dream about Johan. He is the goalie and also the team captain and taller than the rest. Johan is dating Lara. Everyone wants to date Lara and he is the one who gets to call her his girl-friend. Sometimes, Johan makes eyes at me and Lara does not like it. Neither do any of her friends. I think that is why no one wants to hang out with me.

I see the girls meeting in a group next to the poles where the South African flag hangs next to our Stellenbosch Valley high school flag. It feels strange getting used to a new national flag, as though the old South Africa that I grew up in no longer exists. At school, we now learn a whole new national anthem too. I like it, but I might be the only one. Most of the school kids refuse to sing the new anthem, resisting change and holding on to what is familiar instead. The new anthem starts with a prayer that will help us to belong to each other in the same way that beams of colour belong together in a rainbow. Some people do not want to belong, or maybe they already belong somewhere.

I hope that I will also have the chance to belong one day.

When the girls see me passing by, they look away. Lara, who is also the winner of the Miss High School pageant as she likes to remind everyone, whispers to the other girls. They burst out laughing. It is no doubt about me. Sometimes, I wish I could be like Lara, so cute and funny and popular. Everyone wants to be around her. Everyone wants to be her. Lara's high ponytail makes a yellow-blonde swish in the air as she looks my way and quickly turns back to continue gossiping.

I look at the mood ring on my middle finger. It is my first piece of jewellery. My mom says it is for luck. The mood ring glows orange. I open up the colour chart and read about the colour orange. It stands for being confused and upset, restless. It is a mild explanation of what I am feeling.

I miss Audrey. I want to talk to her. I am simply not whole without her, as if I can no longer fully exist since she is gone.

I am because she is. I wonder if she has a boyfriend. I wonder if I will ever see her again. A beam of orange radiates from my mood ring into the cosmos and I imagine it reaching Audrey and calling her to me.

FOR LACK OF FRIENDS, I FIND WAYS to entertain myself at home. My dearest place on the property is the rolling rose garden in front of the house. It starts with a fan of iceberg roses next to the veranda and then merges into neat little rows with all kinds of rose bushes flowering in bright pink and antique purple, burnt orange, sunshine yellow and lipstick red. The rose garden is filled with butterflies and I am fascinated by their fleeting, yet glorious beauty. I am enchanted with their colourful wings and can sit around for hours, watching them dance on air. The closest I ever get to beauty is in the anticipation of having it. I want to touch the butterflies. I want to wear them, I want to own them. I want to be them. I want to fly away with them.

I keep an empty jam jar ready as I watch a basking orange-dotted butterfly intensely until I feel the slow rhythm of its wings. When it closes its wings again, I carefully pinch them together between my index finger and my thumb. It is an extraordinary feeling to have complete control. The wings are powdery. I put the butterfly into the glass jar and quickly close the lid. It is a glorious moment, of holding and beholding beauty.

Shadow stops by, watching me and the butterflies while swishing her tail. She sits around purring, observing me with quiet admiration. It is not that easy to capture a butterfly, but I have done it.

I look at my butterfly closely and, in my own time; studying the fine patterns and colours in its wings. I could press it in my Bible as I do with pansies and then frame it behind glass so I can look at it every day. Yet I now know that capturing a butterfly does not truly gather its beauty. Holding magnificence in a jar takes away its power. A wing without its joyful flutter cannot emanate the glory of butterflies in their element. Perhaps beauty cannot be owned, but only appreciated. It is simply an honour to be in the presence of beauty.

I open the lid of the glass jar and set the butterfly free. Shadow watches with flickering eyes as it flutters on the edge of the jar, before flitting off toward a blood red rose. There is almost more pleasure in the release than in the catch. A butterfly is so much more beautiful when it is free.

"Poppie!" My mom calls from the veranda. "It's time to go!"

I quickly take the empty glass jar back to the kitchen, put on my leather sandals and jump into the air-conditioned car.

"Nothing yet?" She lets the engine run.

The question interrupts my fluttering, rose-scented daydream. "What do you mean?"

"Poppie, come on!" She huffs. "Your period!"

I pop out of my dream into the reality of the present moment. "Nope, didn't get it yet."

"There must be something wrong with your hormones." My mom sighs as she starts to drive me to my first checkup at the gynaecologist. "You should be more regular."

It is a quick, sunny drive out to the practice where I have my appointment, past another school rugby field where a few guys are shooting goals and then beyond a vineyard plump with fruit and down a lane lined with oak trees. The breeze smells of cut grass and wet leaves.

"Do exactly as the gynae says, all right, Poppie?" My mom nudges me as we walk into an icy-cold doctor's practice with no natural light. The air-conditioning is on too high. All the windows are closed.

"Doctor Labia," my mom flirts, "this is my daughter, Poppie."

I am surprised. I thought this was a medical visit. She is showing me off again. I look up at Doctor Labia's translucent face. He has tiny squinty eyes behind thick glasses and a completely expressionless face. My mom, on the other hand, is blushing. He looks only slightly older than my father.

"So this is your first visit here, Poppie." The doctor nods at me the as he states his authority, in a pretend-serious voice. "Your first gynaecological check up, is that correct?"

I nod.

"Good, then, come with me." He is hardly able to contain his excitement.

I look back at my mom half-questioningly, half-asking for help.

"Oh, so enjoy it, you two." My mom takes a deep breath in and puts her hand on her hip, posing seductively.

Either she does not quite know how to act in this situation or there is something going on between her and the doctor.

I go into the doctor's room and sit down. Dr. Labia explains to me that he will do an internal examination to see if my uterus is healthy.

Exactly as requested, I take off my leather sandals and my panties and lie down on the examination bed. It is only the two of us in the room. I am nervous. I wonder if he will be able to see where Jan Bos' fingernails tore at me.

He shifts my dress up over my genitals and onto my belly.

"Bend your knees and open your legs wide," he says.

I hesitate.

He pushes down on my knees until I open up like a frog. "Don't be shy."

It feels awkward when he starts fiddling around down there

with his gloved hands. Not that it hurts, but his heavy breathing makes me feel nervous.

His next comment does not help me to relax. "Poppie, you have the most beautiful pussy out of all my patients."

I have never heard an adult say such a dirty word out loud. So that is really what it means; now I know for sure. I feel like I am in a show. It is all so strange that it cannot be real. I am anxious and it is the last thing I expected to hear. I know that it is inappropriate, but I do not know if this is a way of making me feel more comfortable with doing this for the first time. Maybe he can sense that I am feeling uncomfortable and he is just trying to make me feel better by flattering me. I do not know what to say, so I just say nothing. My anxious heartbeat chokes me up. My consciousness dissipates into a fog.

Doctor Labia takes his time to carefully inspect my "beautiful" pussy, sliding the fingers of his right hand slowly inside and around my labia. Then he rubs my clitoris, making sure that I am wet–before pushing his gloved fingers deeper and deeper inside my vagina. I squirm and tense my muscles in resistance, but I cannot help my body reacting. The gloves are slick and the way he touches me makes me feel sick.

"Just relax, don't worry," says Doctor Labia, "Well, now. There it is Poppie, your G-spot. Do you feel it?" he says matter-of-factly. "You should know where that is. That's so important for a healthy sex life."

With his left hand, he is stroking my inner thigh. It feels as though my mind and body separates. My mind observes that this is out of bounds, but I cannot control my body. It is as though it is not me lying here under his power and filled with fear. Therefore, it does not even occur to me that I can move away. Neither do I acknowledge the heightened natural reaction of my body. I feel suffocated with nausea and shame. Soon, his examination is done and he excuses himself for a few minutes.

My legs feel numb and I am slightly dizzy as I get up and put my panties and shoes back on. What a horrible experience. My brain is jelly.

When he comes back into the room, he prescribes a pill for regulating my periods. "It helps with the skin, which you don't need, Poppie—but it also prevents pregnancy and, you know... you're still too young to get pregnant."

Then he gives me his home phone number, insisting that I call him any time I want, day or night. I push away the bad feeling and smile as I take the piece of paper with his number. I have been taught to be friendly and do as I am told. I am a good girl.

My mom is waiting outside the doctor's room with a big smile. She sees the look on my face and reprimands me. "It's something we all have to go through, Poppie. Come on, cheer up. Why not just try to enjoy it a little? A gynae has to touch you to do his work."

"Mom, I never want to go to the gynae again!" I say with a quiet urgency.

We drive home in silence. I get out of the car as soon as she has parked it in front of our veranda and slam the door.

She shouts after me as I run into the house. "Poppie, behave yourself now! If I leave your father, it will be your fault."

The words come as a complete surprise, even though it should not be after the gynae visit. It is not clear to me if she is talking about a divorce, or if she just wants to be sensational, but the information is too much for me to absorb at this time. I know it is not right to blame me but as ridiculous as it is, the words cut right into me and start to fester.

I go straight to my room and sulk like a wounded animal. I stay in my bed for the whole weekend, sleeping and staring at the wall. The scent of rosemary, mint, fresh tomatoes, and chlorine drift into my bedroom through the high bay window with wooden shutters. It does not manage to coax me outside. I think of that photograph I once saw in a magazine of a magical tower of light that reaches up into the stars—somewhere far, far away. To me, the Eiffel Tower is a beacon of hope, somewhere in another world where I could be happy. As soon as I can get away, that is where I will go.

My mom brings me tea and toast with warm butter and honey. It smells too good to reject. She sits down with me on my bed while I devour it. She wants to repaint the house and lets me choose the colour of my room. She must be feeling at least a little guilty. I decide to paint it blue. Blue as the big sky and the wide, wide ocean. One day, I want to cross it all on a plane and go far away on a quest to find my own true beauty, to a place where I can be beautiful—in full. Not only a beautiful pussy.

Perhaps when I am fully beautiful, I will have some friends again. Maybe the captain of the school rugby team will care to choose me instead of Lara, the high school beauty queen. Perhaps all I need to do this time is to take my panties off. I can at least compete with my pussy. Who knows, perhaps that is all I am good for, after all.

There is a frog in my heart, fraught with warts and croaking back at me from the mirror. It wants to jump out and announce to everyone what a slimy creature I am "down there". I am desperate to hold on to some kind of beauty, even if it is only what I can see everywhere around me. Actively choosing beauty is my secret rebellion. It helps to take the focus away from my own agony. I want to keep moving towards beauty, yet as with the pot of gold at the end of the rainbow, it can never quite fully be attained or owned. Beauty cannot be fully pinned down. It only comes into its own when it is set free. In fairy tales beauty is often liberated by true love. I want to believe in fairy tales.

I escape into the natural beauty of the garden and the orchards and vines all around me, losing myself in the joy of my environment. I am delighted with the discovery of flowers that turn into citrusy kumquat fruit, dragonflies that pop into the rose garden for a visit and rainbows that frame the horizon in all their glorious colours. Swallows come to play in the bird bath as though there is not a care left in this world. These are unique moments that elevate my experience of life. I take the time to notice the golden edges of the clouds as they drift over the valley and the light as it falls into the shadows.

Yet the most fascinating of all is still a caterpillar turning into a butterfly. I watch and learn all I can about the power of transformation.

IT IS NOT ONLY THE BEAUTY AROUND ME, but the property itself, that helps me to change myself. I like spending my time where I can let my imagination run free. There is a small prune orchard next to the house. I am tall enough to reach up high and pick some ripe, deep purple fruit. Sweet juices dribble onto my swimsuit when I take a bite.

Between the orchard and the house is a twenty metre, built-in swimming pool. I swim for at least three hours a day. I am training for the school team. I may not be popular, but I am not a loser. I want to show all the beauty queens and sports jocks that they can no longer make fun of me.

From inside the water, I look up at the pink bougainvillea, avocado trees and a brick wall covered in ivy. I float on my back for a while, allowing myself to imagine that I belong here in the water. This is where I find my power and my freedom.

I turn back around and dive all the way down, feeling the cool water against my face and my scalp. It is fun to swim under the water and see how long I can hold my breath. Today though, something strange happens. It happens, though I am not sure how it is possible. Maybe anything is possible. Or I am just different.

While trying to see how many lengths of the pool I can swim under water without taking a breath, I realise that I no longer need to resurface. I am able to get oxygen while submerged, through my skin. I am breathing under the water. It feels as if it is a game. I go along with it and stay under the water for as long as I like, hanging out right at the bottom of the pool. I pretend I am an abalone. Anything I can imagine. Except being me.

The sun is setting in shades of candy floss when I get out of the water and pull on my towel like a cape. I am surprised at myself. First, I am not sure if I should tell someone. Then I cannot wait to tell my mom as soon as I get inside the house. "Mamma, I need to tell you something wonderful … when I was swimming today I could stay under the water for hours …"

"That sounds great, Poppie …" She gives me a non-committal smile.

"I could breathe under the water." I continue to babble. "I was able to stay down for a long time without coming up for air. I could breathe through my skin."

She is unpacking bags of groceries. "Oh, really? That sounds amazing."

I can not tell if she means it. "Mom, are you listening to me? I can breathe under water."

"Of course you can." She is stockpiling our built-in kitchen cupboards with tins of tuna and bags of rice, even though there is not the slightest sign of war and never has been in all the years since the end of apartheid.

"Ha-ah, Mom." I resist her dismissal, using the tone of my

voice to make her look up. "How is it possible to breathe under water? What just happened to me?"

"Sometimes magic happens." She pours herself some Nuy wine, then hesitates before getting me a small glass of the Chenin Blanc to keep her company—it smells of a spring bouquet and tastes of ripe guava and quince. "Let it be, Poppie, let it be. I'm going to make you bobotie for dinner, my treat."

We should already know how to make this by heart, but it is a tradition to read the recipe for my favourite food from my grandmother's own handwriting.

OUMA'S BOBOTIE
Serve with yellow rice, fresh chopped banana and sunflower seeds, and tomato onion salsa

Ingredients:
1 kg minced beef or lamb
2 thick slices of day-old wholewheat bread (the ones dad won't eat)
250 ml boiling water
2 large onions, peeled and chopped
1 tbsp cooking oil
15 ml butter
1 clove crushed garlic
3 tsp masala or curry powder
2 tsp ground cloves
2 tsp crushed coriander
2 tsp cumin
1 tsp turmeric
1 tsp freshly crushed ginger
25ml peach chutney
15 ml smooth homemade apricot jam
100 ml sultanas (normal raisins are too sweet)
handful of crushed almonds

10ml brown vinegar
3 tbsp freshly-squeezed lemon juice from the tree
2 tsp salt and freshly-ground black pepper

Topping:
7 large eggs
250 ml buttermilk or sour cream
3 tbsp freshly-squeezed lemon juice from the tree
handful of roasted, slivered almonds
6 bay leaves

I collect the ingredients and set them on the table. The lemons from our own tree cast a bright yellow shadow on the light wood. I relish in the zesty fragrance as I start chopping onions and soon the smell of sweet lemon is drowned out by the pungence of the onions. My eyes start watering and I decide that it is a great excuse to let myself cry a little. Tears are a most wonderful release.

My mom chuckles at my red eyes as she preheats the oven to 180 degrees.

"Wait, Poppie." She waves me away, gesturing for me to wipe my tears. Then she gets out a pot for boiling the rice, adding turmeric to make it yellow. "Don't interfere."

She does not see me rolling my irritated eyes. I move to the other side of the kitchen and soak some of yesterday's bread in cold water next to the sink, leaving her to crush up some garlic and spices in the stone pestle. "I'm just trying to help."

We do not really make a good team but we do it together anyway. There is nothing quite like fried onions and spices for creating a homely atmosphere. The aroma has the power to open up both our tastebuds and our hearts, if only we would let it. Oils release into the pan, infusing the lure of fried onions and garlic with the fragrance of cumin, coriander and cloves. At least it whets the appetite.

"Please pass me the meat, Poppie." My mom is getting impatient. "Have you mixed in one of the eggs?"

"No, I didn't ..." I start before she interrupts me.

"Why are you not ready now? You need to be quick. Come on!" She almost loses her cool, as she takes the pan off of the heat.

"You didn't tell me that you wanted me to do the meat." I quickly combine the minced meat with one egg, lemon juice, vinegar, and the apricot preserve in a big orange plastic bowl.

My mom sighs. "Poppie, you're the one with the recipe. You can see for yourself."

"I also can't do anything right!" I rattle a few utensils around on the table for effect before passing my mom half of the meat mixture to brown with the spices. Then I squeeze the excess water out of the soaked bread and add this into the rest of the meat mixture with my hands, using the movement to get rid of frustration. I almost forget about the sultanas and the crushed almonds.

"You always make me do all the dirty work." I do not bother to wash my hands before passing her the bowl with the rest of the ingredients to add to the pan.

"That's why I had you." It is lighthearted but it still burns. She turns down the stove plate and puts the lid on the meat mixture to let it simmer for just a few minutes. "Now can you pass me the oven dish, Poppie?"

I am not amused. I sit down at the table and stare at the dish in front of me, without making an effort to give it to her. It is about twenty by thirty centimetres and at least five centimetres deep so that the bobotie can fluff up nicely.

She reaches over to pick up the dish. "Well then, be like that. I will just have to do everything myself."

I watch her as she transfers the meat from the pan into the oven bowl. Of course, my mom believes in magic, I think, as she presses and compacts, sprinkling the last of the slivered almonds and placing the bay leaves on top in a star pattern. Buttermilk whisked together with the rest of the eggs goes on top of the meat. It is the mystery elixir that completes the spell that is bobotie. She takes a moment to present the dish to me before putting it into the oven. "Abracadabra."

"That's it." She smiles. "That's how magic happens."

My mom looks at the mess that is our kitchen. "The fairies will clean up."

She is referring to our housekeeper, Lena, who moved with us from Namaqualand. Audrey had to stay at school and never gets to visit. Lena cleans our house ever more quietly, retreating to the pool house whenever she is done, as though she is not really here. She drinks only from the chipped cups, which she keeps in the broom cupboard, away from ours.

My mom is the one who raised me on fairy tales, I think again, as she quickly collects the dirty dishes into the sink for Lena to clean up in the morning. She believes in magic even more than I do ... of course she believes that I can breathe under water.

"YOUR HAIR IS A MESS, POPPIE, COME ON, let's get you cleaned up before dinner." My mom walks me to my bedroom and makes me sit down on the chair in front of my antique dressing table. I hardly ever even think of questioning her orders.

She takes my big tortoise shell hairbrush and starts working the tangles out of my hair. I still like it when she plays with my hair. She is gentle with her touch. My scalp is quite sensitive and it tingles as she makes my curls into a neat French plait. If I could purr like Shadow, I would. She takes her time to admire my carefree, sunned summer locks. My hair is becoming so long and so burned.

"I'm going to make an appointment for you at the hairdresser next week." She studies my dry, split ends. "At this rate, it's like you've never seen civilisation. We need to get you neatly cut and styled."

We hear my dad's screeching breaks as he pulls his car into the driveway. It already sounds as though he has had a bad day. Same as every day.

"Poppie, promise me you're never going to get married." My mom sighs. Her words slowly sink in and I make a deep-seated decision to be my own woman. I do not want to make the same mistake as my mom. I want to be free. I look at her in the mirror while she brushes my hair, the image of the wife I never want to have to be.

My eyes are more brown tonight than green. I hear my dad slamming the front door. "I promise."

Dinner is served like clockwork by the time my dad sits down at the kitchen table. The three of us hold hands and bow our heads while my dad habitually says grace. "For-what-we-are-about-to-receive-may-the-Lord-make-us-truly-thankful. Amen."

"Amen," my mom and I echo in a choir of obedience.

It is dinner in silence as usual. I quietly hear the words "Oh, wow" inside my head as my mom lifts the lid of the bobotie to reveal the perfectly fluffed egg whites. A swirl of curried steam whets my appetite. Cooking can, indeed, be a bit like magic.

My mom does not eat anything, but sits with us at the dining table crunching through a handful of breakfast cereal. My dad looks as though he is ready for a fight and we both know better than to ask. Maybe he does not like the bobotie. I am happy that the bottle of peach chutney is standing right in front of me so that I do not have to ask or hassle anyone.

"Poppie," my dad says as he finishes his meal, "I want you to do the dishes tonight. We can't let this bad smell hang around here until tomorrow."

"Dad, but Lena is coming in the morning," I complain.

My dad will not be told. "I spoke, Poppie. Finish, *en klaar.*"

When he reiterates his point in both English and Afrikaans-Dutch, I know there is no point in arguing. I do the dishes.

The sickle moon dapples through the window, dim light catching the blade of a sharp meat knife as I am drying it with a kitchen towel. The eeriness of it mesmerises me. A strange sort of peace draws over me, a numbness. I sit down on the floor with the knife. I cannot stop looking at it, as though I am drawn to it—as though this knife is meant to be my salvation, my final escape. Nothing other than the end seems to exist in the future. My thoughts drift ... how did I get here? Everything is tangled up in my head. I am saturated with pain and I want to leave this ruined body of mine. I want to go away from myself. I want to be free. I look up. Moon, moon, hello, moon.

Shadow jumps through the window, purring. We look each other in the eye for a few seconds, then she jumps down from the basin and starts pawing my lap. Shadow loves me. That is still worth living for. Heaven will need to wait. I get up listlessly, put the knife away and carry Shadow to bed with me.

My mom comes to tuck me in and we look at the new studio photographs of me that are up on my blue bedroom wall. My dad took them in his new photo studio, but I do not remember anything about the shoot or the wine red dress with the lace collar that my mom bought for me. It is confusing, but no one else seems to notice. The photos are framed in elaborate gold.

"Do you like them?" she asks.

I take a closer look. It is not really me. "Yeah. The frames are nice," I say, turning around in my bed, away from the pictures.

My mom is not happy with the answer and so she asks again. "Do you like the photos? You look so beautiful in them … one day, you're going to be a supermodel."

"All right then," I say, swinging my head back toward the wall. "I like this one."

I point to the portrait on the right, a straight close-up of my natural smile. "In the other one, I look like an abalone …"

"An abalone?" My mom laughs. "You don't look like an abalone, my child …"

"I don't like the photo." There is none of me there in the stupid dress and the unnatural pose that I probably had to redo for my dad many times. "They don't look like me."

She pokes me in the ribs, teasingly. "Well … but it doesn't look like an abalone, does it now, Poppie?"

I squirm. "Yes, it does."

"Poppie, you don't look like an abalone, you just have to put on a bit of make-up next time … wait." She quickly gets up and leaves the room.

She comes back with a tiny, twinkly grey box tied with a silky silver ribbon, sits down on my bed and holds it out to me. "I bought you a gift and this seems like the right moment. You're old enough now. I need to teach you how to shop."

I sit up and curiously untie the ribbon and open the box. It is a silver charm bracelet, with three charms: a heart, a butterfly, and a seashell.

"Wow, thank you!" I say, draping it around my bony wrist and admiring the shape of the abalone shell.

She helps me to put it on. "You know, inside a seashell, right at the bottom of the ocean, there is sometimes a pearl. If you're lucky, you might find it. I hope these will bring you luck."

I smile half-heartedly. My mom seems, suddenly, different. Could it be that she actually loves me? Or, is she finally happy?

"Now go to sleep, my angel. Sweet dreams." She smiles and kisses me on the cheek, then takes the bracelet off my wrist and places it on my wooden bedside table.

"You are my lucky charm, Poppie," she says before she leaves the room, "Always remember that. Goodnight."

As she closes the door behind her, I sit up and switch on my bed lamp. Shadow stretches and paws my leg. I cannot find myself in the second photo. I am no longer alive in it. It is simply my silhouette within a reframed reality. If the heart and the mind are expressed through the body, then mine are not shining through. It is disturbing.

I wish she would take it down. I have never done anything for myself and I would not dare.

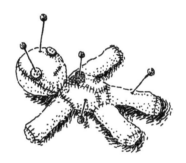

The Voodoo Doll

July 2011, Dubai, United Arab Emirates

THE DUBAI SHOPPING MALL IS EERILY EMPTY as I walk down its fashion avenue in my, ever-so-slightly turbulent, stilettos. It makes me feel nostalgic for my short stint as a ramp model. I started my modelling career too late, but I am glad I had the chance to experience the haute couture catwalk for once in my life. Better than never. Now I am living in this desert city, working as a flight attendant for a private airline. I want to keep travelling, discovering, exploring—and now I can, while using the airplane aisle as a catwalk.

It makes me feel alive to see how societies around the world can be constructed in different ways and still work. The world I grew up in is not the only truth. There are many other ways of being. I do not want to build my life on what I am told. I do not want to see myself through the eyes of my parents, my bosses, or my boyfriends. I want to find out for myself how the world works and which parts of it I want to keep. I want to choose what I believe and how I live, without being controlled, abused, or manipulated. I know that my life will not fall miraculously into place the moment I get on a plane, but I also know that travel can take me away from the restlessness inside me.

I imagine cameras on me as I walk through one of the largest shopping malls in the world, pretending to be a movie star wowing the silver screen. The mall feels even bigger when it is so empty, as though it is a neatly primed yet deserted film set. I flick my meticulously-styled hair, smile and wave. When people give me strange looks, I pop into a cosmetics store to touch up my make-up, just to be sure that I still look my absolute best. The worst thing that can happen is for people to see the real me, without my face on. Fashion and make-up provide me with a shield of protection from the blemish on life that is myself.

With batting eyelids, I look for a coffee shop where I can sit down and pose for a while. The waitress pulls up an extra chair for my handbag and shopping bags, because "designer bags should never go on the floor."

I like that.

She quickly comes back with my caramel latte and smiles sweetly. "Sales have been really bad during this year's shopping festival. People are leaving the city very fast as projects close down and people's jobs are terminated. We thought it would never happen, but the recession eventually hit Dubai."

"No wonder the discounts are so good here in 'Do-Buy' this

year." I deliberately pronounce the two syllables separately, but she does not get it. "There are less people and more things to add up."

The waitress is very pretty. Her hair and skin have a silk-like sheen. She shrugs. "On designer wear, the price is still a bit high, always."

I look at her with new eyes. "Tell me, do you have any insider tips on designer shopping? I absolutely love how designer wear fits. Never mind people holding on to their money. Not me. I spend what I earn. It's my life. It's my money. I can do with it what I want."

Her tiny eyes open wide.

"I don't need to own every piece of clothing I touch, but almost." I lower my voice, secretively. "The way the luxurious fabrics feel against my skin, the tailoring that fits just right. It makes me feel special ..."

"Shoes?" She cackles behind her hand, uncontrollably yet composed.

"I always allow myself to buy shoes." I conspire. "Some things are simply not possible without good shoes. I do wear them, all of them—and they make me happy."

She needs to attend to another table, so I do not get to tell her that fashion helps me to put myself back together. The clothes I wear change who I am. When I know I look good, I feel more secure. More assembled. More everything. When I wear good shoes, especially a certain kind of high heel with a slight platform, I feel elevated above the world—as though I have an advantage on achieving my goals for the day.

I watch the handful of people walking by as I sip on my latte. Everyone is carrying at least one little bag, or two. I spot an elegant older lady walking with no less than five pretty designer bags, a look of pure elation on her face. It may be short-lived, but shopping is true pleasure.

Suddenly, the smell of smoke fills my nostrils.

"Fire, there's a fire," I shout. My chair squeaks as I push it out across the lustre of the polished tiles. The people at the other tables all turn to me in confusion.

The waitress comes running over. "How can I help you, madam?"

I am in flight mode and looking around like a mad woman to find the location of the burn. "There's a fire, I can smell it!"

"Madam," the waitress speaks calmly and gently, "sit down."

She shows me to my chair nervously. Her mouth turns into a cautioning pout. When I sit, she comes closer and whispers. "You'll get into trouble. It's Oud."

"Oud, who's that?" I look around to try and locate the source of the mysterious smell. Some of the restaurant patrons are still staring at me.

"It's resin perfume." She is talking softly, desperate to keep the attention away from us. "This one is definitely high end."

The smell intensifies, becoming earthly sweet, before I see the group of local ladies following their husband. They are wearing the full Gulf-style abaya, loose robes that cover all, but the hands and feet. Their heads are swathed in elaborately jewelled niqab, with only their eyes showing. The female energy underneath the layers of fabric sparkles even brighter than the crystals. Their eyes are highlighted by bold kajal and bright eye shadow. One of the ladies turns to glare at me. It is impossible to look away. I can spot the shopping dazzle right from where I am sitting. As we make eye contact, an ominous feeling passes through me. It tingles in my cheeks and shivers all the way through to my toes. I feel strange, as though something foreign has taken hold inside me.

"Can I have the bill?" I have the urge to stand up and shake the shiver.

The waitress answers with a cute nod and disappears. After being so fast with the coffee service, it is astounding that this one last task can now take so much time.

I continue to stare at the group of locals outside the coffee shop. Another lady in the group is wearing a metal face shield, an extra covering that also hides her eyes. She is completely hidden under the veil and face mask, as though she is a shadow of herself. I notice that she is also wearing satin gloves, hiding her hands.

The waitress interrupts my frightful stare and explains. "A woman who is covered in this way is honoured very highly in the culture, in an almost saint-like way. Usually, it would be the mother, or an elder, but it can also be an honour bestowed upon the first wife, or any other woman who is highly praised by her husband or family."

These women are hidden and unreachable; thereby winning respect. I hide behind myself too in a way, behind veils of myself that allow me to be safe. As long as I do not expose my true self, I can avoid being hurt. These women are not so unlike me. Perhaps I would feel safer underneath a *niqab* too. Yet ...

I shift on my chair. "Wow, the most self-expressive these women dare to be is to show off a handbag. Or a pair of fancy shoes ..."

She leans in a little closer before she speaks. "Since they take so much care selecting these items, I often take my style tips from them. Do yourself a favour and observe their handbags and shoes."

My eyes seek out the finer details of the shoes worn by the fully-veiled woman. I give the waitress a generous tip before rushing off.

I no longer need to wander the mall. I walk straight up to

the shop assistant at the designer shoe store in question and ask for exactly the same signature style, but in red. Dainty pin heel. Overall smooth lines. Trying on new things helps me to reinvent myself. In the shop mirror, I stand and stare. Changing my style. Changing my life. I escape into another self once more. I look and look until I become the new look. Then I march out of the mall with my designer shoe bag, feeling an immense sense of achievement.

Shoe success.

AFTER QUEUING AT THE TAXI STAND inside the mall for half an hour, the euphoria dissipates. While the shops may look empty, there are more people out and about today than I thought. The expat culture in Dubai revolves around shopping after all. It is the best distraction from the blazing desert heat. When I finally get to hop in a car, I ask the driver to take me to a small French hotel bistro. I am running late to meet my neighbour Priyanka and a few other girls from my apartment building. It is forty degrees outside. I should be almost used to it after growing up in a half-desert, but this is a real desert, after all.

My skin burns as I step outside, same as when I sometimes stand too close to a boiling kettle and the steam hits my face. Nevertheless, a sense of relief passes over me as I walk away. I did not even realise that I was holding my breath for the entire ride. I am always grateful when a driver brings me safely to my preferred destination. I cannot shake a certain sense of paranoia when I am alone with a man. Anywhere, not only in a taxi. Yet it is not something that I can ever avoid completely.

I soak in the air-conditioning as I walk into the shelter of the restaurant.

"Poppiiieee!" Pri shrieks as she gets up to throw her arms around me.

"I'm so excited to see you, Poppie! Come, come, sit down, the others are already here." Pri leads me by the hand to our table. She uses her sing-song, girl gang voice. High-pitched, attention grabbing and accompanied by the most dashing smile ever. No wonder she gets to make so many friends so quickly.

"Ta-da!" She announces my arrival to the rest of the girls as we get to the table by the window. Beyond the girls' dashing faces lies a yacht marina, with a Ferris wheel adding a festive touch in the distance. The curtain is slightly drawn, dimming the light inside the room.

"Hi, Misha." I take care to remind myself of her name as I greet the girl closest to me. We do the cheek kisses thing and I get it wrong. In Dubai the local custom is three kisses, but we end up in an awkward nose rub situation.

I feel inelegant and embarrassed. "I'm sorry, Misha. I always mix it up. In Paris, it used to be one kiss on each cheek. I know it's three here, I know."

She bursts into laughter, too. "Yeah, it's weird. Happens to me as well. Nice to see you again anyway. You are Poppy, right?"

"It's Poppie, like the doll. Not Poppy, like the flower."

"Ah ..." She smiles and tests out the slight nuance by pronouncing my name again. "Poppie."

I notice that her nails are freshly done this time, as per required duty for each flight. I take her hand to get a closer look. She got caught out once. A chipped nail has a way of ruining a career quickly around here. Then again, a good gel manicure such as this can be the very basis for a successful professional image as a private flight stewardess.

Alicia looks up at me from the other side of the table. I step over to her and repeat the festive gesture, getting the count of kisses right this time. She throws her honey-streaked hair around, posing and checking who is looking as she greets me. It is a bit pretentious, but she is gorgeous. She can get away with anything.

Pri pulls out my chair for me with a big smile.

As soon as I sit down, I quickly order a *soup de l'oignon* and *vin blanc* while overlooking the yachts and the sunset. I have been here for lunch a few times and already know the menu. The others take a little longer to decide. I blur out the first part of the conversation. It is a constant blabber of small talk and competition for the spotlight. Might as well be a reality TV show with a couple of flight attendants who think that they are models just about to hit the big time.

I stare into the distance until my second glass of wine arrives, perfectly timed to match the rich indulgence of my onion soup. After a sip or two I am ready to jump in to the conversation. "I always thought being flight crew was just a glorified waitressing job. I mean, we serve people and clean toilets, but we also get to live our lives in private resorts all over the world and earn a tax-free salary. I thought it does not get higher than the Paris catwalk. Then again, the sky is the limit. Literally."

"Ooh, it looks like our doll here has her head in the clouds." Alicia traces the outline of my figure in the air, making a smooth and rhythmic curve with her index finger. "Welcome home, Honey. Life's so much better up here."

"No, but I mean, there are quite a lot of very practical, responsible things that I am learning right now. Safety and emergency procedures. Service. Grooming. Especially grooming." I stop short of telling them that I have never owned hairspray before, or stuck a whole pack of pins into my hair to ensure that no single strand falls out of place. I have never had to reapply lipstick over and over, making sure not to forget after drinking coffee. These are magnificent life skills. I have become a real expert at hiding, or even reviving, my tired face when I strut down the aisle after too little sleep on layovers. I can, in fact, invent myself with make-up on a day-to-day basis.

"I think I have to vomit." Misha interrupts as she pushes away her full plate of steak frites. Her face is as pale as her long, platinum hair.

We stare at her in amazement, almost asking at the same time. "Are you pregnant?"

"No!" She half-laughs with a cheeky longing in her lifeless eyes. "For that you need to do something which I haven't done in ages."

"So much for the Mile High Club." I huff. Life as cabin crew can be lonely. There is not much time for close relationships with travelling all the time. People do things in other countries that they will not do at home. The temptations that get served up are often irresistible. What happens in Vancouver, Vienna, Vegas ... does not always stay there and, even if it does, who really wants to have a relationship with no sense of loyalty or trust? Without those basic building blocks, I would rather have no relationship at all.

"Oh, come on," says Pri, shaking her impeccable locks, "if you need a shag just go and flirt a little in the cockpit. Before you know it the pilot will drop his wedding ring under the seat—and, oops, he suddenly can't find it anymore ... I honestly think that's what the space beneath the cockpit seat is for: losing the wedding ring. It happens too often to count." She pauses for a private thought. "Not all pilots are married though."

I feel compelled to justify myself. "It's not for lack of opportunities, Pri. On my last flight, the drunken business man who commissioned the jet gave me his card before disembarking. I smiled politely and then threw it in the bin right away. Not interested."

According to Alicia who has four boyfriends, each one living in a different city, the trick is to "use what your mama gave ya and never ever feel bad for being adored."

She reprimands Misha, who is still looking queasy. "What about that diamond merchant who kept calling you? You didn't get it on with him?"

Alicia flashes the two engagement rings that she kept from former lovers. "You need to carry your beauty with you, or neither you nor anyone else will ever notice it."

Her diamonds catch the light as she takes a sip of red wine, leaving a luscious, red lipstick stain on the glass. The big stone must be at least a couple of carats. The way she holds her body—even sitting down at a restaurant with the girls—oozes confidence.

"Ugh, no way. I am no carrier of beauty today." Misha changes the topic back to herself. "I hit my head on a container during my last flight. It's not good."

Alicia reminds us that Misha has a history of disaster. "The last time I saw you, you had been slapped by a fat bald man. Remember that one? He was upset that you didn't have any vegetarian meals on board."

Misha's cheeks remain as colourless as they were before.

"Maybe people should bring their own food on board." Alicia continues, as true as ever to her audacious self. "Or feel free to step out onto the 'over-wing restaurant'."

It is funny enough but none of us are laughing. Our jobs are well paid. Our clients are flashy. In the luxury service industry, I take whatever comes and keep smiling. I choose to have no voice. It is a conscious, trained effort to feign a pleasant facial expression. My smiling muscles are so fit that my default expression is a smile, even if I am not really happy. It is my job to not get frustrated at people's demands.

Alicia takes another sip of her red wine, diamonds glistening, before she continues, slightly more pensively this time. "Maybe it's the evil eye. Someone must have shot an evil eye at you".

Pri's face shades over. She looks completely afraid.

"What's the evil eye" I am curious why I am the only one who does not know.

"When someone gives you the evil eye," Alicia says ominously, "they shoot tiny little evil arrows at you with their eyes, turning you into something like a voodoo doll. It's a curse," she hisses, "that can stem from anything, from jealousy to revenge to simple meanness."

"And all they have to do is just look at you?" I think of the lady in the mall's eerie stare.

"Oh, it's not 'just a look' at all. It comes from somewhere deep inside." Alicia makes big, theatrical hand gestures. She is delighted that she got us all entranced by her knowledge of this magic.

I decide not to take it seriously and flash a big smile at Pri, who looks like she needs some cheering up. It helps a lot to smile when trying to keep others calm, especially in an environment such as an airplane where people are stuck together in a small space for hours at a time. Today our small dining table simulates such a small, closed environment. We are stuck with each other, by choice, despite our diverse backgrounds.

"Passengers can be dangerous, absolutely they can, but I don't believe in voodoo." I say it louder than I think, as if I am trying to prove something to myself.

Misha looks down at my empty soup bowl, visibly relieved to see that I have already eaten. She grabs her shawl and arranges it around her shoulders, indicating to the rest of us that it is time to get going.

"Come on, how old are you, thirteen? Poppie, don't be boring." Alicia waves at the restaurant staff to come and clear our table, all the while keeping our attention on her. "Don't you have any airplane horror stories?"

Sometimes, I do feel like I am thirteen compared to some of these streetwise ladies. It pains me that I have to spend my mental energy thinking about bad things happening on board. "Not my own, but I've heard some. A colleague who works for a commercial airline once tripped over a stray leg in the aisle and broke her ankle."

"Yup," Alicia turns slowly as she speaks and lets her voice travel across the restaurant for public effect, "so next time you all are about to give your empty meal tray to a trolley dolly who already has her hands full and looks like she can carry it on her head like an African queen, please at least have the decency to shake up your spouse who is sleeping with his or her head, arms, feet, legs, or whatever, in the aisle."

She does not get a reaction from any of the other restaurant patrons, but we give in to a laughing fit amongst ourselves, within our own little bubble.

Misha is not looking good at all. She notices the question mark on my face and addresses me directly. "I felt fine when I woke up after my last flight, but as soon as I got in the taxi today … I'm sorry I don't want to spoil your fun."

"Don't worry, that hot Latino guy in the SUV was still checking you out on the way here!" Alicia pouts and looks around teasingly, unsuccessfully searching for an audience in the restaurant.

"Even on your worst day most women would still dream to look like you," adds Pri, "and most men would still want to sleep with you."

Misha shows no hint of a smile. "I wonder if it's all worth it. I just want to go home."

Alisha shrugs and adds another touch of drama. "Where is home, anyway? Ah, the things we put our bodies though … of course it is worth it, for the chance to jet off to a massage on a private island one day and do a shopping spree in New York on another. By the way, ladies, I've decided to get my lips done. I found a special discounted deal with a doctor in Johannesburg."

"Alicia!" I laugh in disbelief. "You're like, what, not even thirty?"

She is serious.

Alicia holds her chin in the air. "If it goes well I might get my nose done too."

We look at each other and then at Misha, who should really be our focus, rather than cosmetic surgery. We agree to take Misha home so that she can get some rest.

In the cab, I feel remote from everything and strangely aware of how displaced I am, driving through this unlikely city in the desert, with this random bunch of people. Between each skyscraper, we pass wide open spaces. Nothing feels crammed. There is room for possibility within this elaborate dream. It takes almost two hours in the traffic to get back to our building, in a semi-developed area on the outskirts. Away from the razzle, the scenery becomes so dull. Everything looks like sand. Everything. Today, there is even sand in the air. I am not able to see far and get nervous for the driver trying to find his way through the sand storm. No wonder it is such a big deal here to keep cars clean—it is to make them more clearly distinguishable from the dust.

As we get out of the taxi, Misha pulls her shawl over her head, as though it is a veil of protection. The perverse stares from the group of men lurking at the entrance of our apartment building makes me grab for my pashmina, too. I do not want to be exposed and reachable. Not for these types of eyes. I wrap my pomegranate pink pashmina around me before we head for the door. Hiding behind veils of myself are not enough at all. Sometimes I actually need to cover up physically in order to feel comfortable.

Pri intuitively puts her arm around me as we get to the entrance. I do not tell her that I notice one of the guys in the group moving his hand up and down in the area of his crotch, thinking that he is cleverly hiding his action behind his cloak. She either does not notice, or does not care. Still, it is so creepy. I wish they would not hang out there.

"I will take care of Misha but only until I have to get ready for my date this evening." Alicia ruffles Misha's hair as she speaks, her perfect red nail polish set off by the platinum blonde. "I'm sure she will be fine by then. She has to be. This guy has po."

"Po?" I stop and turn as soon as we are safely inside the door.

"Po-tential." Alicia is all pleased with herself for knowing something we do not.

"Aha." I can see her reflection in the shiny floor tiles as she throws her arms out into the recycled air and pulls up her shoulders.

"He has potential," she explains, enjoying my confusion, "I came up with that myself."

"Keep us updated." Pri cocks her head towards them.

I turn to Misha, but before I can speak, she interrupts.

"I will let you both know if I need anything." She quickly rushes off.

"Come on, Poppie, let's go out tonight," Pri pleads as we hop into the elevator together. "I've been invited to a party; it will be fun! No excuses, I'll come around later to pick you up. Dress up a little, hmm?"

My face in the mirror says no, but I nod approvingly as she holds the elevator door.

I HAVE BEEN LIVING IN DUBAI FOR ALMOST A YEAR NOW and hardly go out clubbing. I do not feel comfortable letting my guard down. Tonight though, I am making an exception as, perhaps, I am overly cautious. I should make time for a little fun.

Besides the essential shopping excursion now and then, I do not leave my air-conditioned apartment next to the mosque. By now I have grown used to the entrancing sound of the call to prayer. The supermarket downstairs delivers for free. As do the Pakistani kitchens in the area. The restaurants here are mostly filled with construction workers, who stare as though they never see women. Maybe they do not, as most women are veiled, out-side of the expat areas. Either way, delivery is the better option for staying out of sight and having a good meal before going out partying in this city will keep me out of trouble. I am already dialling the number for a chicken tikka masala with chapattis before I change my mind.

"A woman is always allowed to change her mind," I tell myself, echoing the words of my former ballet teacher, Miss Blom.

I excitedly head for my spacious kitchen and put my new plan in motion. Kashmiri rice is something Pri often makes and has become one of my most-cherished dishes. I add two cups of rice to a bowl and fill it with water to soak while I prepare the rest of the ingredients according to her recipe.

KASHMIRI PULAO

250 g basmati rice
1 cup milk
500 ml cream
handful of chopped apple or pineapple
1 tsp sugar
1 tsp ghee
2 cloves
1 bay leaf

piece of cinnamon
2 cardamom pods
1 tsp cumin
some saffron strands
dash of rose water
pinch of salt
optional crispy fried onions as garnish
decorate with well-rinsed rose petals
roasted nuts optional

I pick out the whole spices and the bay leaf, smiling in anticipation as I lay them down in a neat line next to each other on the wide kitchen counter. There is no ghee in the fridge today, so I add a dash of vegetable oil to my pretty, spun copper pan. I add the spices to simmer on medium heat, while chopping an onion. No tears this time.

When the fragrance of spices start to fill the kitchen, I turn up the heat and add the chopped onions, stirring swiftly. Even though I am not all that hungry after our girls' lunch, frying onions always helps me to work up an appetite. It inspires me to get creative and I decide to add a few cashews and almonds to roast in the same pan.

Once the onions are nice and brown, I take the pan off the heat. Then I drain the rice and add it to the rice cooker together with the milk and the cream. I intuitively feel that it needs just a small dash of extra water. Saffron, onions and the spice mix goes on top. I add the rose water before I close the lid. My rice cooker is smart enough to let me know once my meal is ready. All I have to do is press a button and wait.

I find a little bit of leftover pomegranate to use as garnish instead of rose petals. It is not only going to be delicious, but lovely. Intentionally making things pretty is an act of freedom, a refusal to give in to the ugliness of the world. I call Pri to ask if she wants to come over and grace me with her presence, for a beautiful dinner.

"You're cooking?" she squeals, "Poppie, you know how long it takes me to get ready. I'm going to need at least three hours for my hair and make-up. Maybe I'll have a quick bite when I arrive, but don't count on me. Besides, we just had lunch!"

"Don't stress," I try to calm her. "I just thought it would be nice to have some company while I line my stomach. It's always a bit sad to sit down to a feast alone. Not a big deal though, take your time."

Pri does not entertain my self-pity. "*Khalas* Poppie, never mind food, we'll have a drink together later!"

While the rice is cooking, I entertain myself by making a cucumber raita to complete my dinner. I take half a cup of yoghurt and mix it with a handful of chopped mint, half a cup of grated cucumber, and a tablespoon full of finely sliced spring onion. An extra little grind of cumin and coriander and it is done.

The rice cooker reveal is always a special moment and I breathe in as I open the cooker. First the steam, then the fragrance of spices, rice, and onions fills my being. All excited, I sit down to the company of one of Dubai's excellent movie channels, watching a classic favourite as I inhale my tasty, pretty bowl of food.

Of course, I do not eat all of it. It has been ages since I have worn my little red dress and I do not want to get bloated. I have to make sure that it still fits me later.

I always wonder if it is too revealing for Dubai and, yet, this is who I am. I like to dress sexy. It makes me feel good. Besides, the dress is a perfect match with the new designer shoes I bought today.

I run myself a bubble bath and keep my head under the water so long that my lips become wrinkly. I figure this is what I will look like when I am old. Water relaxes me, holds me, cleanses me. Reincarnates me.

Once I am all dressed up, I take a turquoise silk pashmina and wrap it around my shoulders. That should be demure enough for this occasion.

I am about to check on her, when Pri finally arrives wearing an even shorter pink dress and high heels. Her eyes are beautifully done in a purple pigment framed with slick liquid eyeliner.

"Come on, I'll help you with your make-up." Pri masterfully draws a smoky cat eye that adds the final touches to my party look. "You really should wear more make-up, it makes you look so pretty—just like a doll."

I let her draw on my face, enjoying the care and attention. When I look in the mirror, I am someone else. I cannot look away, even as Pri is calling from the front door, ready to get going.

Audrey's face appears next to mine in the mirror. She is nonchalant today. "Ai, Poppie. What pretty girl in her twenties doesn't like to look at herself in the mirror? Take your time. Do things that make you feel beautiful, but remember that if it doesn't come from the inside, it is wasteful. If you don't yet feel it inside, it helps to look at yourself until you do. Until you can see that you're beautiful and internalise that. Keep looking into the mirror until you get there." She tilts her head as though she is waiting for me.

Pri calls again. "Come on, Poppie, our taxi's downstairs already!"

I look away from the mirror and turn off the light.

WE ENTER THE NIGHTCLUB VIA AN ELEVATOR in a private part of a hotel resort. The door opens onto the rooftop of a skyscraper, where we are greeted by a large bouncer who looks us up and down and then approvingly lets us through.

There are some familiar faces in the pool. Models I saw at castings in Paris a few years ago. No one greets me though. They would rather point and whisper as I pass. I recognise a very famous runway model on the arm of the host and I can hardly believe my eyes. Funny how I never got to mingle with anyone like that in Paris and yet now I am standing here on top of a skyscraper in the desert with my role model. Every now and again I have to pinch myself. Is this real or am I only dreaming?

Further, beyond the pool area, some of the guests are arriving by helicopter. I can not see right away if they are celebrities.

I look around to assess the reality of my surroundings. It is an interesting combination of rich royals and beautiful girls in gold bikinis. Out there in the streets of Dubai, shoulders and knees can almost be seen as pornographic and it is believed that a woman should know better than to show any skin. I take a pashmina with me everywhere I go. For the purposes of this evening, however, it seems wholly unnecessary though.

Pri is preoccupied with a British man who makes her laugh out loud. She has the expression of a big screen actress in the middle of a musical love scene with her face bobbing flirtatiously from side to side. It looks like I have lost her for the night.

I spot someone else from our private flight crew group called Jinfen. She is standing on the steps that lead out on to the well-lit rooftop pool. She could not make it for lunch at the French place today, but she also lives in our building. She is wearing her iconic blue silk dress and platform heels, looking like an antique Chinese painting with long hair hanging to her waist. She is talking to another stewardess from Australia who I have seen around.

"She doesn't belong here," I hear Jinfen say to the girl as I walk up behind them.

It makes me pause.

"Poppie is not one of us," Jin continues, "she doesn't fit in. She doesn't belong."

They are so deep in conversation that they do not even notice me. I walk past them out into the star-covered night. The sky is clear. No further sign of the earlier sandstorm. Two pretty women are having cocktails in the pool with a man who looks like he could be their grandfather. They are hanging on him as though he is famous. Maybe he is.

Behind the pool, the host's private helicopter sits elevated on its pad. The story goes that he once had a fight with a supermodel he was dating and chased after her with the helicopter as she tried to get away from him on a yacht. I wish I could fly away in that helicopter right now. It would be a faster way out than taking the elevator.

Instead, I take the time to breathe deeply and push the words away, without judgement and pain.

I always have this sense that something is absent from my life—as though I am hollow. Perhaps that is what Jinfen means—that I am neither fully present in my life, nor really doing what I want to do with it. Jin is intuitive, with her psychic nature and palm-reading abilities. Her face was struck with fear the first time she looked at the lines of my hand. She refused to tell me anything. At least now I can sort of figure it out for myself.

The club is full of people and yet I feel more alien than ever. I do not fit here, or anywhere. Is there nobody to love me? Somebody with whom I can belong?

I start to feel dizzy. The music and the buzz fade out as I swirl upwards outside of my body. It is as if my mind is weightless and hanging somewhere above the crown of my head. I look across the dance floor from left to right and back again. Then I spot him. Our eyes lock. I slide back into my own head, settle back into my eyes and look at him.

We are drawn to each other across the dance floor and that is that. I move through the crowd toward him as though possessed. He does not take his eyes off me. As he gets closer, I gaze intensely at him. He has a large hooked nose, foxy hair, and lively, light blue eyes—like the sky on a very hot, misty day. It is the eyes that get me-they burn into me and start a kind of fire that I had never felt before. We dance and look into each other's eyes. I feel his big shoulders and hard biceps next to me.

"Paul, *je suis* Paul," are his first and last spoken words for the night. He gives me a business card with his phone number and excuses himself.

I find a seat for myself at the small bar and look around, wondering where he went.

A scruffy voice catches up to me from behind. "Can I get you something to drink, *habibi*?"

Turning around, I see bright eyes and a rugged beard framed by an Emirati headdress. He is using the local term of endearment.

"Oh, no, thanks," I say politely.

"We don't have a barman here tonight, but I'll fix you something. Paul is a good friend of mine. I saw you dancing." He ignores my response as if I do not have my own mind.

"What about a glass of Champagne?" His local dress flaps around his legs as he walks behind the bar and has a quick look around.

I had considered not drinking at all, but who can resist Champagne?

He notices my hesitation. "Or a whiskey? He has quite a nice selection of Japanese whiskey."

"I'll have a glass of Champagne," I give in, only partly because I want him to stop talking.

"There you go." He places the drink on the bar and draws much too close to my side. "I'm Khaled."

"Poppie," I respond, without saying thank you.

He continues trying to make small talk. "You are living here? In Dubai?"

I feel obliged to respond. "Yes."

He looks pleased, in spite of my lack of enthusiasm. "How long?"

The people around us start moving away to create some privacy for us and I want to call out to them to stay, but only shift uncomfortably in my chair. "Just a few months."

"Ah, it's nice so far?" He puts too much emphasis on the "r".

"Yes." I look over my shoulder and around, searching for Paul.

"There's no point waiting for him. He's not coming back tonight." Khaled is already turning possessive and the tone in his voice elicits fear.

I smile sweetly, using my long-lived strategy of keeping the peace. Good thing we are in a public place.

Khaled does his best to capture my full attention. "Any place can be nice if you know the right people. And now you know the right people."

The music changes to percussion.

"Oh, the Lola show is starting," Khaled looks delighted. "Stay here. You've got a good seat—and I can keep topping up your glass."

The name sounds familiar, but I cannot quite place it. A ripple of fuchsia silk stirs the air in the room as a dancer with long, curly hair and caramel skin enters. She makes a large round to create some space for her voluptuous self while enchanting the audience. First, she flutters like a butterfly; then she teases with little rhythmic accents of her hips and chest as she looks individuals from the audience in the eye coyly. Her veil sends some cool air my way and I welcome it gladly. Then she swiftly lets go of the veil and purposefully sends it my way. I recognise her face from Cape Town. Perhaps she wants me to pick up the veil, but I do not want to divert attention from the show by moving.

While she is blonde and pretty, the generous proportions of her body topple the Westernised idea of beauty. She celebrates all of herself as she moves to an energetic Egyptian drum solo with lots of undulations and shimmies. I am impressed at how she really dances from her belly, using all the little muscles there. She has a very good technique. Most belly dancers I have seen here dance mostly from the hips. That is only the start—and then it takes time to train the belly over many years, Lola once told me.

I completely lose myself in the performance. Every twist and turn, every graceful ripple of her belly draws me in as though it is a secret language of the heart that streams from her body to mine. I vow to myself that I will find a teacher here and master the art of belly dance, so that I can learn to love and celebrate every part of my body in this way.

The belly dance scene in Dubai is mostly underground though. They do not advertise shows in English newspapers. You have to know the locals to know where the private parties are held. I would like to chat to Lola about it, but I know she will have to leave as soon as possible if she wants to avoid a proposal. Staying and socialising would draw the wrong kind of attention. Belly dance is very much associated with the sex trade in the Middle East and, as a dancer, one is expected to be available to the men after a show. I wonder if I would be able to find a teacher without being thought to be a prostitute. It would probably be best not to tell anyone that I am even interested in belly dancing.

Indeed, someone approaches her as soon as she has done her little bow and sent some air kisses to the audience. She is on her way towards me to pick up her veil when the man stops her and makes a request. She looks me straight in the eye as though to gain some strength from our shared womanhood.

"I'm sorry, I already have an appointment for the evening," she lies, deliberately looking away rather than looking into his eyes.

He looks annoyed as he turns away and leaves.

Lola takes a few long, graceful steps toward me.

"Thank you for picking up my veil." She emanates nothing but kindness. "That's so nice of you. What's your name again?"

"I'm Poppie". A scattering of glitter gleams behind her on the floor where she was dancing.

"Of course, yes, Poppie." She pulls me closer by my hand and gives me a big hug. "You never came back to my class again in South Africa. What happened?"

"You were wonderful, Lola, and I wish I could dance like that. I just, I guess, I'm travelling a lot." I catch on to her smile.

"Come to Egypt and I'll teach you. I'm based there now." She laughs, tossing her hair back gently with her hand.

I want to say it is a silly idea, but I can not speak. Her words linger between us until it becomes something concrete, a clear plan that I am compelled to fulfil. I know right away that I will be going to Egypt to be Lola's student. When it will be I do not yet know, nor do I want to worry about the details. The important thing is that I feel the weight of her words, the invitation; the vibrating thrill inside my body. I want to do this and I will.

She thanks me again for picking up the veil and then retreats to her room. Lola does not socialise with her audience after a show, except if they are close friends. It is one of the rules that she taught me long ago, in my first belly dance class. "You simply perform, pick up your money and move on."

I take a moment to send Paul a message and he responds right away.

I had to go. Will explain. Hope you will never forget this moment, I am already dreaming about you.

There are good men in this world. Not everyone wants to take advantage of me.

Khaled, on the other hand, soon appears at my side again and fills up my glass with Champagne. I like the attention, but I do not want him to come too close.

I quietly reflect on the wonder and the power in Lola's performance. Other less famous dancers can be less fortunate, such as some of the Russian girls doing a jiggle on the 4x4 desert tours. The dancing itself is not as good, but it is a scene to behold; watching these girls shake their hips in glitzy costumes under the stars. The experience of leaning back on Arabian cushions in the desert and sipping sweet tea while the dancers set the mood, is enough to transport an audience to a faraway place. That can also become a dark place for some, as soon as night falls. These dancers are often underrated, underpaid, and under-respected. Making money with your body is seen as inferior to doing it with your brain. It has been like this throughout the ages.

When the power of feminine beauty cannot be contained, it can always be exploited. If a woman chooses to dress in a more revealing way than the local custom allows, as I have done tonight in my little red dress, then it is her own fault if a man cannot contain himself.

Right?

Right.

After only two glasses of Champagne, I space out.

THERE IS A CONSCIOUS MOMENT WHEN I REALISE that Khaled is sodomising me, but I am unable to move or feel or regain the mental structure to resist or be angered.

When I wake up, what must be hours later, it is as though I come back from the dead. The presence of a strong man next to me in the huge four poster bed is comforting.

He holds me and smiles at me as though we are a couple. The dry skin on his face creates scutes that make him look like a crocodile. "You're finally awake?"

I do not smile.

"You were so sweet last night," he says, "you fell asleep in the car."

The vomit creeps up in my throat. I get flashbacks of being dragged to a big four wheel drive against my will. Out comes a needle. A ghastly type of voodoo.

After that, I remember nothing.

He rambles on about the restaurant owner who did not want to cook for him at 3 am. My brain is mush, but I pick up on "fight", "police", and "jail".

"You didn't wake up at all?"

I shake my head in disbelief.

"Wait, I will show you." He gets out of bed and grabs a blood-stained, tattered white shirt from a heavy desk chair. What the … I feel like I cannot breathe.

He says he had a bloody fight with the Syrian restaurant guy over food he wanted to pick up for us on the way back from the club. In his anger he then phoned the police and asked them to lock him up, so the poor guy is in jail now.

"I don't have to give a reason," he says, "if I say lock someone up, they will lock him up. And he deserved it. Now he can stay there."

I smile. The old trick. Trying to stay on his good side, although I feel like running as fast as I can.

Suddenly, his face changes and he looks at me in disgust. "I have to go and shower."

I still feel like I cannot move, my limbs flapping as I try to get up. I am a butterfly in a jam jar. There is a hissing sound in my head. I did drink a bit last night–but this … total blackout, I have been so careful …

As much as I want to get up, I can not get my body to move properly. When Mr. Khaled, all-showered-and-ready-for-his-luxurious-life, comes to run his fingers through my hair and says, "You can stay as long as you like, I'll be downstairs," I doze off.

Life can not go on as usual.

It is the woman's own fault if a man cannot control himself. A woman should be more careful. More conservative. More unapproachable. I should have known better.

It is my own fault.

I have no core, no self. I am a stale apple with a worm inside. I can be anything I want to be. Except me.

DISRESPECTED, DISREGARDED, DISSED. I want to change that, starting with myself. By considering how I present myself, how I move, how I act. Yet, at this time, I only want to pretend that it never happened.

I feel grateful that he lets me go, as though he is doing me a favour by not keeping me locked up in his villa. When the taxi finally drops me off at home, my neighbour Jinfen passes by with wide eyes and says, "Poppie, you look great. I've never seen you looking so beautiful!"

Looking good is a perfect façade for being cursed.

I look my best when I feel at my worst inside. The right look.

176 / LIZE DE KOCK

I finally found it and yet it is not what I expected. The right look is merely a popular illusion behind which I can hide the raging chaos in my heart.

Audrey, are you here?

She is sitting on my giant designer couch when I enter my apartment, a tiny girl tucked in between trendy scatter cushions. I can never tell anyone the truth about what happened. Except Audrey. I feel like my soul starts stumbling. I laugh a little louder and dance a little harder in order to cover the scars inside. I want to hide in my room and close the blackout curtains. I want sleep a little more, a little longer. I do not want to wake up anymore.

Audrey looks at me as though she knows that I need to talk more; that I need her to listen and believe me. She skips up close and gives me a bear hug. I exhale and collapse onto the couch next to her.

Why is it always a fight to find the light? Why am I always fumbling for the switch when the night is pitch black?

Breathe. I try to breathe through the dust. It is the lack of air that wears me down. Oxygen is a must. My soul suffocates in the sand. Please. Someone? Hold my hand. On this battlefield, my heart is my shield. Only love knows the way when the sun sets at the end of the day. I can not find love. I can not find my way. Why is it always a fight? A fight … to wake up and find the light? I do not want to wake up anymore. Please, please take me away, somewhere far away from here.

I hear Audrey's voice as in a dream. "Poppie, you have to pick up the past before you can let it go. You have to remember."

I feel myself tighten. "Remember what?"

She sits down next to me and plays with my hair. "There's more to the men in your past, Poppie. How far back can you go?"

I am not going back there. Or anywhere. Neither can I stay here. I want to get away. I want someone to take me away. I do not want to think about this, or that, or anything. Especially not about Lena's boyfriend. What did we ever do to deserve what he did to us? I will not say his name. Not now. Not. Ever.

I feel Audrey's hand running gently down my neck, finding the small of my back. "Bringing secrets out into the open takes their power away." The weight and the warmth of her hand calms me. "Besides, it wasn't our fault."

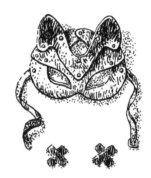

The Love Doll

September 2012, Venice, Italy

VERY DEAR STUDENT,

I dare to send you some French homework before we see each other again.

1) Translate these sentences:

My French teacher is a very rich and handsome man.

He is 27, but he looks much more wise and mature.

I long to see him again and have a romantic dinner together.

His kisses are absolutely perfect and I want more of that.

2) Refuse to practice any French with your guests on board, or with anyone else at all, as it could terribly damage your accent in progress.

Paul is an in-demand entrepreneur and it is always a busy time. It makes the days that we get to spend together all that much more intense. We do not meet often enough. When he is free, I am flying. When I am off, he is working. I want more than just French lessons and love notes.

Je tu rate xxx

He writes that he misses me. It makes me lovesick, Audrey. There is too much distance between us. Physically, if you can imagine what I mean. We do not talk much when we meet. Perhaps due to the language barrier. We communicate through our eyes. This is how I want to feel all the time. He can see me. Right into my soul. He recognises the best of me. I am reeling with tantric love energy, perhaps also because we have not had sex. I feel like I can extend my heart beyond all the corners of the earth.

Paul is both good looking and charming. Of course, I say yes when he invites me on a weekend to Venice. I am addicted to Paul. I do not eat or sleep well until we meet, until I once again feel that rush that binds me to him on such a deep level. I cannot imagine letting go or saying no to his eyes. With Paul, I have no boundaries. His sense of adventure has me exploring surprisingly naughty things and I miss the thrill of it.

"Every woman puts a man through some sort of test," says Audrey. "To see how much he loves her."

Paul must love me if he invites me to Venice. He seems to love me. He just has not said it yet. Venice will surely do the trick and make things click for us. The only way to find out is to go to Venice and see what happens. Besides, I have never been there and what better way to experience it for the first time than with a lover. Audrey, I want Paul to do everything possible for me, to spend time with me, to be with me. If he can do that, then I will open my whole life to him.

When we meet at the boarding gate at Dubai airport, I notice that I am running. I can not wait to throw my arms around him. He is coming off a connecting flight from China, where he does regular business. Paul looks displeased. Perhaps he does not like the pink dress? I decide to let it slide.

"I just found out that my friend, Amy, is in Venice for a fashion shoot," I say to fill the silence. "Maybe we can meet up with her. It will be fun!"

He looks even more annoyed. "Poppie, no, I want you all to myself I don't want your friends around. That's not good for us."

The way he says my name, pronouncing the "ie" with a near-smile, can make me agree to anything. I nudge him gently. "You missed me."

As soon as our flight takes off, I make a sexy suggestion. "Come to the restroom with me." I can see that the WC sign is lit up green and want make use of it early on in the flight while it is still clean.

"No," he says determinedly in his heavy French accent, while shaking his head. "No, we save it for Venice."

I am devastated. I am suffering and longing. Maybe he finds sky sex boring. We need a bigger fantasy. Try it on a gondola later ... or sneak under a boat cover.

From Venice airport, we take a quick detour to Mestre, a red light area on the mainland. Paul slips a few Euros into the sleek hand of a woman in an inky lace dress with a high collar. She has short curly hair, the same colour as her long eyelashes, and thick eyebrows. Without a word, she tilts her head slightly to the left and her blood-red lips pout into a plump strawberry shape. She turns around flirtatiously and beckons us to follow, hips popping from side to side as she leads us along the dirty, industrial main street to an unassuming side shop with studded leather outfits in the window display. I feel soothed by her sweet pout and fluttering eyes as she leads us inside the sex shop.

On entering, I see bondage-style lingerie and corsets. In a glass case at the back of the room, there are very large glass dildos in pink, purple and bright yellow, next to boxes of candy panties. It is my first time in a sex shop. I always imagined cute stuff, such as sex dice, masks and fluffy pink handcuffs. It is rougher in here and I am rather fascinated. What do people do with those long metal pins? Is it used for sexual torture? How on earth does a woman handle that huge orange plastic dildo on the top shelf in the left corner? It must have been modelled on a monster.

The lady in lace introduces us to a petite, platinum blonde shop assistant. I do not know where to look because it is hard to keep my eyes off her breasts—simply because they are so unusually large. She winks at me and takes my hand, then leads me down a narrow staircase to the shop basement. It is small, about twenty-five square metres. The walls are painted a bright shade of red and latex outfits are hanging from metal rods on all sides.

I am not convinced about wearing plastic. I have never been a fan of synthetics, but I am willing to try the latex dress she picks for me. It is nothing special; a simple shift. A dusting of powder makes it less likely to cling so it is easier to put on. I do not think it does anything for me. It is not very wow at all. Even the petite blonde with the big boobs looks at me slightly disapprovingly when I step out of the changing room to present myself. I feel a sting of discomfort as she disappears for a while. Paul and the lady in lace are nowhere to be seen.

I am not sure if I feel all that safe here on my own. Alone, in the basement of a sex shop.

I am relieved when the tiny blonde comes back with a lace-up corset and I am distracted again from my true self. She pulls it over the dress very gently. I can feel her warm breath on my neck as her fingers trace a line across both sides of my waist, from the front to the back of the corset. She starts slowly lacing it up and then pulls it tighter and tighter. Her breath becomes heavier as she starts pulling the laces harder and rougher. I want to say stop, but then she yanks it really hard another time and pauses to catch her breath before she ties a knot at the small of my back. I can hardly breathe. My lungs feel trapped and restricted. Does suffocating equal sexy?

When I look up. I see my breasts spilling out of the dress. I never expected that they could look that luscious. With the corset pulling in my waistline, they are accentuated. I like what I see. It kind of turns me on. Never mind being able to breathe; even I can look hot. The blonde behind me is spellbound. I catch her eye in the mirror and she looks down shyly, then back up at me again full of invitation. I am surprised. I have never tried to date a girl. I mean, girls are not my thing, but I am flattered that she wants to flirt with me. I smile at her warmly and let her take my hand and lead me back upstairs.

"*Signora*," says a tall man in a teal T-shirt, rudely interrupting our little moment as he appears at the entrance of the store holding a slick black box.

He steps inside as though he owns the store—and maybe he does. "*Magnefico, molto magnefico*! It looks great on you, *signora*, but I have something even better. It's couture."

He dips his eyes down to the black box and winks at me secretively. The box is decorated with intricate, over-the-top pink and white swirls and a big silk bow. He puts it on the shop counter and slowly lifts the lid.

Inside the box is some charcoal crêpe paper. It rustles as he pulls out a top and skirt. They are the colour of tar. The top has a big oval hole with a frill around it, clearly meant to frame the breasts. The skirt has a similar cutout at the back.

He holds it out to me, as though he is trying to picture me in it. Our eyes lock.

I gasp for air—and at the thought of putting it on—but struggle to fill my lungs in the tight corset.

He steps in behind me without a word and starts unlacing me. Our eyes lock again in the mirror in front of us. Being able to get more and more oxygen again as the corset loosens up feels so good that it is close to an orgasm. I can see that it gives him immense pleasure to release me slowly, holding me in his power for a fraction of a second longer than he needs to unlace the corset, bit by bit. When it is all undone, he holds the corset at my waist and we stay in the moment for a little while longer, our eyes remaining locked in the mirror. Then he slips it off and the spell is broken. He fetches the box with the second outfit from the counter and holds it out to me.

I put it on in the changing room. The frill frames my naked breasts in the front, while pushing them slightly up and together. In any case, my breasts look firmer and sit higher. I adjust the skirt a little until it sits well. Wherever my hand touches the latex, it sends a ripple of excitement across my skin. I am surprised at how the latex magnifies my senses. With each touch of skin on latex on skin, the feeling of being touched continues to spread spontaneously across my body, as though an invisible lover is caressing me further and further. The latex multiplies the sensation and it slowly spreads until I feel like I am tingling all over. I turn around and look into the mirror. The frill at the back reveals my bum cleavage. It makes me feel a bit nervous, but Paul might actually like that. He always tells me that my bum is my best asset.

When I walk out into the store, I am glowing. The shop guy

gives me extended platform shoes to put on which are probably about ten centimetres high. Ridiculous. Like I can walk in that? It actually takes me a few moments to realise it is not meant to be funny. I am the only one smiling. He takes out the shoes and I slip in my feet. I can stand on the platform and maybe shuffle a little, but that is about it. Then he takes my hair and makes a loose ponytail on the top of my head, so it falls over my face like a fountain. I look dumb. I want to laugh and make a joke, but everyone is dead serious.

"That's good," says Paul as he appears in the doorway, almost as suddenly as the owner did earlier. Perhaps he was smoking outside.

"We'll take it," he says, slightly out of breath and looking at me with a radiant smile. I notice a trickle of sweat on the side of his face. Then I see the little red mark on the shoulder of his T-shirt. It is the same colour as the lady in lace's lipstick. I manage to isolate my perception of this discovery to my sight only—and push the realisation of what it might mean away from my consciousness.

Instead, I start to question my own reality. I feel like I am losing my mind. How can I even think of doubting him? I trust Paul with all my heart. I swallow the tinge of anxiety and smile at myself in the mirror as I take off the latex outfit in the changing room. Even when I am no longer wearing the latex, I feel as though little feathers are caressing my skin.

MY HEAD IS RUSHING AS WE TAKE A TAXI to the Piazzale Roma, where the buses from the surrounding areas terminate. Paul puts his strong, tattooed arms around me as we cross the Grande Canal on the way to the Piazza San Marco. The water is the colour of iced peppermint. I feel a wave of heat crawling up my body as my imagination flashes back to the sex shop. The flirty assistant. The attractive shop owner, who looked me so deep in the eyes ...

We are sitting on a hard wooden bench as the boat rocks rhythmically up and down, up and down. The rocking movement further turns me on and I quickly move over onto Paul's knee, straddling my legs around his and pressing my vulva into his strong upper thigh through both of our clothing. I catch his hands in mine as he holds on to my bum from behind. I look away across the water and start having my first real orgasm. My gasps are blown away in the wind and crowded out by the sound of the boat engine. I did not know that wearing latex could have this kind of after effect. I still feel the caressing sensation on my skin, brought on by my hypersensitivity to the latex fabric.

Though I squeeze Paul's hands hard one more time, he does not realise what is happening with me. I have never had a completely fulfilling orgasm before—and now this, without Paul's dick (or any man's body parts, for that matter). The flattering Italian light, the water, the candy colours and vintage architecture all come together in sights that perfectly please my eyes and heighten my very own little secret moment. Nobody ever has to know. This is for my pleasure only.

As soon at the boat stops, we get our feet onto solid ground, although I still feel like I am floating. We cross the Bridge of Whispers and I see the gondoliers singing to lovers and Chinese tourists alike. I look at Paul and almost say "I love you," but then I drop my camera and the moment passes. We get a little lost in tiny cobbled streets and eventually find ourselves at the Rialto Bridge where we stroll through the market and discover heart-shaped pasta, amongst other, rather pornographic, shapes.

You do not have to be rich to impress your beloved in Venice. Paul has not spent a whole lot and I am already enchanted. Neither do you have to be as good-looking or charming as he is.

186 / LIZE DE KOCK

The city itself commands love. It simply has this way of stirring the heart. Venice is a fantasy island of love, so very far removed from my usual world. That is, until now. I am still reeling from my orgasm and the feeling of owning my pleasure.

We take a pause from our lazy stroll at a pink public bench. It is perfect for catching a breath and, perhaps, a kiss, underneath the pink street lamps. Yes, in Venice the world is, indeed, rose tinted.

"I'm getting us an ice cream," Paul says.

I do not like ice cream. It gives me a headache. It is the combination of cold and sweet and creamy that do not work for me. Give me a sweet, iced sorbet instead. Or a creamy panacotta, but not cream and ice together.

Yet, how can I say no when we are on the island of gelato? Paul always says he chooses his women by the way she eats an ice cream cone.

He sits down on a bench next to the canal and holds his pistachio ice cream between his thighs. He is wearing black shorts. His legs are tanned and shaved.

"Go down on your knees and beg," he says.

I feel compelled to sink my bare knees into the ground in front of him. I look deep into his eyes, ignoring the small crowd of tourists surrounding us. His eyes are a light, dove blue colour with a tiny speckle of an iris, as though he avoids letting too much light through.

"Please can I lick your ice cream," I say, to everyone's entertainment. People stop and stare.

I can pretend. Even though I want to roll my eyes and walk away, I can play the little doll performing for his pleasure. I can do it so well—and so I do. I have been acting all my life, after all.

Paul looks down at me. "How much do you really want it, Poppie?"

"I would do anything," I say, dramatising the words with a lot of breathiness and batting my eyelids for extra effect, knowing full well that I no longer need any man in order to have my sexual pleasure. I am glad I got the false lashes done before this trip.

"Anything," I breathe, my acting skills fully coming into their own.

I eat so much ice cream that it makes me feel sick. Sick, but happy. Happy that Paul is pleased with me. It is important for me to win his favour. I want to earn his love. Good food is always his little reward. We will probably have an amazing meal together later. I do not mind playing a little ice cream game in order to make him happy.

The flavour of deep, pistachio kisses linger on my lips. He holds me in his arms for just a moment. He looks at me as though I am the most beautiful thing he has ever seen. I feel so special when he gives me his full attention. Never mind what I like. I feel loved.

We walk to the top of the bridge and watch the candy floss sunset with a crowd of other tourists. Hordes of gondoliers take off from there and the tourists jump at the chance to surrender to the nuances of love. Venice is so out of time and out of place in today's world that it somehow fills the empty spaces.

"Do you want to go on a gondola?" Paul asks.

I look out across the rose-lit canal. "Yes!"

Paul's face hardens. "Hmm, actually. It's too expensive."

I decide not to indulge my disappointment. It is clear he is only doing it to annoy me. Never mind, there is going to be a delicious dinner coming up soon. The restaurant he wants to try is not much further away anyway.

On the way, we pass a shop with the most exquisite Venetian masks I have ever seen. We walk inside and I am drawn to a golden cat-eye one, decorated with pink feathers. Instead, Paul buys me a full face mask with slanting indigo eyebrows dotted with glitter and big pink lips lined in gold. I think the expression looks a bit sad, but Paul likes it.

"Sadness is beautiful," he says.

By the time we get to our food, I am starving, but it is worth the wait. We try the typical Venetian squid ink pasta and, having been quite skeptical, I am surprised at the exquisite taste. Our chef certainly knows the art of pleasure. It is a messy, fishy fusion of garlic, wine and olive oil that goes rather well with a classic Chianti. Italian wines are lovely to guzzle with food since they are usually mild and low in alcohol. This Tuscan red complements the sauce so well, without overpowering the fish flavour. By the time we finish our *biscotini* and sweet wine, it is dark and cold outside and I am glad to have someone with me who can keep me warm.

When I turn to take the route toward our hotel, he grabs my hand.

"Where are you going, Poppie? Not so fast *ma fille* ..." He stops me.

"Don't you want to go back to our room?" I flirt a little.

It does not soften him this time.

"Take off your dress," he says, "You can leave it here in the street. We'll come back for it later."

It takes me a few moments for the words to register. I feel anxious, but at the same time, compelled to do exactly as he says.

"It's going to be cold down that alley," I say fearfully, not daring to challenge him directly.

"Poppie, I could love you if it just wasn't for that face you're making now. You should be beautiful. You've got all the right features. But you're not."

I feel myself doubling over, submitting to his words as I hold on to my abdomen, trying to comfort myself. I already know that I am not beautiful, but I so want him to love me. I obediently slip out of my dress and let it fall on the sidewalk. I take off my bra and my panties and then I let him look at me. There is a thrill in the air.

My voice vibrates as I speak. "Then why are you with me, Paul?"

"Because you've got the perfect *derriere*," he says, walking toward me and grabbing my arm.

He pushes me really hard down the alley and away from him. "Turn around."

I turn and keep walking with my back toward him.

"That's my girl," he says.

He catches up with me and pushes me carelessly against the stone wall.

I protest. "I love your hands on me, Paul, but it's cold out here tonight—and, besides, someone might walk past."

"Stop complaining, Poppie. You should be grateful that you are here with me in Venice. Now just stay like that. Don't move. That's it. That's good, *ma cherie*."

My heart is anxious. It is cold against the stone wall in the narrow street. Somewhere at the end of it, dark figures are getting out of a gondola. I sense him getting more excited at the thought that they may come closer, but they do not and I am relieved.

I do not know what he is using to hit me. Is it a branch, or some sort of whip that he found on the ground? Or did he arrange for it to be placed here? The same way he arranged for our suitcases to be taken to the hotel?

I am shocked, unable to fully register the moment or accept what is happening to me, unable to speak, move or fight Paul in any way. Through it all, I focus on my breath. Deep breath in. Long breath out. And again.

Later, it takes me a while to realise that it is over and I find my dress lying in the street a few steps away. It stings my back when

I put it back on. I realise that my raw welts must have glistened in the light of the single streetlamp.

"I'm proud of you, Poppie," Paul says, as we walk further through the night. "*Bravo*, you did well."

OUR HOTEL IS DECORATED IN A VINTAGE STYLE, with heavily-printed wallpaper, and a beautiful red velvet tufted couch. I am relieved to be here and able to relax in a safe space. Yet our adventure is not over yet. Paul brings out the black box and unpacks my new latex outfit into a smaller bag.

"Don't get too comfortable now Poppie," he says as I tuck myself into the corner of the velvet couch, "we don't want to arrive at the party too late."

"What party?" I ask as I sink a little further.

Paul pierces me with his eyes. "Come on, Poppie, I didn't buy you couture for nothing. Did I?"

He rounds up the bags with our latex outfits. "So are you ready, Poppie?"

I grab my handbag and follow him out the door. He is carrying my outfit in a small leather duffel bag. We walk only a few blocks before we arrive at our destination, not exchanging a word. It looks like a small, unassuming bar from the outside. On entering, it is quaint and ambient, with crystal chandeliers multiplied in the mirrored walls. The host shows us to the changing room. A few people are hanging around there, changing into their costumes, or relaxing and chatting. Everyone seems to be quite familiar with each other.

Paul strips right down and puts on his latex shorts. He has a ripped body, I must give him that–dimples at the hip bone and a flat six-pack stomach, with his big broad shoulders crowning it all. I put on my new latex couture and try to balance in the shoes.

Then I shuffle over to tie a thin silk ribbon around Paul's neck and make a little bow, not right in the front, but slightly to the side.

I look down at his crotch. "Why are your latex shorts so much shinier than my dress?"

His latex has the colour of wet tar, while mine looks kind of dusty.

"Oh, of course." A small spray bottle instantly appears from his bag. He shakes and opens it, aiming for me as though I am an insect.

"Wait, what's that?" His skin brushes my arm as I try to stop him from lifting the bottle into the air. It evokes a hunger to be touched. I lower my eyes when I start blushing. "You can't just spray me with something without telling me …"

He suppresses a smile. "Relax, it's the spray for the latex, Poppie, you need to spray it when you put it on the first time. Otherwise, it won't shine."

"Be nice," I warn him, "I'm not a cockroach."

He gets the idea that I do not just want to be sprayed at and does it gently, as though he is painting me. The latex changes to a wet look and starts clinging tightly to my skin. I feel a rush as I turn around so that he can spray the back of my dress. My wounds start burning as the outfit clings into it. I embrace the pain as part of the pleasure. I can be tough. I do not want Paul to think that I can not take it. No one here has to know about the scars. It is only my pain. For now, no one can see the scars beyond the lines of my dress. My back is completely covered.

Two people in gas masks and blue full-body catsuits are staring at us. I smile back at them. It all seems quite relaxed and easygoing. At least in the changing room. By the time Paul is done, we are both feeling high. I can see in his face (and in his shorts) that spraying my latex has turned him on.

"Come on," he says hoarsely as he takes my hand.

I follow Paul out into the bar area. It is as small as I thought. There is a shiny wooden bar that makes a curve across the mirrored room and around twenty people are spread out across it, so that it looks neither empty, nor full. On the couch in the corner, a sporty topless girl in a short latex skirt is giving a fat guy a blowjob. I feel someone staring at me and look toward the other corner. A rugged guy in long suit pants with scales tattooed across his upper body is making eyes at me. He is surrounded by five pretty blonde girls, who treat him like a god from all sides. At the bar, there is a woman with fiery hair and a red dress. A man in a full suit walks up to her and, without a word, takes out her breast and bites her nipple.

Paul walks up to the woman in red and greets her with a kiss. The other guy is still busy with her nipple and does not flinch. Paul does not introduce me. However, the woman gently asks the guy to give her nipple a pause and takes a step toward me, all the while leaving her dress undone. She kisses me full on the lips, slipping her soft tongue into my mouth playfully for just a fraction of a second. She steps back. Her right hand follows her eyes to my naked left breast. She caresses the side of my breast, where it protrudes from the frilled frame of the latex top and says, "You're beautiful."

Then she leans back onto the bar and pulls the nipple guy into place at her breast again before I even have a chance to respond. My own breast is still tingling and I can feel my nipples hardening. They probably look better in the frilled latex frame when fully erect anyway. The woman in red has a short conversation with Paul, seemingly about the people at the party. Do they all know each other?

Suddenly, I feel someone poking me from the side. When I turn my head, I see a sweaty, hairy man who seems to be hyperventilating. He is only wearing long black pants with a belt.

"Can I kiss your feet?" he asks in an accent that I cannot place.

"No," I say firmly.

The guy looks devastated.

"Will you whip me?" he asks again, pulling out a small whip behind his back.

Is that what Paul used earlier? Did he tuck a small whip into his pants too?

"Most definitely not," I say.

From his expression, I get the feeling that getting rejected is part of the excitement. He is sulking and yet it looks as though that is exactly what he was going for. The other alternative would be pain. I guess I would rather choose sulking too. The wounds on my back are stinging against the plastic top, but I am beyond pain. I do not feel myself anymore at this stage of the night.

I look back toward Paul and the red lady. They are kissing. The man who was fondling her breast is now giving her oral pleasure. Her dress has a slit right up the front and the guy has opened it up fully to expose her smooth and hairless genitalia. At first, I do not want to believe my eyes. I look away. Another guy comes up to me and asks if I want to go to the playroom. I ignore him and he moves on to another woman.

When Paul is done kissing the woman, he takes my hand and leads me to a dim room at the back of the bar. There are some beds and chill areas where people are having sex. I see the big fat guy having sex with one of the tiny blonde girls, while the guy in the scale tattoo watches his property intensely, his eyes filled with pleasure at watching her with another man. For a moment, I am worried about her, as it looks like the fat guy might break that tiny little body of hers—but then I hear her sounds of pleasure. Behind them, a small group of guys is having an orgy, adding to the chorus.

"Are you having fun, Poppie?" Paul says as he takes my

hand and makes me feel his erection. It is a rhetorical question. He pulls me further into the dark room and sits down on a bed, while moving my hand up and down over his latex shorts.

It reminds me of my first sexual experience and so many others—being forced, rather than men waiting for me to be ready, or caring at all about what I might want.

I am still hurt from seeing him kiss another woman and I am not sure that I feel comfortable with doing sexual acts in public. I pull my hand away subtly, but as soon as he feels my hesitation, Paul gives me a vicious look and steps away from me. He does not waste any time to follow through on his arousal though. After doing a quick scan of the room, he walks up to the guy in scales and, after a few mutual nods, he gets on top of the tiny blonde as soon as the fat guy is done with her. Not only does she comply, but she seems to like Paul even more than the previous one. Perhaps, the guy in the scales will take the final honour upon himself and make sure to claim his property at the end of the night. Instead, the scaly guy turns around and approaches me. He admires the back of my skirt and runs his index finger along the top cleavage of my bum. He shows me the single drop of sweat that he collected there, as though it is a precious elixir. Then he snorts the drop of sweat up his nose and makes a reeling sound, like a pig.

"Argh, you're a tasty little thing," he says, as he turns me around and starts lifting my dress. I do not feel centred enough to know what I want, or to object to what is happening.

"Bend over," he demands.

I follow his command blindly. Just like that, I flop over and hold onto the bed in front of me as he starts fucking me hard from behind, knowing fully that in this moment I am saying yes to being violated. I am hurting myself. I am willingly allowing myself to be raped. I am even inviting it, welcoming it. It is as though I am filled with the power of a demon that is devouring me from the inside. I am hurting so much emotionally and psychologically from all I have seen and experienced here in Venice with Paul that I just want my body to hurt as well. In fact, I would be happy to destroy myself or be destroyed right now. Paul is breaking my heart and that is a lot more painful than anything else that can be done to me. I am feeling so messed up. Watching Paul inside another woman, seeing him betray me … it makes me realise how deeply I feel for him. I do not care what happens to me anymore. I am worthless anyway.

As soon as the reptile is done with me, I go back to the changing room and get all that plastic clothing off of me. It is enough. I change back into my normal clothes and wait for Paul on one of the couches. I am half-asleep by the time he finally arrives.

He gives me the disappointed look. "What is this, Poppie, you're so *stupide*, wasting the night."

I am too tired to respond. Back at the hotel, he still has the cheek to try and get all sweet with me. I do not want him to see me cry, so I pretend to be asleep in our king-sized bed. He does not stop trying to kiss me. My body is defeated. Even if I could try to rationalise a reason to get close to him, I am not physically able. I am hurting. Both inside and outside.

"Paul, Paul, stop," I say through tears, "I can't do this. I'm too much in love with you. Please just leave me alone."

His discontentment sounds like a grunt. I can feel the moment deflate like a week-old party balloon. "Ah, now you've ruined my weekend."

He gets up in a huff to go to the bathroom. Then stops and turns around. "I'm not letting you off the hook that easily. I paid for all this. You owe me and look how you're treating me now. I don't even need a hot girlfriend like you, Poppie. I need someone who is tough enough to take this."

He picks me up from the bed and carries me to the bathroom. The pus in the wounds on my back sticks to his sweaty skin. Pain is secondary to this forced removal from my slumber. He kicks open the bathroom door and puts me down, keeping his hand on my upper back so that he can easily stick my head into the toilet bowl. It smells like his shit. I am not scared when he flushes. I do not resist. I do not struggle or writhe. I can breathe under water. I let the water wash over me. Over and over again. Then he drags me back to bed by my hair, pulling out clumps at a time and shouting. "You're fucking crazy."

I am shaking. It is not a shiver. It is a full body shaking. It is an earthquake. It is a tsunami rising up inside my head. Paul gets back into bed without touching me, turns his back and instantly starts snoring. It is the sound of a wild baboon, a beast beside me in this ornate Venetian hotel bed. I stare at the wallpaper all night, escaping into the intricate moonlit patterns, finding solace in the symmetry of flat flowers.

In the morning, my flight leaves a few hours earlier than Paul's. I grab a quick espresso before I go and feel compelled to give him an uninspired last kiss goodbye, too tired to defy his control. When I get to the airport, I receive a text message that he decided to go on a gondola without me and that it was "really super."

I have to run to the restroom. Relieved that there is no queue, I kick open the door. My tears flood into the toilet bowl, together with half-processed pieces of my breakfast and a despicable slithery creature that I do not want to describe. I feel like fainting, but I have a plane to catch, so I wipe my mouth and flush.

When I turn around, Audrey is there. I did not even bother to lock the door. Or did she find a way to open it, the way she always finds me when I need her most?

"Audrey," I cry, "I've just spent a weekend in the most romantic city in the world with a man who would rather screw a stranger in a sex club and take a gondola on his own. It is quite the riddle that he is even with me at all. I just don't get it!"

She looks down in an attempt to avoid telling me what is on her mind this time, but then she has a change of heart and looks me straight in the eye. "It's so much easier if girls can be groomed for sexual abuse. If women can be coerced into prostituting themselves, as if they chose it. If rape can be normalised. That leaves a lot of room for predators to operate without any trouble. Our societies have been propagated into an abuse culture. It looks all shiny from the outside. We don't even know."

Her words go over my head. All I can think about is my own agony. "I just want to understand why it has to happen, to me?"

She is confident when she speaks. "You think you are alone but you're not. There are so many others. It happens to you and all around you. Why does it happen? Eish, who knows? It has become trendy to disregard love, to turn sex into pain. Trends are often used to sell something. If you want to find the why behind anything, it usually makes sense to follow the money ..."

I roll my eyes at her over-the-top wisdom. "I don't care about money. I just want to be loved. Is that so wrong? Am I doing something wrong?"

"Ai Poppie," she sighs. "Sometimes, it's the lessons you need to learn to find your own destiny and sometimes the wrong man prepares you for the right one. If it is not yet the right one, you can change yourself to reflect him as best possible, or you can change the man to reflect you better. You can force it if you're both committed. Or you can focus on yourself. Choose yourself. Love yourself."

The bright airport light is unflattering, but Audrey is still the most beautiful thing I know. "One of your riddles again. What does that even mean? I have pushed myself far enough in trying to meet his needs. I can't force it further. This man will never do anything to reflect on my emotions."

She does not move the tiniest muscle, not even a smile. "The other option is to wait for the right one. Someone who sees you; who feels the joy around you and wants to be with you all the time. If it is that easy for a man to turn away and be with another woman, then there is not enough commitment for anything lasting and meaningful. A man has to love a woman in spite of troubles, because when it comes to love, a woman tends to fall deeper in love and a man, more out of love as the years go by. Ai, Poppie, but a man is not the answer. Neither is travel."

When I look up again, a woman and her teenage daughter are standing in front of me in the airport restroom looking concerned for my sake. I excuse myself and quickly wash my hands and mouth before rushing to my gate.

"YES, OF COURSE I DID IT TO ANNOY YOU," Paul writes a few days later via email. "You know how much more I like you when you are sad. It is the first thing I ever noticed about you. Your sadness. It is why I was drawn to you in the first place. It was boring for me when you started to look happy in Venice. *Bises*."

I break up with him via text message and delete his number. Yet deleting him out of my mind is not as easy. The whole experience makes me think a lot about who I want to be and how I want to be treated, but I do not know how I can make myself more lovable. I try so hard. I would give up anything.

Audrey's words echo in my ears. "Giving up your boundaries won't make someone love you. Everything has to change, starting with yourself. You need to stop trying to please men and please yourself instead. Respect your own sex. Respect your own body. Take ownership of your body. You buy good make-up and think that it means taking care of yourself, even loving yourself. Yoh, that's not it."

This is annoying though. As a flight attendant, I get discounts at airport duty free. I own the latest fashion from all over the world. My shoes are from Italy. My bikini is from Brazil. All these things that I own, they are my armour against being unloved. Above all, my branded items are a mark of approval from those who know. Wearing high-end labels makes me part of an elite inner circle of people who just, get it. That is so much better than being alone. You just do not understand, Audrey.

She interrupts me, still keeping a straight face. "Industry loves to play on this idea that loving yourself means buying yourself things, but it doesn't have to mean spending money. Putting a price on love takes the beauty out of it. Loving yourself comes from inside your heart, does not cost anything and, most of all, it should not hurt."

So far love never did not hurt, I think, as I shrug her off. The wounds on my body sting all over with every move. "Then the beauty of love is something that does not exist. Not in my reality here on earth, Audrey."

I continue to hide behind my shopping spoils and my lip-lined smile and yet, inside, I am shattered. There are many chatty, crew girls around me all the time and yet I no longer connect with anyone. I try to call my model friend, Amy, but she is busy at a cover shoot in Milan. Her success no longer leaves room for listening and laughing. As with many things in life, friendships can be fleeting too.

If only I could be adored by the world the same way she is. I spend so much time and energy on perfecting the right look. I am pretty enough to be used, but I am still not pretty enough to be loved. Beautiful people are easier to love. I want to be beautiful.

I pick up a postcard with azure island impressions in my

mailbox. It is from Lola, written in elaborate curvaceous letters with lots of twirls.

> *I am doing a belly dance gig on a cruise ship in Greece and thought of you. How are your travels going? When are you coming to Cairo?*

That seals it. I do not need to be invited a third time. It is time to embrace the divine feminine.

The Dancer

March 2013, Cairo, Egypt

FOR THE FIRST TIME SINCE I LEFT HOME, I dare to call my dad. I just want to hear his voice and be acknowledged, even if it may turn out negatively. Maybe I will never stop hoping for his acceptance. His phone barely rings when someone picks up. "Hello, it's Lena speaking." Her melodic, nasal voice is the last thing I expect to hear. "Lena? You're picking up my dad's phone these days?"

"Hello, Poppie, let me quickly see where your dad is." How is that for trying to dodge a conversation.

"Lena, slow down, I think the two of us should talk first." I hear her swallow. "I don't really care if there's something going on between you and my dad, Lena, but I want to know where I can find Audrey."

The silence is scratchy.

"Where's Audrey, Lena? Why would no one tell me where Audrey is? I keep seeing her in visions, in my dreams. I need to know where I can look for her."

Nothing.

"Lena, please." I beg.

When I am on the verge of giving up, she speaks. "Audrey, she was ... she, she died, when she was twelve. She was killed by my boyfriend, the one I was with all those years back in Springbok. He was drunk. He hit her over the head with a broken bottle. When I found her she was already dead. We did not want to tell you. We could not. Do not ask me to talk about it again, Poppie. I do not want to resurrect that ghost. Her murderer is in prison. It is all done and dusted."

The words come down on me with a boulder's weight. *I won't say his name.*

Her voice quivers. "It is not like I really had a choice. I was only with that man to cover up for loving your dad. This love destroyed everything in its path. None of this would have happened if he did not marry your mom, if we did not have to lie, if we were not forced to separate because of apartheid..." Lena sobs in tiny bursts, a tap opening and closing. I can feel her heart expanding over the phone line. "I am sorry, Poppie, I am sorry. I love him. I mean, I love your dad. I have loved him all my life. Let me call him for you."

My whole body vibrates with tears. For Audrey, for my family, for everything. I forgot why I wanted to speak to my dad in the first place. "No, Lena, just leave it. I will call back again another day."

TIME AFTER TIME, IT IS WORTH getting as far away as possible. To a place where I can feel closer to myself. Some places have more healing power than others. It possibly has something to do with cosmic alignment—the pyramids were not built to mimic the stars for nothing. I want to be a light, not a mirror of society or the pain I have seen. Being in Cairo, with the most famous belly dancers of the city, gives me the chance to gain strength from their beauty so that I can learn to dance to my own authentic drum. I will stay as long as it takes to cultivate that ability within myself.

"Look!" The majestic and gorgeous woman next to me in the taxi beckons me to look out of the window. Amalia is speaking in a cooing voice, her face unfolding like an ivory garden rose. She is even more beautiful when she is completely relaxed. She has been on this earth longer, but she looks younger.

I turn my head in the direction that Amalia is pointing and catch the sun going down as our taxi crosses the Nile.

"I love this view every time," Amalia vows, "no matter how many times I come back to Cairo." It is lack of stress more than anything that makes her so attractive, as though she imprints on her surroundings, instead of being drawn into the restlessness of the world.

The last drop of gilded sunshine melts into the horizon. I hope its sparkle will find Audrey in the afterlife. Her soul never had the time to create the things she yearned for. As long as I am still alive, nothing is final. I am still becoming. The question is who am I becoming? What do I want to be? I still have no idea who I truly am.

"Thank you for coming with me," I say over the cacophony of car hooters, "Amalia. I feel like I've known you forever."

She points out our matching evil eye charm bracelets, a talisman against that damning stare. I am wearing mine layered with the lucky charm bracelet my mom gave me years ago. Double protection.

Amalia toys with the charms. "Shopping together well can do that to women. You get to know what makes the other's heart beat faster. Which either divides you, or you become friends. It transcends culture or personal differences. Shopping is not only a beloved pastime in Dubai, it's a universal love. Not that I've been to Dubai. Tell me."

I take off my sunglasses and hold them in my lap, playing with the ears while I speak. "Nothing much to tell. Just that, when I saw Lola dancing in Dubai, I felt this sense of belonging. Something in her was calling out to me. She was, sort of, drawing me into her. She told me to come to Cairo and I decided to do it. Things fall into place so effortlessly sometimes. Then she led me to you. I feel like I've known you forever."

"Instant friendship." She smiles. I inhale the sweet scent of her lotus oil perfume. "It can happen like that when you recognise a kindred spirit along the way. Besides, you attract the right people into your life at the right time, when you have a clear goal."

My heart contracts. It is time for the beginnings of a new friendship. I suddenly feel clumsy. "So, how long have you been coming to Cairo?"

She takes a moment to reply. "I was married to an Egyptian. For eight years. I lived here with my husband before I moved to California. The women use belly dance to connect with each other. Over time I learned that there is something to be said for dancing with other women. It is social and inclusive and all kinds of wonderful."

I smile, encouraging her to continue.

"Dancing together can be healing. It is a means of communication. Validation. A celebration of femininity. We used to meet in a group to dance together. Just us women. Sometimes with a drummer, or a band at bigger parties. The dance is the one thing I wanted to keep after my marriage ended. I have been back for five years now, but I still come to Cairo every year." She holds out her hand to the window, as if to present the scenery of street vendors and stray cats outside the car.

Our taxi driver swerves to the right, swearing. He makes a detour and interrupts our conversation to explain something to Amalia in Egyptian Arabic. Then he turns up the radio to hear the latest news. I close my eyes to the deafening sound of tires screeching and hooters honking, as the whole world suddenly turns up too loud. I have no control over my own safety and I have to cup my ears to hear my own voice as I scream.

Amalia moves closer to me and translates calmly. "He says that some of the roads are blocked again due to protests on Tahrir Square. He is going to get us to the apartment a different way. A safer route, so we can avoid getting stuck in the mob."

I have seen enough to know that the world will not change to a better, more peaceful or harmonious place. "We have to change," I mouth as she tries to read my lips, "Things are getting worse."

Her look does not convince me when she finds a quieter moment to speak. "It is not as bad as it is seems. We are going to be fine. We are free spirits."

My cynical laughter is muted by the traffic chaos outside. "You, maybe yes. I would love to find the freedom I long for inside my own self and bring it to the world." My eyes involuntary roll up before I continue. "Instead of waiting for answers. But I have to be able to survive. Do whatever. How do you manage to be so sovereign in the face of all this? Will you teach me?"

Amalia pouts as if to dare me.

My words come rushing out, furiously defending my fear. "Women are getting raped on the square. People are dying. Things were not this grim when I booked my trip." I compensate for myself by talking faster. "I didn't want to miss the chance when Lola invited me. Coming to Cairo is one of the best things I've done. I just wonder how it will continue. Right now, we are driving toward the danger, not away from it. We live on top of the problem."

She steadies herself as we cross a few potholes in the quieter backroads. "Don't you worry. We are going to keep holding on, keep moving, keep dancing." When she laughs, it sounds like singing. "Dance, Poppie, dance."

I sit back to observe Amalia as I would a bird in a tree.

Her green eyes are smouldering crystal balls lighting my way. "Dance is the ultimate way to deal with any challenge, threat or disaster. When all else fails, just dance. It is a philosophy for turning your life around. You wait and see."

I feel the rhythm of my heart responding to her words. If I have the power to reinvent myself, I now also have the partner and the props. "I've just shopped for a boot full of belly dance accessories at the Khan al Khalili. I might as well learn how to use it. Every single thing at that market had my name on it. Four floors of dance costumes, silk veils, headdresses, jewellery, finger cymbals …"

"Shop till we drop." Amalia flutters her hand light-heartedly. "It is a non-stop dancer's paradise. Belly dancers spend their entire budget on their next costume. It is a commitment to yourself. To celebrating your beauty. See, you now have everything you need to feel like a dancer. We are almost ready to go and train with Lola."

I am a woman who no longer has anything to lose. I might as

well take the chance to learn from powerful, independent women how to regain some of what I have lost already. I will soak in all there is to learn on being delicately powerful.

THE DRIVER DROPS US IN A SMALL, DUSTY STREET at the back of our apartment building. We are staying in Lola's city loft, where Modern Egyptian art is matched with vintage furniture and silvered mirrors set in elaborate golden frames. Our pad has two bedrooms, a spacious lounge with a French balcony and a kitchen so tiny that we have to squeeze into it sideways. The bathroom is decorated in regal North African tiles. It is the only room with a proper mirror where we can do our make-up.

Amalia likes my dramatic kohl from Dubai and I am enamoured with the stage make-up pigment that she brought from the United States. We quickly freshen up for our evening appointment.

Then we go all the way back through the same traffic chaos, to the edge of the Nile. I focus on the scenery. Twilight is a beautiful time in this desert city. The sand gives a red tinge of drama to the rising moon and the sky. Flickering lights add sparks of colour to the bland hues. There is a definite power in the air, when I look beyond the thick layer of dust.

By the time we get there, the cruise boats are casting twinkles on the river water. The closer we step to the dinner boat, the more quiet it is. We stop to take in the serenity of the moment, before getting on board via a walkway lined with festive fairy lights. Inside the boat, dining tables are prepared with formal table linens, making a half circle around the area reserved for the band and dancers. We sit down at our table and watch as the boat fills with mostly locals.

"In Cairo, dance is celebrated by a large part of the community," says Amalia. "Fans are plentiful, given that dancers honour local techniques. Lola is convincing enough and the city accepts her as their own."

The band starts warming up as we walk past to grab a snack from the generous buffet of falafel, salads, cold meats, flat bread, grilled vegetables and dips. A group of elderly men are tinkering with local instruments, including percussion and strings, as well as wind instruments. The Egyptian drum, or *tablah*, as it is called here, quite literally moves me, as it provides the beat for doing strong hip movements. The band has two drums, both elaborately decorated with intricate Egyptian patterns inlayed with bone. There are also several tambourines, smaller and larger kinds, to add some jingle. Romance is infused by the *kanun*, an enchanting stringed instrument that sounds similar to a harp. There are also flutes and oboe-like instruments to complete the traditional Egyptian band. The men do sound tests and start playing background music to set the scene.

Lola lets her band play for longer than I expect before she enters. It heightens the suspense and allows us to still our first hunger, before she captures our attention. Her large, curly blonde figure appears hidden behind a golden silk veil. She gives us only little hints of her voluptuous shape and couture costume as she swoops around the show area. She makes deeply sensual veil movements before gracefully letting the veil go to the ethereal sound of the *kanun*. The whole room gasps, as she circles the tables, making eye contact and smiling. It is a wonderful way of honouring the audience one on one. When Lola returns to the dance floor, the boat smells of myrrh. I look across the tables and notice that most people are smitten. That is how she sets herself up for success, winning her audience over by acknowledging each individual before she even starts to dance.

Back in the spotlight, Lola has the luminosity of one thousand and one stars. She is wearing a crystal-embroidered top with a

209 of the Nile, Amalia

matching silk skirt. A high slit up to her hip, reveals her long legs as she does a few hip drops and bold poses to the sound of Egyptian drums. There is power in her body. It is not simply dance training and skill. She is animated from the inside. When she opens her heart in dance, the audience cannot help but fall in love. I feel my own heart, mesmerised, by the time she exits.

Later, at the dessert buffet, Amalia introduces me to one of the local guys. "He is a regular at Lola's shows, coming to see her every night on the cruise. He always gets the same table and has become a sort of patron of hers. Right, Ammon?"

"*Aiwa*, I can no longer get her out of my mind." He picks out a few sweets. "My blonde Egyptian, she gets better and better with every show."

WHEN OUR BOAT DOCKS BACK AT THE EDGE of the Nile, Amalia explains that Ammon is a wealthy Egyptian and his zeal for Lola has helped to elevate her status in the city. "He is her personal ambassador of sorts and often accompanies her around town."

"Join us for a nightcap?" Lola is already waiting for us outside, with a big smile. She has endless energy.

I look toward Amalia, relieved to see her shaking her head.

"Not tonight, Lola." Amalia yawns. "Thanks so much for a wonderful evening. You're magical, as always! Enjoy the rest of your night."

"Okay, *meeshi*." Lola gives us a group hug and plants a kiss on each of our cheeks. Then she waves Ammon over.

I briefly shake Ammon's hand before flagging a taxi close by. He is fixated on Lola. My own bad experiences of men watching over me makes me uneasy as we wave goodbye—and yet it gives me comfort to know that she will not be alone in making her way through the unrest in the city tonight.

As soon as I crawl into bed, I fall into a deep sleep. I dream that I am dancing filled with pure light that radiates from my heart around the world. Protection is given to me in the form of a crystal bracelet. It holds the gift of time and eternal youth. I twirl in gratitude for this feeling of wholeness, for the pieces of myself that I am able to revive. The ripples of my circle skirt send vibrations of healing to all humanity, as I keep turning.

WHEN I WAKE UP, I KNOW THAT I HAVE RECEIVED a spiritual gift. I want to dance until I can realise this dream of harmony and wholeness—but first, coffee. In the distance, I hear echoing noises. Then I smell the tear gas. The clashes on Tahrir Square are continuing. What a contrast this violence poses to my dance experience of the city. There is a spiritual realm beyond the soot. Cairo is a heart place. Even if it is a rather troubled heart, full of complex emotions. Stirring these emotions can evoke wonder, or disaster. I am filled with wonder, even while disaster reigns.

"Oh, you're up!" Amalia appears in her leopard print kimono while I discuss Cairo with myself in the hallway, as though it is totally normal. Her hair is a messy bird nest on top of her head. "I was just going to make a coffee. Do you want one?"

I nod and sit down in our cosy kitchen, pulling my legs in under the table with its synthetic lace tablecloth. She does not seem to think it is weird that I talk to myself—or perhaps she is not yet fully awake. I am glad to let it slip.

"Hmm. I'm wondering if we should get out of here." She brews our kahwa in a traditional kanaka. "I've been keeping an eye on the news."

I stare sullenly at the kitsch vase with plastic flowers in front of me, pushing the angst in my heart down and out. "Yup. Let's do it. I can work on not being afraid, but I don't want to be reckless."

She puts a perfectly foamy cup of traditional coffee in front of me. A whiff of elation. "Let's think about it. We can read our cups."

Amalia's Egyptian coffee has grit. I am getting better at seeing the patterns and symbols that are formed by the thick coffee residue. She is teaching me how to do coffee reading and I find that I have a knack for this kind of thing. It takes me a while to relax and let things flow, but then it comes. Amalia turns her empty cup over on the saucer and waits a few seconds. When she turns it back over, she slides the cup my way and looks at me expectantly. At first, I see nothing. I study the patterns of the residue from the handle of the cup clockwise. It is almost like an optical illusion, the images only come to me when I let my eyes look beyond the obvious. The answer is not in what is there at first sight, but when I look through that, more meaningful images start to appear.

"Oh, there it is, I see a pyramid." I turn the cup back to Amalia. "It's pretty clear."

Her eyes take on a deeper shade of blue as she looks into the cup. Then she shakes her shiny onyx hair and takes a deep breath.

I look again, trying to find more clues. "There are also some ripples, could be the ocean … or, the skirt of a dancer. A dancer. It's definitely a dancer."

"There's something else … an eye," I add after a short pause.

Amalia fiddles with her bracelet. "The evil eye. Good thing we got these."

"Or perhaps just the eye of the tiger." If the truth lies in the eye of the beholder, I may as well speak into life something beautiful.

Amalia seems pleased with my alternative interpretation and her rosy features ease out visibly. She can do that-simply let go of the anxiety brought on by stressful surroundings. From one moment to the next, her mood turns upbeat. "Let's go and dance with Lola, next to the pyramids. Hey, it's all in the cup."

IT IS ANOTHER COMMOTION on our way over to Giza. People are shouting. Taxis are moving along in a rush. Cairo is a city of opposites. Men at street cafés quietly drinking their *kahwa* and smoking shisha pipes while the unrest gets bloody in the background. Banana stands are juxtaposed with propaganda posters on the side of the road. Dirt and a pile of rusty metal next to glamorous dance factories full of dyed chiffon and rhinestones. People are slamming on their hooters in road rage.

We seek out the soul centre of the city around the pyramids, to shimmy and shake in protest of all that is brutal. To use our bodies in praise of beauty. In glory of the magnificence of the female body. I want to choose love where others choose anger. To shake off all signs of worry and pain. When all else fails, I will dance.

Our taxi conquers the Giza traffic and drops us as close as possible to Lola's house. We walk down the sandy pathway scattered with kittens. Laundry is hanging in makeshift lines from the windows across the cracked ochre walls of the buildings. The olive green wooden shutters are closed up to keep out the heat of the day.

We walk up seven flights of stairs and end up a little out of breath, which makes it all the more wonderful when we step into Lola's rooftop dwelling. It is a dancer's den full of drapes, marble details, and carpets. A magnificent turquoise alabaster vase in Lola's foyer lures me inside, as do the cats who greet us curiously.

"Hi, Lola," calls Amalia. She is nowhere to be seen.

We walk through the mirrored dance studio full of photos of Lola in the rapture of dance. The next door leads us into the kitchen and out onto her balcony, where she is sitting wearing oversized sunglasses, with the backdrop of the towering Great Pyramid.

"You're early." Her voice is syrupy. "Sit down, let's have some tea and catch up."

When I hug her, I smell sandalwood. It lingers in my hair when I sit down, making me feel alert and stimulated. Lola offers us strong tea boiled with a lot of sugar, then passes along a glass bowl filled with sprigs of fresh mint and slices of lemon. I put mint in my tea and Amalia adds a squeeze of lemon to hers. The tiny glass cups are decorated with gold patterns. A grey kitten looks for a cuddle on my lap.

"That's Sequin," says Lola, "she's a rescue."

"She does look like she needs a little love." I count as many as five other cats swirling around the balcony.

"Rather, a lot." Lola casts adoring eyes at Sequin as the kitten jumps up and starts pawing my knee, all the while still managing to keep our full attention. Lola flashes me a proud smile. "There's so much cruelty to animals here. They don't deserve it. Animals also need love and they can't always help themselves."

It is not only what I see that makes Cairo a magical place. It is an unseen realm, a city filled with dancing angels in a dusty mirage.

Audrey steps onto the balcony out of nowhere, props herself up on to the wall and bounces her legs so that her whole body hops. My first reaction is to get up and embrace her, but I do not want to kick off Sequin and then I remember that she is just a daydream.

Amalia chimes in with a clear, wide smile. "Poppie, helping animals, or other people, is not unusual for the dance community here. To be called a true belly dance artist, the dancer has to be a good person, because of the potential connotations. You can only reach the artistic level Lola's at if your energy is pure. It's not only training. Belly dance is a personal journey and at some point you have to make an important choice."

Audrey pulls her face and swings her legs to and fro. The next time I blink, she is gone. I hear her fading giggle like a naughty child running away.

"And what happens if you're not a good person? I mean, not every good dancer is a good person?" I look from Amalia to Lola.

"Oh, people feel your energy," says Lola sweetly. "You have to be spotless. On the inside. If a dancer doesn't have a good heart, but only skill, it doesn't truly move others. Great art flows from a great heart."

Lola tucks in a few strands of hair and gets up from her chair. She beckons us inside to start our lesson. Sequin moans gently as I lift her tiny body from my lap. She stays as close to my feet as possible, tiny claws pricking. I try my best not to step on her.

"That's not going to work, Sequin, you know you need to stay outside," says Lola, as she picks her up off the studio floor and leaves her outside the room. Before Lola can close the door, Sequin slips inside again and hides between my feet. She's fast. It takes us a while until we have the room to ourselves.

"Time to shimmy," says Amalia with that peaceful glow that belies her age.

We remove all our excess clothing so that we are only wearing dance tights and t-shirts. I tie my new red hip scarf, from the Khan al Khalili, around my waist and watch the bright colour move from side to side in the mirror as we warm up.

"When the heart dances, it moves others," says Lola, as she prepares to teach us some provocative belly accents, as part of the choreography we are learning. When the classical Egyptian love song starts, it transports me to a world of intense longing. I can feel the poetry and emotion from the very first note. My body is filled with yearning. A yearning for who, or what, I am not sure, but I have to dance to express it.

Lola is not really dictating, but she looks at me all surprised and bobs her head from side to side in one fluid, sliding movement. It is the most natural thing in the world for her to move like this. I, in turn, do as much as I can in the lesson but some of the moves are beyond my ability.

"I know, Lola, I have to train harder. I'll keep practicing." I can not but commit to Lola's clear eyes. I am getting to know belly muscles that I never knew existed.

I feel the power in the women on either side of me and respond to their movements in the mirror. Soon I forget about myself and let the music move me as though by a spell. Amalia, Lola and I are in tune, opening our hearts to one another without saying a word. I am able to say things through the movements of my body that I can not express otherwise. Things I know the others can understand without knowing how or why. It is one of the most intimate of human connections. It is the language of dance.

"Relax your foot, Poppie!" Lola's voice brings me back into the room. "Relax completely. Keep your feet natural. There's no pointing of toes like in ballet. Belly dance shouldn't be forced, or hurt."

In life, I am often forced and hurting. In belly dance, I can just be myself. I let go of the tension in my feet and shake it out all the way to the tips of my toes. This is my permission to throw off the restrictions I learned as a ballet dancer at school. Lola is offering me the space to be expressive and revive the bones of my original self. There is no system in belly dance. While there is a basic technique, the movement is free. I can go with my own passion and interpretation of the music. It is not only my body, but my whole being vibrating and releasing, renewing itself, resurrecting the mummy in me.

For the first time in what feels like forever I move out from my hiding place behind all the personae that help me to fit in. I let the little girl in me shine through every part of my body, as I shimmy and vibrate using all the belly power I have available to me at this stage of my training. I dance for all of me and for Audrey. I am, finally, free.

"You train and train and train and then you simply allow your body to do what it wants to do." Lola teaches us about the importance of a strong core stance before putting on some harmonious cooling down music. "First you have to have the muscle fitness. You've got to be in top form".

She accentuates our last stretches with soft arms. "Then you listen to the music and let your heart lead you. Move with your heart".

AFTER CLASS, I BREATHLESSLY PAGE through Lola's books in the corner of the studio. The great belly dancers of Cairo have strong bodies, strong hearts, strong minds. I have so many questions but wait until Lola is fully dressed and turning towards me, expectantly, before I start. "Don't you ever feel vulnerable to say you're a belly dancer? What does it take to express your sensuality so freely, without losing your honour as a woman?"

Lola makes her neck long and lifts her chin when she answers. "It's not easy. A *raqs sharki* dancer can bring a lot of shame to a local family. Belly dance is seen as a sinful profession and since family reputation is very important, your second cousin twice removed may have problems marrying well if there is a belly dancer in the family. In fact, the shame can be so overwhelming that a father would go as far as killing his daughter if she confesses to being or even wanting to be a belly dancer."

She pauses until her words take on their full meaning.

"The truth is," she continues, the softness in her face contrasting with the steel of her determination, "I had to flee Egypt at a young age with my mother's help. That's how I eventually ended up in South Africa. I had to build up my dance school as a teen and make a name for myself before I could afford to come back. Now I live in between countries and I love it. It took a lot to pursue my dream and remain an independent woman."

I want to be like that. Fully individualised and accomplished. Soft on the outside and strong on the inside. I think out loud. "What happened in between fleeing and South Africa? How did you do it as a young girl? What exactly does such a journey entail?"

Amalia looks up at me from where she is sitting on the floor and almost starts to laugh. "You mean, the one where your intentions as a woman are seen as corrupt just because you are who you are?"

Lola is not smiling. She waves a strand of hair from her face and sits down on a plush cushion, steadying herself for the next part of our conversation. Sequin is moaning pitifully at the door.

"Well, no," I say and then decide to reframe it, "the one where you finally become, and remain, a strong, independent woman—and succeed."

We both look toward Lola expectantly.

She answers with all her grace. "It takes a lot of strength to be true to yourself and stay on that path even when everyone around you sees you as immoral. You have to fully claim yourself. Everything you feel, everything you are. Every tiny muscle in your belly and every lock of hair on your head. In the end, a woman standing inside her full power is a phenomenon to be reckoned with. It takes time and conviction, but it's worth it."

I am suddenly feeling cold and pull on my jersey. "Phew, I don't even know my truth. You risk all to live yours ..."

Amalia has her arms wrapped around her knees, as though she is holding herself. Her hair is draping all the way down to her fluffy sheepskin boots. She continues another thought. "Why does a local mother even support this kind of rebellion in a woman?"

For a moment, pain cuts across Lola's eyes and then settles into a wise kindness. "A lot of women are jealous of others' freedom. They envy the fact that they have submitted and denied their own souls, whether by their own will or by often violent force. And they hate the others for being allowed or insisting on their freedom. My mother supported my free spirit because freedom is something she never had. She loved me and she wanted me to have a better life than the one she chose. Yet, there's a catch. Freedom comes at a high price. It's a lonely, narrow road and I am lucky that it eventually led me to success. It doesn't work out for everyone, but if you have that kind of spirit, it's the only way to be truly fulfilled and happy. Everything you do must be true to your own soul, from the heart—and not dictated by others. Not even by a man or by your own family."

Amalia is now sitting legs crossed on the studio floor, with her mouth wide open. "How do you stand up to your family, Lola? It's tough with my parents already judging me for getting divorced. There are so many expectations. I do not want them to look down on me for choosing to wander, instead of having a family and a stable job."

"Every now and again, I think that maybe I am doing something wrong," Lola smiles, "and then, but no. This is who I am and I have to be true to myself. It takes a lot for a woman to commit to herself, especially within a very conservative environment.

Everyone wants to be liked and it is hard not to care about what the people say. Especially if it involves the people you love."

"Do you still have contact with your father?" I ask, as Sequin competes with my voice for attention. She is so tiny, but she knows how to make herself heard, announcing herself so loudly from behind the door that we cannot possibly miss it.

"In the end, my father is very proud of me, but it took a long time of being in a sort of exile until I reached the kind of status that won over his respect." Lola says it with a sense of achievement, as though she has overcome an impossible challenge.

Amalia closes her mouth and dusts herself off. She moves over to sit next to me on the bench. "Lola is the big boss of her own show now, Poppie. She is the one who hires the male members of the band. Is it ten or twenty, Lola?"

"Oh, it's about eighteen at the moment. Yes, I get the gigs and they work for me. They play the music to suit my movements. They follow my body. Not the other way around. The belly dancer leads the performance." Lola speaks with a neutral expression, open and humble. She gets up from her cushion in the studio nook and heads for the door.

The story changes me and a jolt of energy makes me jump up and twirl. "It doesn't happen often that a beautiful, sensual woman who makes money with her body also gets to be completely in charge of her own thing. You're an important woman."

She pats her heart area just below her left shoulder. "Everything important starts here," she says, pushing her chest forward and relaxing her shoulders. "If it doesn't start here, it is not important."

Her words settle, like a silk veil floating slowly to the floor.

I comment dreamily. "What a beautiful story."

"The beauty is in your own eye." Lola's smile comes from her heart. It is important.

Amalia smiles this way too and now I cannot help but to join them. A smile that comes from the inside brings relaxation to the face. A relaxed face is more beautiful—and stays beautiful for longer.

When Lola opens the door of the dance studio, Sequin is still sitting there waiting. Lola picks her up and she starts purring. "I love you, my little Sequin."

I have angels on my journey, no doubt. I have Audrey and Amalia and Lola and, yet, I keep getting caught up with the same devils every time.

ON THE WAY BACK TO OUR PART OF THE CITY we stop at a French patisserie. Amalia knows people here. Their faces shine when she walks in the door. She knows the secret of being quietly powerful in a room. She can be the same woman who sits in the corner unnoticed, or a goddess if she chooses to be. Powerful beauty is more than a state of being. It is a decision. Amalia, for one, fully inhabits that space.

"Amalia? Of course it's you!" I hear the raspy voice from behind me. "You're back in Cairo? How have you been?"

"Ehad, what a pleasant surprise," says Amalia politely. "This is my friend Poppie. We are taking some dance lessons at Lola's."

He grins as I turn to face him.

Ehad is athletic and handsome, with his courteous eyes and rough beard stubble. It surprises me that I want to blush. I get up quickly and shyly shake hands. "Hi Poppie, I'm Ehad. I mean, hi Ehad, I'm Poppie."

His grip is binding and I notice that his arm muscles are solid and saturated by sunshine. Ehad looks at me with a firm focus in his eyes. I freeze as I sometimes do in front of a camera. I am self-conscious and unsure what to do or say. He moves over to my side. It is too intense for me to talk properly, but I find out two things about Ehad: that he has connections to the military and that he has known Ammon and Lola for many years. He drives us back to our apartment and invites us for a street food dinner of traditional *koshari*, a mix of rice, vermicelli, lentils and a spicy tomato sauce.

Afterwards, we meet Lola and Ammon at a *raks sharki* night-club. They play belly dance music all night. Amalia heads for the dance floor right away. I catch on to the excitement as soon as the DJ puts on some popular drum solos. A quick nod and Lola joins us on the floor, drawing the attention of the whole place with her. We let our shimmies free, aware that all eyes are on us. None of us is small or cute. Amalia and I are both tall and Lola is a large lady. We are also not young. Yet we are, in this moment, the most alluring women in the club. I take the moment in and imprint it on the floor of my mind, where I intend to keep it as a stronghold for the rest of my life.

I have some way to go in learning to thoroughly relax and enjoy myself, without holding back, or hiding. Belly dance makes that possible to an extent. Not only the movement, but I feel protected around Amalia and Lola. They know their way around in Cairo—and tonight they have the guys looking out for us too. Ammon and Ehad sort out mineral water and seats for us at the bar as soon as we leave the dance floor for a break.

"What a nice dance club, Lola, thanks for inviting us out." I feel my body thanking me for the rehydration too as I sip on my water.

"This is a good one." She smiles. There is no trace of strain in her face, which gives her a youthful appearance that has nothing to do with cosmetics. Taking joy in life must be a woman's best anti-ageing cure. "The best one was unfortunately burned down a few months ago."

"What?" I slip onto my bar stool.

"Ach, it's all the stuff going on, you know." Lola shrugs. "Some people feel that belly dance is immoral. Women are showing too much flesh, expressing too much sensuality. It's too provocative for some."

"I'm sorry that happened, Lola," I say.

She laughs half-heartedly. "Someone even sprayed 'Sorry Lola' in graffiti all over the burn site. They knew it was my favourite spot. Sorry still doesn't make it right."

I take a moment to honour the weight of the moment before I respond. "I hope no one got hurt."

She opens up to me even further. "No one I know got burned in the fire, Poppie, but it hurt me that someone would do that to a place I love. I used to go there a lot and I liked to perform there too sometimes."

I try to change the slant of the conversation. "I've heard belly dancing in nightclubs is less respected than the formal shows on the Nile cruise boats and at hotels. Some even say dancing in clubs is sleazy. Why was performing at a club your favourite gig?"

"Sometimes it can be less respected to dance in clubs," says Lola in a non-committal way, bobbling her head, "but it depends who's doing it. Who's dancing and who's looking. Some women want to make money by being seductive or sensational in spite of their own selves—and some people will always look at a dancer and disrespect her. In the end you decide. How you feel and how you allow yourself to be treated. You can only control yourself, not other people."

There is still something about it that bothers me. I pour some more water into my glass and take a sip before asking. "Why do people disrespect dancers at all?"

"For belly dance to be respected, sex would have to be respected. However, we do not live in such a time." She says it as though there is nothing left to say on the topic and looks away across the club. I sense that my time for questions is done.

"To you, Poppie!" Lola turns back to me and raises her glass. Indeed she must have been born beautiful, but at this late age her beauty is to the credit of her own soul. "It's lovely to have you here, in Cairo. What are your plans. Will you stay?"

I grab at a sense of purpose, but I do not have one. I have no plan, no immediate future beyond admiring and learning from the dancers. I quickly make something up to avoid the telling truth. "Actually, I was thinking about going to Europe next."

"I know people." She narrows her eyes. "Maybe someone can hook you up. You can ask Amalia. Or, Ehad." With the wave of a finger, she swiftly has all of them standing around us at the bar.

"Ehad, can you organise a gig for Poppie." She guides him my way gently.

"You?" He cups his ear, straining himself to listen to my voice under the music.

I lean in so close that my lips brush his earlobe accidentally. "I'm looking for a job in Europe." I go along with my story as though I really mean it, until I really do. "Anything really. I have some experience in the restaurant industry, fashion, travel, film."

Ehad stares into my eyes as though he owns me. "I have connections in France who owe me. I'd like to get out of Egypt myself. We could elope."

Amalia rolls over and saves me just in time. "Lola says you are looking for work, Poppie. What about a film agency? I know a guy in Munich. He's a bit hard work, but they do some great projects. Most of their clients are in the hospitality industry."

I follow my own plot to somewhere new. Somewhere I have never been. "Why not? I've done some food documentaries. I'm sure that counts for something."

"YOU CAN'T LEAVE CAIRO BEFORE you've been to the pyramids."
Ehad calls me every day now, treating me like a girlfriend. "When
can I see you again? Tell Amalia I am coming to pick you up."

It is too much, too soon. I've been too overwhelmed. Too
friendly. I want to be wanted, but I am unable to open my heart
to Ehad. I shudder. "Amalia needs me."

There is a long silence on the phone before he speaks again.
"I need you too, Poppie."

My distant approach makes Ehad forceful. He knows that he
does not have me. "Don't go around wearing short dresses like
that other night again? I don't want other men looking at you."

Our conversations make me feel cramped. I have been doing
what I want all my life. Yet Ehad makes me doubt myself. "Poppie, just don't assume that people will respect you if you dress
like that."

I put down the phone and disappear into the couch next to the
heavily-foxed mirror in our Cairo apartment. Amalia still sees
me, even though I no longer feel present.

"He looks like a good man," says Amalia as I go through some
of my thoughts with her. "Egyptian men can be really passionate.
Sometimes, it happens like that. Some people can fall in love in
a split second. It happened to me. I was married to one for eight
years, remember. Those were some of the best years of my life."

Amalia shines as she thinks back to the happiest days of her
marriage. "Those moments were my whole life. They still are.
That's what connects me so deeply to Cairo. You should take a
chance, Poppie. If you don't try it, you will never know. Even if
relationships don't last forever, they can hold some of life's most
precious moments."

Everything in me rebels, but I look up to her advice. "You
decide if you want to go on a date with him to the pyramids or

not. I can't tell you what to do. You have to find the answer inside yourself. You take the chance or not. Up to you."

"EVERYONE WANTS TO KNOW the true history of Egypt. Everyone wants to own it." Ehad is kicking at the desert sand.

"I studied History in college." I look at him but he does not seem to be interested in what I have to say. I continue anyway. "It fascinates me that the ancient Egyptians revered women so much. They believed in the protection of the female emotion and intuition. They were right. People got along better and because of that men stayed safe and dynasties survived. There must be something to it that our modern society is missing."

Ehad stops and points toward the structures around us, waiting for my reaction. Next to us are giant boulders and, in front of us, the Great Pyramid of Giza.

"It's so much bigger standing in front of it than looking at it from Lola's balcony." I throw my scarf over my hair and take in the scene. It reminds me of my insignificance. In comparison to the giant structure in front of me, I am only a grain of desert sand.

"It's all yours today, Poppie." Ehad hails me as the queen of the moment and I spin around on my right foot in an attempt to turn the moment into my favour. It is only the two of us here. Tourism in Cairo has completely stalled due to the unrest. I feel grateful for this when we climb up the very narrow staircase inside the pyramid. I follow Ehad upwards towards the King's Chamber, taking care not to hit my covered head. It must be completely suffocating to do this in a large group.

After a while, I give up counting the stairs and continue in an automated way, staying in rhythm with Ehad's footfall in front of me. The climb to the top feels like an eternal push upwards, a bit similar to life itself. I feel as though I can no longer continue, but I keep going anyway.

When we get to the top, we enter a very small chamber inside the tip of the pyramid. As I squeeze inside, I remember the small cave I used to visit with Audrey, back in the Klipkoppie behind our house in Springbok. The size of it is irrelevant because it is not about about the physical structure of it. This is the kind of sacred space where I can let go of all rules. Where I can get in tune with myself and turn completely inwards. There are no windows to the outside, no view of what I am supposed to see.

Ehad does not speak, but only gestures to me to sit down. The granite floor is cool after the sweat of the long climb. I close my eyes. It is not possible to see much here in the dark anyway. My breath slows. I take a moment to honour Audrey inside this ancient tomb. My mind empties.

Time becomes as fluid as a belly dance artist. I let myself sink into it. All the way, deep into a sense of expansion, I discover a pearl. I feel a confirmation of truth inside my torso, a serenity that fills my body from my lower abdomen to the bottom of my chin. The revelation that comes to me is, that knowing my truth is this feeling. I can trust the physical sensation in my body to show me the way. It does not matter what anyone else believes or not. I feel the knowing and it is true. I am true.

A hand on my shoulder brings me back to my body. At first, I believe I am being touched by God. Then I notice that it is Ehad. We have to go, he gestures. Time. He helps me up and his hands are suddenly everywhere. It is as though he has arms like a squid, sucking and slinging all over my body. I feel smothered, resisting his advances, so aware of the fact that we are alone. Is this all there is? I close up my heart and my body. The true feeling disappears and I am no longer fully inside myself. No one will hear me if I scream. I slap his hands away and head for the staircase. He lets me go, but not without an expression of graciousness, as if he is doing something special for me.

It is a long way down, to freedom.

"YOU MADE A LOT OF STRANGE NOISES while sleeping last night," says Amalia over a cup of her special coffee. "I came in to your room to check on you and you were sleepwalking. You said, 'I am true as a pearl,' in a strange voice."

"It's probably my experience in the pyramid. Resurrecting my inner truth or something." I laugh it off and she does not push for more.

Thanks to Amalia, I have a good job prospect. It takes less than a week until I have a video interview for an English secretary position at an agency called Brezel Films in Munich. They value my travel experience because they have many international hospitality clients, mostly hotels and resort chains. I can take care of communication in English and have some idea of film and fashion too. It is a match.

I successfully avoid Ehad until I can tell him that I got the job and will not be staying any longer. "They want me to start as soon as possible. Thanks for everything!"

He sounds genuinely happy for me. "Congratulations, Poppie. Let me know when you want to leave. I will take you to the airport."

IT COULD BE JUST ANOTHER NORMAL NIGHT in Cairo, which makes it easier. It is not *goodbye*, goodbye. My suitcase is already in Ehad's car so we can head directly for the airport. We drive in silence. No talking. No radio. Nothing.

When he stops at the airport, he opens the glove compartment and casually takes out his gun. "I want to come with you," he says, as he strokes his weapon like a lover. "Let's get married, Poppie."

With his left hand, he scratches around in his glove compartment until he finally finds what else he is looking for.

"There it is!" He holds out a chunky silver ring set with an oval tiger eye.

I do not say anything. I am so aware of the pistol on his lap.

He takes my hand and pulls it closer. The rest of my arm flops as though it belongs to a rag doll.

With his other hand, he compresses the metal to make the ring smaller. The thick silver ring easily yields under his strength. Yet it still does not fit on any of my fingers.

"My flight is leaving soon, I have to go," I lie.

He hits the dashboard of the car with the ring folded in his fist. A single drop of blood starts to form on his knuckle. The ambient sound of airport comings and goings seem out of place in the background.

"I want to give you this ring—and I will come and find you," he says, ring in one hand, gun in the other.

I hold out my hand this time and let him put the ring on my wedding finger, where it hangs, loosely.

"Thank you," I say, "also for driving me."

Feeling partly paralysed, I move in slow motion to gather my things. I have to get out of the car. I am feeling confident that he will not shoot. It is an airport, after all, and, even if I am wrong, I am not afraid to die. By now, I am used to it. Almost dying. Dying. Not dying. It all happened before. It happens again. So what?

He grabs my arm and pulls me back inside, as I open the passenger door. I feel like a butterfly about to escape from a jam jar. Almost, but not quite. He wants a kiss. I oblige, smilingly, pretending to be happy.

"I'm coming to see you and then I'm bringing you a proper ring," he says, "call me as soon as you arrive."

It sounds like an order.

"Yes," I respond firmly as I slide out of the seat into the warm night. Exhaust fumes never smelled so sweet.

I run around to the boot of the car, but, of course, he is there to help me get my luggage out. No gun this time. At least not where I can see it.

"As soon as I can, I'm coming for you," Ehad says aggressively.

One last obligatory kiss and then I rush off as fast as I can, disappearing in between the cars and the dust and the people making for the airport terminal. As soon as I am through the gate, a vibration ripples through my chest and I shake it, ignoring the weird looks I get as I shoulder my way through duty free. Only when the flight takes off does it hit me that I am really free.

I survive, once again, without any visible scars. Best rush ever.

The Tumbler Toy

I STEP UP CLOSE TO THE MIRRORED WARDROBE and look myself in the eye. Could it be that I am getting younger? Thirty-five and not a single wrinkle. My reflection stares me out until caffeine emergency alarm bells start going off in my head. Deep engine rotations from somewhere above the roof pulsate through my being. Am I somewhere inside a nightmare? A yawn backfires as I slowly turn around to blue lights flitting across the silk-embroidered summer duvet that lies crumpled at the foot of the futon. The moment stretches. I stay very still. It is not clear if I can trust my senses. I have been known to resist reality in favour of my dreams. At least until my first cup of coffee.

Another vibration pushes through the small studio apartment where I find myself. It rings in my ears and makes me clench my pelvic floor. Another blue light, now tracing the shape of my body against the whitewashed wall. They can see me, whoever they are. Or worse: shoot me. I am not sure if I am awake. Or, if I am still in Cairo.

I thought I moved to Munich. I thought that would be the safe choice. Yet I do not hear any of the usual squeaks of the tram coming and going, or the kids playing in the park on a Saturday morning. Even the church bells are quiet. I put my index finger to my lips and hold my breath. The panic in the face of my reflection sketches a small crack that starts with a single chink in the mirror and then splits into the shape of a crow's foot. As soon as the pointers stop targeting me, I flop on to the bed. A strained tear splatters into the corner of my mouth. I want to live. I pull the summer duvet up to my chin and feel my eyelashes caress the pillow as I curl into the feathers. It feels like a hug.

Seven. Eight. Nine. I count ten helicopters before I get up. One foot in front of the other. Three steps across the parquet floor to the kitchen nook. I briefly glance toward the mirror, unsure of what I might find. Am I still ... here? When I catch myself behind the cracks, I am surprised at how serene I look after all that. Do I even know this woman with the big glittering hair and the juicy lips staring back at me? How did I become her?

My phone beeps as soon as I have put my mocha on the stovetop.

Poppie, are you safe? LG, Hans Ritter

It is my new boss. In Munich. I am half-relieved at the

confirmation that I am where I think I am. Hans Ritter is not my favourite person, but at least he cares enough to check on me. The sound of helicopters drills down my spine until I reluctantly check social media for clues. A quick browse through my mobile reveals posts about a shooting at the shopping centre in the north of Munich, close to the 1972 Olympic stadium. The police report encourages citizens to stay at home until further notice. This is why everything besides the rotor noise is muted outside. There is no movement on the city streets, apart from the official search party. I pull back my single linen curtain and open my window wide to let in the scent of the blooming linden and lilac trees on the corner. Not even the birds are chirping today.

The latest update says that the killer is hiding at the Isar riverside, close to where I live in the Lehel neighbourhood, right at the edge of the old town. I know that is not true, because he is dead. I know that the killer is dead because a part of me is dead too and that dead part of me is starting to knock at the back of my mind with all the things I prefer not to know. The dead part of me desperately wants to live.

The images of the killer's tiny body flash through me, as though there is a live screening in my head. He is only a child acting out his trauma. My chest fills up with emotion for the kid and his victims. Something unimaginable must have happened for his life to come to that hopeless place where death is the only option.

I understand the utter desperation to escape, to get away. Anywhere. Even into the abyss. Yet I still want to live. Age has taught me to hope. Time has a way of revealing options, even within the extremes of life and death. There is always something new around the next corner. Something worth living for. No matter how bad it gets. I am still willing to take a chance at finding what matters to me. There is always something.

All I really want is a safe place to be. A place where I can be enough.

My stomach starts to rumble, bringing me back to the present moment, to the part of me that is alive here, today, in this tall, lean body of mine. Today, I am still breathing. I am still trying to make my life work.

At the very least, thanks to Amalia, I have a job.

I respond to my boss' message.

I'm fine, thanks for checking, Mr. Ritter. Hope you are OK too.
Two seconds later, he writes back.

I stayed on the couch in the office last night. Missed you ;) *Pity you left so early* ;)

The whole national army is out and about hunting for a killer and Mr. Ritter still finds the inner fire to try to seduce me. I am going to have a hard time trying to douse that flame.

I decide not to answer his message. It is my prerogative.

The coffee is bubbling and calling for attention from the nook. I pour a double espresso into a gold-rimmed porcelain Arabic coffee cup, a memento from my time living in Dubai. Then I breathe in the aroma and relax my shoulders. I absolutely need coffee to be all right.

Several different kinds of sirens pass through the streets below. When I look out of the window from the fourth floor of the neo-baroque apartment building and down the narrow, cobbled alley, I see ambulances and police cars driving in a convoy all the way past the Saint Lukas church and the Mariannenplatz tram stop and then further toward Isartor, one of the original Munich city gates. More blue lights. More alarm. No chance to pick up my favourite German rye bread with walnuts from the local bakery.

"So then, what's for breakfast?" I muse to myself while opening the fridge. "Nothing in here, but white wine."

The girl in the mirror peeks out from behind the cracks and
winks at me. Her lashes are long and luscious. She flutters and
pouts. "Come on, Poppie, let's do wine and bread. We can even
bake a bread. The toasty wafts will comfort us."

It happens when I am anxious these days. My reflection starts
to change into a version separate from myself. There are different
sides to my reflection. Right now, I can only see the dancer. She is
my favourite part of me, soft and feminine and quite the opposite
of the tough girl I have to be in real life most of the time. My skin
tingles and my heart beats like an Egyptian drum. I am relieved
that I am not alone, that I have someone to talk to.

When my body starts to tremble at the events of the day, I
turn it into a silly shimmy on the spot. I shake it all out, letting
the vibration flow through and through me. I need to release
the adrenalin bottled up in my veins as though they are made
of tiny bubbles, waiting to pop. I purposefully make my jiggle
stronger, trying to gain a feeling of control, until it feels as though
my entire body is screaming. My breasts wobble underneath my
favourite, ragged, orchid pink-purple Thai silk nightgown that I
bought while travelling as a flight attendant too many years ago.
It turns my awareness to my generous curves and I save a tip in
my mind to always wear a bra when dancing. The rest of my bits
are toned and tight. I undulate in shimmying circles from my hips
to my chest as though I am a wine cork unscrewing myself. My
reflection continues with a chest shimmy finale and nicks at me to
copy her movements. "Come on, dance, Poppie, dance with me."

We laugh. Dancing with my reflection is the closest I get to
feeling loved and accepted. A gentle kindness builds between us
until it spontaneously bursts from my heart. It is the only time
that I allow myself to feel like a woman, rather than a bruised

and battered survivor. It is the only time when I no longer find myself ugly. My reflection ends in a power stance. Back arched upwards toward the ceiling in one smooth, slow curve. Chest forward. Long neck. Chin up. Eyes gently gazing down. Arms flicked high above my head, shaking my hands outwards into a strong, proud end pose. I continue with a final chest shimmy before doing a curtsy to the mirror.

My reflection takes a bow. "So, Poppie, shall we bake a bread for breakfast? I'm getting hungry."

"Since I finally have a kitchen, why not? In fact, let's celebrate!" This is my seventh rental apartment in less than a year. It is the smallest space I have ever lived in. Yet it is a place where I am free to show my original face, albeit in the mirror, that one authentic version of me that lies hidden beneath all the personas I have been trying on over the years. This is where I can relax and allow myself to grieve for all the parts of me that I have lost, without filtering or framing it. Blocked photographs of my travel adventures remind me that there have been happy moments, even through it all.

I take the chilled bottle of Chablis out of the fridge and place it on the small marble kitchen counter. The wine is a gift from my boss. Something special, for me to try. I pull out the cork. It smells like a meadow full of wildflowers. As I swirl it around in my wine glass, I imagine a picnic with ripe pears, goats cheese, and daisies. The sensation of a sea breeze so close I could almost turn toward the body of water and listen to the waves. What a great pairing this wine would make with scrambled eggs, but since there are no reserves at the moment, bread and butter will have to do. I quickly find my old recipe journal from the foodie books I stack up against the teal tiles that frame the kitchen surface. Then I flip to the messiest page and check that I have all the ingredients.

LENA'S HOMEMADE BREAD

4 cups whole wheat flour
1 cup rolled oats
15 ml honey
15 ml olive oil
15 ml salt
10g sachet instant yeast
Handful of mixed sesame seeds
2-3 cups of warm water
Extra olive oil and sesame seeds to sprinkle on top

Preheat oven to 200°C.
Mix the ingredients together and place in a greased bread tin.
Top with olive oil and sesame seeds and let it rise for 45 minutes.
Bake for 1 hour, then turn off the oven and leave the bread in for
another 10 minutes.
Let it cool.

My heart sashays as I take in the recipe. Lena used to let us mix the bread dough every week, even when we sometimes covered each other in flour for fun. I miss Audrey, my best and only friend, my sister from another mister. I miss her every day. No one knows me like Audrey and no one else has ever made me feel like home.

I take out a big mixing bowl from the traditional Bavarian oak kitchen cupboards, throw in the ingredients and mix it with my hands until the dough gets spongy. Once I cover the inside of the bread tin with butter, I fill it with the dough and sprinkle oats on top. No more sesame seeds in my cupboard so I have to improvise. Forty-five minutes on the phone timer to let it rise.

Military choppers keep buzzing outside above my roof while I try to hold on to a sense of normal, whatever that means. My life takes on a pace of its own, a shimmy to the drone of heli-copters. The rhythm of my existence can no longer be altered. I keep dancing and moving with the changes, hoping to keep up, to stay safe.

When the timer goes off on my mobile phone, I put the bread tin in the oven and soon a reassuring smell fills my apartment. This is my tiny rebellion against the world. I bake my own bread, I decide what goes into it, what goes into my body.

It is my small freedom. The difference between doing what I am told and doing my own thing. A little flour, yeast and water is all it takes to fill my small dwelling with the warm smell of home. Despite the bitterness of the day, I consciously fill my place with the cosy feel of fresh bread. A humble attempt in trying to determine my own life. It soothes me, but not as much as my second glass of wine.

By noon the news of the Munich shooting is all over the inter-national news. On social media, the idea of a mystery killer on the run is out of control. My mom is posting video footage of the recent shootings at her local mall in Cape Town, passing this off as evidence for the #Munich #shooting. I pick up my phone to call her, but then decide to write instead.

Mom, what are you doing?

I get an answer immediately.

Poppie!! Good u were not shopping last night. U no shopaholic like your mother.

She could have checked on me rather than staying glued to her apps.

You're R8 mom. No shopping. At home. All fine.

Right away, I can see her typing a new message and it feels good to know that I am not only hanging out with my reflection. There is a real person at the other end of that message. One who is meant to love me.

In the Cape we've mall shootings every wkend now. By u they bring the entire army out!

It gives me a chance to take her on.

Mom, there's a diff between mall shootings in CT and Munich. Why mix it all up now?

My mom cannot resist telling me off.

Dunno bout that Poppie. Only diff is that you make the headlines. We need coverage too!!

I know that there is no convincing her. I can almost see her blonde bob swishing from side to side in a flat panic.

Stay outta the shops rather Mom, OK?

She plays it back.

OK, Poppie. You too :)

When I take the bread out of the oven, I can not wait for it to cool. I loosen it from the tin with a butter knife and carefully pop the bread onto a wooden board. The first slice steams and crumbles onto my small kitchen counter. Then I try to cut a more generous slice in an attempt to keep it together. Leaving it to set first would help, but I am too hungry. My phone beeps again as I take a first bite of chunky, melty, buttered bread.

Messages from over the world start pouring in, from my belly dance teacher Lola in Cairo and from my modelling buddy, Amy, in Paris.

Even Pri, from my flight attendant days, writes to me from Dubai.

OMG just heard about the Munich killer. Please tell me you're safe, doll! Love, Pri x

I have not heard from her in ages. Fancy death being a trigger for human connection.

Thanks, Pri, I'm safe. At home, having coffee. Love, Poppie x

There are people who care about me, but they do not know me closely. They also do not live close to me. I am torn between a globe of people who are all connected to different sides of me. Everywhere I go, I am only a piece of myself. Every time I relocate, I no longer see all of me reflected back in the eyes of those around me. Everywhere I go, I am less known and more alone. If anything would happen to me here in Munich, I would have no one to turn to. Least of all Hans Ritter.

The mid-afternoon media statement confirm that the killer is, indeed, dead. They encourage people to go back to their normal lives as the streets are safe once more. The city is back to business as usual. Within half an hour, public transport is running, kids are playing in the park again and church bells chime into the crisp sunshine. The people of Munich fully claim their city, trusting the police and getting on with their lives. I am hesitant to go out though. I first need to shift back into the tougher version of me. The one who can face the world. I want to leave the gentle dancer at home. The soft little feminine girl in the mirror will not survive out there.

My phone beeps.

Freedom! Though I still wouldn't mind getting stuck with you ;)
Hans Ritter

He likes writing his full name at the end of every text.
I do not answer.

DURING MY TIME IN MUNICH I meet three kinds of people: those who are kind, those who take advantage, and those who seem to be kind, but boldly lead me to my ruin. My boss falls into the second category. Hans Ritter is the type of person who complains about the lack of restaurant stars at business lunches and will never lower himself enough to fly economy class. It is a mystery where he gets his cash. From the agency accounts, I can see that Brezel Films is not profitable. Either he has a family stash, secretly looted from the Second World War, or there is other funny business going on in the background.

When he is not showing off, he complains. Being grumpy is a popular pastime for Mr. Ritter. "What's with this *scheiss*, shitty summer rain today?" He waddles and groans, curls jumping. "I want to drive my cabrio." He tucks his thick grey locks behind his ear with greasy fingers, fiddling with his sleeve just long enough for me to notice his designer cuff links.

There is no emotion in his face when he speaks, but it is not because he does not feel anything. It is cosmetic neurotoxin injections that make him look empty, expressionless, and without any sign of human character. Despite investing in expensive beauty treatments, the extent of his abundant life shows. His neck is rough and scaly, sagging ever so slightly under his chin when he approaches me at the reception desk.

"First world problems," I remind him. "Mr. Ritter, there are many people less fortunate today. Not only in terms of the weather—and, yes, I do mean that the kids in Africa are starving. It is true, even if it exists far away from your daily luxury."

He has a smart answer for everything though. "The kids in Munich are dying, they're killing each other." He points his index finger at me, thumb in the air, then lifts his hand to his mouth in the same pseudo revolver position and blows on it.

I do not like his humour. "In Cape Town, there are people dying from gun violence every week. There are mall shootings every weekend. We are still extremely privileged here," I insist, "I'd rather live in a place where the whole European army is out to protect me than down there where nobody seems to care what happens to people anymore."

Hans Ritter pretends not to hear and looks me up and down with a stunted grin that makes me want to gag. With his new sneakers squeaking across the polished wooden floor, he slides around to where I am standing behind the reception desk. His eyes become hazy and large as he focuses in on my behind.

"Look, Mr. Ritter, some post arrived for you this morning." It is a dumb attempt at keeping his attention on work. My personal space panic button is going off, but I do not know how to make him keep his distance. It would be impolite to say no. A diversion tactic is my only option right now. "I've also completed the invoices you've asked me to do."

It is no good. His tongue starts flicking in and out of his mouth in a pointed manner. All my muscles tense, yet I am not able to do anything but freeze. Mr. Ritter keeps slithering toward me until he is so close that I can smell his armpits. At first, I pretend not to notice as he brushes his body up against me. I continue to flip through the paperwork on the table until I actually do stop noticing. I space out when Hans Ritter pinches my bum, as though I am welling up with a poison that pacifies me and allows me not to feel humiliation. I escape into a meditative state and pretend that everything is good the way it is, that it does not matter when his bad breath wets my neckline. I block out all of the unwelcome closeness and, as he hangs himself over my chair to slide his hand down to my breast, I finally stop registering the reality of the moment.

"The invoices are wrong, Poppie. They always are." I vaguely recognise the low ceiling and the bright office lights I am look-ing up at when I become aware of his reprimand. "You should stick to what you're good at, you know. You're only good for one thing. That's why I have you here." He lifts his hand off my breast and grants me half a step of breathing space. Yet he keeps me wound within his perverted stare. Mr. Ritter tucks a strand of loose hair behind his ear and the corners of his mouth curl slowly upwards as he gloats. His face has a green sheen to it. "Just accept who you are."

The words fall over me as though they are a sticky poison that prevents me from standing up and defining myself. There is absolutely no challenge to what I do—answering a few phone calls from clients and keeping his calendar up-to-date. Even doing invoices is an easy job for me and I know I am capable of more. The expectation is that I should act according to his will and not according to my own inner pilot. That I should contribute what is expected of me and not what could be valuable to the company. My skills set, after all, is not important to Mr. Ritter. I would like to contribute something more. I want to learn something, perhaps even use my brain. Yet I am not who I am. I am expected not to have ambition. I am nothing more than Hans Ritter's office toy.

DAYS MERGE INTO EACH OTHER in such a way that I can no longer recall what happens. Everything becomes automatic. I am present, but only physically, when Hans Ritter asks me to work late to help him "plan his travels" and catch up on the "workload". It is not as though I have a rocking social schedule, so I do not mind staying in the office. It turns out there is not much work to do after all, so I sit around to keep him company.

He has that look on his face, full of expectation. I am forever amazed by his male ego, how powerful the belief that any woman he desires should want him in the same way or be conquered by whatever means necessary. He flips back his curls, sticks out his tongue and hisses from his desk, "Let's have a beer, Poppie. There are some cold ones in the fridge. Will you get them for us?"

I do not like beer. Nevertheless, I go to the office kitchen and fetch two local Munich cult beers. I notice that we are the only two people left in the office. All the other desks are empty. No one else is hanging around for a beer tonight, but me. I do not want to drink beer with him alone in the office. I hate that I have to be nice to him to keep my job.

"Here you go." I flash him a fake smile as I put down his beer.

He takes a guzzle and shakes his curls. Then he slithers around to the front of the desk and holds a pose. He grabs me by my fingers and pulls me toward him. His other hand reaches for my breast as though it is the most normal thing.

"Look, I am not going to sleep with you." I pronounce each word slowly and clearly. Perhaps I do not even need courage. I am tall. All I need to do is to stand up straight, relax and speak up. I have a voice. It is about time I used it.

"Well, then, you might as well leave the company," he answers matter of factly. He turns his back to me and picks up his cell phone.

Suddenly, I am filled with shame. Standing up for myself feels like suicide. In this case, job suicide. I am only safe in this world when I cover my authenticity, when I hide behind the perfect façade of a submissive smile. I leave both beers on his desk, round up my bag and my jacket and make my way home. Though I am embarrassed and scared, I know that this is a secret victory. Regardless of what happens next.

One small step for Poppie. One giant leap for womankind.

A NEW DAY. A NEW ME. There is only one thing more stressful than trying to look perfect and that is trying to make myself invisible. I want to be so unexceptional that Mr. Ritter will no longer want to get close. I grab whatever baggy clothing I can find and go easy on the make-up. My German colleagues do not notice my upside down smile.

They expect life to be difficult. Being troubled is the status quo. It helps me to blend into the background, even though the office reception desk is strategically placed in full view of both my boss' office and everyone who walks in the door. I keep my head down and update my filing as best I can. For the first time, I am grateful for the extent of German administration. Perhaps that is exactly the point of all the paperwork. Less idleness. Less chance for pestering or getting pestered.

Or not.

"Poppie," my boss' voice rudely interrupts the monotonous rhythm of preparing today's post. I look up to see him beckon me with a cigarette. He likes to discuss the most important business while smoking, which is why I picked up smoking at the office as a habit too. I do not even like smoking, but I still need the job. I do not want to make any further moves that can put my livelihood in danger.

There is a young girl in the office next to Hans Ritter. It must be the working student who is meant to start today. She looks smug and trendy. I follow her clicking heels down the stairs and out onto the sidewalk in front of the historic office building. In front of us stretches the full Isar River, shining turquoise through the lush chestnut trees.

Hans Ritter's shadow is exceptionally large today, extending beyond the sidewalk out across the glimmer of cars and into the street. He talks without looking me in the eye. "This is Hildegard, our new intern."

The little student accepts the cigarette that he holds out for her with a grateful smile. Her eyes shimmer like two dollops of dew. Neither of them look my way. Hildegard's smaller shadow is trapped inside his, as though his ego has claimed her space.

She closes her luscious red lips and takes the cigarette between her coral-lacquered nails. The light catches her orange fringe as it falls across her face. She does not bother with it. Every time she takes a drag, she kind of gasps, as though she is not getting enough air—and then bats her eyelids at my boss from between her hair.

She could not be much older than twenty-three or twenty-four. He is turning sixty this week.

I want to protect Hildegard. I want to tell her that Hans Ritter flirts with everyone. That he pinches my bum when he passes by reception. That he grabs my breasts when he gets drunk at work. That this fat slob is self-justified and without any shame. That no one says anything because he has power and money and provides our sustenance. I want her to know the truth that he will never change. I want to tell her that she is beautiful. That she deserves better than throwing herself at a depressed, alcoholic psychopath. That she, too, can take that step and say no. It took me much too long to learn that.

"Shall we go for lunch?" I ask her as she squishes her cigarette butt graciously underneath her sparkly kitten heels. She does not look up.

"Poppie," my boss bites, "why don't you go and finish that filing you've been so busy with all morning?"

She takes a step closer to him as he slides his arm around her tiny waist and guides her to his luxury SUV, which is parked on the sidewalk in front of us like an accessory. From the idiotic smirk on his face, it looks like they may not be back for a while.

HILDEGARD PITCHES UP AT WORK AROUND NOON the next day, wearing designer shoes and a neat silk neck scarf. She looks good, I must give her that. She shakes her blood orange hair and sneers at me as though she owns the place. "Can someone bring me coffee?"

The producers in the open office next to reception strain their necks at the new eye candy. Gerard, Florian and Basti all jump at the chance to serve her. This time, I am off the hook.

"Poppie is thirty-five and single," she tells them, while looking me straight in the eye. "Nobody loves her."

As soon as they are out of sight, I make a dash for the ladies bathroom. I look at myself in the mirror. I need this job, despite the fact that they have the worst office coffee. I cannot afford to annoy the boss. Or his girlfriend.

My reflection is kind. "That sort of bullying says a lot more about her than about you."

It hurts nevertheless.

Single.

If she only knew how much worse it really is.

Single, unprotected, and afraid.

"Go and make yourself a double espresso and pretend not to hear her. Don't show her your despair. Put on a cool face, like this." The lady in the mirror does not smile. Neither does she look sad. Her face is relaxed. "They must have discussed you in quite a lot of detail on their little shopping trip yesterday, judging by her bad mood."

I nod and sigh at the confirmation. He is playing us against each other, but I refuse to take part in this game. Slowly and steadily, I sublimate myself. Remove myself from the equation. Hide behind Hildegard like a coward. I dim my light to show her that I am no threat.

"POPPIE," SHE COOS A FEW DAYS LATER, "will you plan Hans and myself a nice holiday to India?" It is more an order than a question. "I've heard you know your way around. You know, the world and so ..." She giggles and then continues with a list of priorities. "Silk sheets at all the hotels and a bottle of gin on arrival. It's his birthday, you know, we will need to celebrate. Also apples, I need a fruit basket with apples."

"Apples? In India?" I blurt.

"Of course. Apples everywhere." She says it as though apples are something erotic.

I look from Hildegard to Hans Ritter, who simply shrugs as though it is my own fault that I am not the one sleeping with him.

"Imagine what I could do for you, Poppie," he says as soon as she is out of earshot. I pretend not to hear him.

IT IS STILL LIGHT OUTSIDE when the film producers gather opposite the reception desk, all leather jackets and studs. I am astonished at how late the sun sets here in summer. They are getting ready to leave for the boss' birthday party tonight.

"You joining us, Poppie? Maybe you can find yourself a nice guy there tonight, huh?" Gerard's tongue ring clicks on his teeth.

I look away from his mocking eyes. It is too late now to sneak away, I should have done a better job at disappearing today. "Oh, come on Gerard, I don't want a man."

He raises one eyebrow. "You mean, you like girls?"

"No," I try to snub the assumption before it becomes a rumour, "I ..."

"Don't worry, Poppie." Gerard laughs. "That's hot!"

I straighten up and huff. "Why can't a woman be alone? Why do there have to be consequences for that?"

Florian pitches in from behind Gerard and pulls him by the shoulder. "Whoa, you two, relax? So, Poppie, are you coming with us or not?"

I switch off my computer and pick up my handbag. "Yup, guess I have to be there. I'll be back in a wink."

I slip into a simple sky blue dress and the standard party heels that I brought in a small bag. It is only a short walk to the Fesch, a tiny bar close to the office. The guys are giggling about the boss' new young thing. Gerard is playing with his tongue ring. "I wouldn't mind a bite of that little snack, Hildegard."

Florian drags hard on his cigarette and chokes through his response. "I bet she digs in her teeth. She's exactly the kind of flaming vampire I like."

Basti blocks them. "The boss will bite you both in the ass if you go there. While the three of you fight it out, I'll quietly abduct her and tie her up with guitar strings in my music room."

Determined to stay out of it, I manage to hold my tongue until we get to the bar, staying with them as we walk, but keeping to myself. They hardly notice that I am there.

When I step into the Fesch, I take off my coat, greet the rest of my colleagues, and, as I look up across the small crowd, an intense pair of blue eyes hold my gaze and will not let go. It is an arresting stare that startles me because it is so unexpected. He sees me. I am here and I can no longer look away. A thrill enters my body and coils itself into the pit of my stomach. It is disarming.

Hans Ritter looks up from Hildegard's voluptuous breasts to give me a bright smile. She threatens me with her eyes.

I mingle for a while, making small talk with some of our office suppliers, partners, and business contacts. Even though I do not like 80's music, I manage to shake out a few moves with the producers on the dance floor underneath colourful disco lights. Some random guys at the bar are buying me expensive whiskey and cigars. I like neither. We move over to the smoking lounge where I smell cocaine. The vibe changes quickly and I decide to leave. My wrist watch says it is 2 am. Time to get some shut-eye.

Hildegard rolls her eyes at my bottle of sparkling water. "Why are you not drinking, Poppie? What's wrong with you?"

I am not prepared for the question and make a stupid face. "I …" I try to say something, but break into a stutter. I want to say that I am in for the next round. I want to say that I am not that boring. I want to fit in, but I do not get the words out.

How many versions of myself do I need to invent in order to please everyone?

She turns to whisper something to the agency guys and orders another round of beers for everyone, except me. I am overcome with a silly sadness and leave without saying goodbye to anyone.

Almost immediately, I start wondering if I will ever see the man with the piercing gaze again. The best and worst things in life happen so quietly that you might miss it completely if you do not pay attention.

"YOU'RE QUITE THE WILD ONE NOW, aren't you, Poppie?" It is 10 am which is early for Hildegard to show up at the office. Her cheeks are as flushed as the skin of the single apple she is carrying. In her other hand, she is holding an energy drink. She looks at me with roving eyes, her tongue popping on her palate. "We should go clubbing together sometime."

"Are you still drunk Hildegard, or am I?" I cannot take her seriously.

"So what if I am. Hans took someone else home last night. Now I am in the used goods box, like you. We might as well make friends." Hildegard walks toward her office without taking off her sunglasses.

"Hildegard," I call after her, "I never slept with him. Just for the record."

She stops and turns around slowly, making that clapping sound with her tongue again before she speaks. "He said you were … he even told me your favourite position." A harmonious faux scream fills the foyer. Then she walks away, throwing her hands up in the air and shaking her head.

Even more surprising is the person that walks in a short while after Hildegard. My hangover is certainly messing with me. Those blue eyes immediately take over every other thought in my mind, dominating my attention. I cannot look away as the thrill enters my body once more. He addresses me, but I do not react. Not because I do not want to, but because I cannot speak. My throat closes up, as though the slithering feeling is strangling me. I want to run as far as possible. Instead, I stand mesmerised.

THE NEXT FRIDAY, HE IS BACK IN THE OFFICE. When I get up to make espresso, he is there, in the kitchen, waiting for me. I avoid his eyes, then I seek them out and dare to look further. His face is as smooth as his shaved head. He is wearing a light grey T-shirt that reveals a single red rose tattooed on his left bicep. He has big hands and clean fingernails. It has been a long time since I felt anything else, but disgust for a man. Perhaps it is now finally time to move on, to open up again. Maybe he can protect me from Hans Ritter. I could finally be safe in those strong arms.

"Poppie! Can you quickly check that our beer fridge is filled up and make an order if necessary?" My boss interrupts and so we only have the sensational silence, the energy crackle between our hidden glances.

As I put the beers in to chill, I feel the slithering coil twisting into my body until the man with the blue eyes becomes all I think about. Everything. Every. Wonderful. Thing. I am going to suffer every day until I get my kicks next Friday. His eyes.

Those eyes.

I feel seen for what I am unable to see in myself. I feel noticed for the woman I aspire to be.

I LIVE ONLY FOR OUR EYE CONTACT until we run into each other in the foyer one morning. It is not chance. He arrives at the same time, on time, every Friday. All I have to do is take a calculated step out to meet him. I linger at the heavy wooden front door of the office building for a few moments. When he gets inside, he looks up from his phone. The morning light behind him casts a dappled glow.

Our first private moment is as wordless as the others. He almost says something, but hesitates. The unspoken words hit me like a fifth glass of wine. I know that he feels the same. He just cannot say it. This feeling is a fire. And a flutter. It is beautiful. And terrible. Our silence is supernatural. To me, it is a bolt of lightning that ignites me from inside. To the outside, it is shy, like the hush of a summer stream.

There is no one and nothing else, but him. It is time now for me to believe. Love, at last.

I DO NOT EAT OR SLEEP UNTIL WE FINALLY manage to talk. He finds me in the copy room and looks at me for a long time before he speaks. "I'm Michi."

The moment is so overwhelming that I fail to understand his name. I find his German accent difficult to follow and I am not ready for any of this, but I so much want to be brave and take a chance on love.

"Michi." He pronounces it slowly, in two long syllables.

"Poppie," I shudder without meaning to. It is hard to hold his gaze because I am afraid. I am so afraid of this love.

"Poppie, I'm picking you up for dinner. Tonight at seven." I can hear from the tone of his voice that he knows what he wants. He is in love with me just the same way that I am in love with him. I know it. It is all perfect. This is my fairy tale.

Hans Ritter is on holiday with Hildegard, so I get away with leaving the office early to put on a face mask and paint my toe-nails. I wait around in a plunging little red dress until I get his text message saying that he is an hour late.

As usual, I escape into the mirror. "He's just busy, Poppie, it's not that he disrespects you."

Going out with him dressed this way might be a mistake.

My mirror image strikes a pose. "Poppie, don't put on something else. This is who you are. Got it, flaunt it!"

Nevertheless, I change into a more conservative outfit of long beige pants and a colourful satin shirt with an Asian collar that buttons up to the top of my chin.

Then I change back into the red dress.

"Yes!" The dancer in the mirror does a happy twirl.

No.

In the end, the need to hide wins. I cover my body with the long pants and button-up shirt. It would be wrong to throw myself at Michi under any circumstances. Especially when he is so late.

Michi arrives in an oversized four-wheel drive. I see from my tiny window that he can hardly fit his car into my tiny street as he pulls up to the apartment building. He does not get out to ring my bell, or to pick me up at my door. He does not look up or wave. He simply waits in the car revving the engine down the narrow alley until I finally run down and jump into the passenger seat.

"Where shall we go, Poppie?" He is fidgeting, avoiding my eyes, putting the pressure on me to decide.

"You're the one who grew up here, Michi. Why don't you show me something?" I nudge him against the shoulder with my fist.

He is stressed. Uncertain. He runs his eyes up and down my outfit with a frown. Then he drives until we get to the centre of the English Garden, the biggest park in Munich. We stop at the Chinese Tower, a traditional beer garden set under chestnut trees around a multi-level pagoda that is popular with tourists and locals alike.

I want to ask him why there is a Chinese Tower in an English Garden in this German city, but my heels do not do well on the gravel and there is hardly a seat free that does not have beer spilled all over it. We move in on the benches next to a rowdy group of female drinkers. I pretend not to notice the wet patch under my bum. In turn, he feels right at home and proceeds to flash his eyes at every woman at the table who looks like she is potentially open to it. A tiny, tattooed blonde gasps and stares at him, mesmerised, just like me. He looks back at her for a while without saying anything. Then he gets up to fetch us two beers without asking me what I want.

"I'm sorry," the girl says to me as he walks away, "I'm sorry." Then she turns her head all the way around to follow his whereabouts as he heads for the beer counter. She does not respond when her friends try to get her attention.

All this time, I have wished for the moment where we could be alone. I have waited for his first private words. It comes as soon as he gets back, under the giddy gaze of his newest fan on the other side of the table.

"Heya, Poppie, first I have to say this, I'm still kind of seeing my ex-girlfriend. There is also a new girlfriend who I am currently dating. And while I was on holiday recently, I fell in love with a married woman and I talk to her on the phone every day. But—I really, really like you."

It is as though he is a kid in a candy store who wants the lollipop, even though he is already sick from too much sugar. He wants to keep me, but put me away in a drawer for later. With my heart wide open and receptive, I am so vulnerable that I want to cry, but I do not. I am not afraid to be weak, but I am not too proud to be strong. I take a deep breath in the hope for us to be happy together. Then I hesitate. And he hesitates. And the moment is lost forever.

He asks for the blonde girl's number as soon as we finish our beers and then drops me off at home.

"Let's do that again soon, Poppie." On his face is a look that I can only interpret as love as I know nothing about love and I lie to myself. I have probably never loved or been loved. I have experienced other things, but I cannot sugarcoat that something in me is broken as a result. I am missing what life is about, but I do not know how to fix it or know if it can be fixed. My concept of love is only a fantasy of what it might be.

I am Michi's pick-up-and-throwaway toy, a rag doll of a human, unraveled at the seams and missing a few pieces. I go through the motions of a daily routine, but, inside, I am tattered, dragging myself along. I do not know how to mend myself. Except with coffee.

On the street corner in my central Munich neighbourhood, lies a beggar holding a dog on a leash. He is the most handsome man I have ever seen. I wonder how someone this good-looking can end up in rags. His perfect square shoulders show through the tatters. His eyes are red and glassy, as though they are a mirror of my own.

I collect the fractions of pain in my soul into a heap, scoop it aside and keep smiling. Then it comes. The darkness. Oppressing. The heart brings darkness to the soul. The thrill becomes a slithering demon that takes hold of my being, tearing the life out of me.

The way men look at me only gets me into trouble.

I collapse onto my futon, wrap my hands tightly around my knees and rock myself from side to side. I know that sleep will not come, but I am trying to find some comfort anyway. I would do anything to be able to speak to Audrey right now. My best childhood friend. I keep baking Audrey's mom's bread week in and week out, in the hope of luring her back. My heart aches for her presence, for a kind of love.

AS SOON AS I START TO DRIFT OFF, SHE IS THERE. A sparkle of light from the window catches my eye and then I spot her, sitting on my bed and looking at me with big, seal eyes. She is always aged twelve, always perfect. Audrey sits with me for quite a while saying nothing, as though there is a warm sun-ray hanging between us. We do not even have to talk. We simply look at each other and what is unsaid becomes more eloquent than words. There are times when silence is more meaningful than anything else.

Yet she does not pass on the opportunity to challenge me. "Poppie, get up. You have to keep moving."

I want to ask why, but then she is already gone. So are four slices of bread and a good chunk of butter. If the heart makes or breaks a human being, Audrey makes me.

THERE IS NOTHING WORSE FOR A WOMAN LIKE ME than to be single in my thirties, when my hormones are raging. I look around. There is no one to love me. All that is left is to accept being used. It is the normal natural maturation of the female body to have a heightened sense of sexuality when the time starts running out to have a baby.

You will not know this because you are still a kid, Audrey. You do not know how lucky you are that you never had to grow up. I am not in a relationship, or in any position to start a family. It is a dilemma to try and deal with it in a respectable way. All I really want at this stage of my life is a penis. In fact, I cannot think about much else these days. Can you believe that after everything we went through as children with your mom's boyfriend? After what he did to us, you might have thought I would never look at a man again. Perhaps I am possessed.

It is a sick, desperate feeling, Audrey.

The dating scene in Munich is tough. I do not meet many men. No one dares to talk to me. Never mind asking me out. I do not even have a chance to show off how quickly I picked up the German language. Perhaps the men are afraid of me here.

My height can be intimidating. Maybe they do not want to date women from other cultures. Or it could be that I am simply not as beautiful as the gym-styled local *Maedels* with their milky skin. Bavarian culture and language are tougher to crack than a chestnut. I have had to learn to be a stranger again, as a foreigner and as a woman, in Germany. Whenever I flirt, men seem elusive and confused about what to do, as though I may be trying to trick them. When I do not, they do not do anything but look.

If only I could find another friend like you, Audrey, maybe then things will get better. Why did you have to die? Was it as bad for you as for the kid who went on an amok shooting at the Olympia shopping centre? What really happened? Were you unable to find a way out? I am still searching, for a friend, for love, for everything.

"GERMAN MEN ARE VERY PASSIVE," Hildegard advises when I ask about the dating scene. "Prostitution is widely accepted in Germany, so men don't have to try hard to get a woman into bed. You need to loosen up, make it easier for them. We should go dancing. Why don't you come out with me to a techno club? You can catch someone when they're drunk—and then just sleep with him. Decide if you want to keep him in the morning."

Her strawberry locks are deceiving. She has deep wrinkles around her intrusive eyes. "In Munich, making prolonged eye contact with someone is the unspoken code that you're open for being sexually approachable. Remember that, Poppie."

We make a good chunk in a bottle of gin at the film agency before hitting the club. She orders rounds of energy shots, but I have never been able to handle a lot of alcohol. I throw the next drink over my shoulder. The guy right behind me is annoyed, but he cannot quite figure out where it came from—and he is too drunk to care.

The longer I stay in the nightclub, the more I get the feeling that a thousand devils are collecting on my skin. It makes my hair stand up. Hildegard disappears somewhere with a guy that she met shortly upon entering the club. I do not even catch a glimpse of him. When I look again, she is gone. I walk through the entire nightclub to try and find her. Yet she is not at any of the bars or dancing on any of the floors. I get myself another gin and tonic and I am so thirsty that I down it. People are not dancing. I do not get it. What is the fun of being inside a dark nightclub listening to deafening bass without dancing? It makes me feel restless.

It is a lonely experience, losing myself in techno music. An unusually tall guy comes up to me. We speak a few words, but I do not know what he says. It is too loud inside the club. Then I see it. The demon in his eyes. He has a long, pale face and yellow eyes with tiny slits. There is nothing human about his presence except for his manly shape. I drop my drink on the floor and start running down the steps.

I remember picking up my jacket and getting a taxi and I remember him beating hard on the boot of the car as we drove away. Besides that, I remember nothing.

I WAKE UP GASPING FOR AIR. It is only a nightmare. I hold onto the walls that lead to my kitchen nook and go through the motions to prepare a mocha. Something. Anything to flip the switch of my conscious mind.

A double espresso is not enough. I sit down on the brown leather couch in my one-room apartment and stare at the blank wall in front of me. The light is dim, despite the open window. My hair smells of smoke and sweat.

I wish my mind could stay as blank as this wall. As clear. As clean. As empty. A sharp feeling starts building in my heart and then suddenly drops down into my pelvis. It makes me curl and cuddle my belly. I feel so nauseous. What happened? Did I? Did he?

I pick up the pieces. My handbag is still lying in front of the door and my stilettos mark a trail to my bedroom. It looks as though I made it without losing anything, but that is not true.

It is the yellow eyes that scare me. I leave the nightclub really quickly in order to get away. Too much liquor is rushing in my head. It is because I do not like techno music, so I drink more. He follows me down the stairs. I try to go faster and fall down a few steps. It smells of ash and dirt. He helps me up. I wish he would just leave me alone.

I start running down the rest of the steps, across the other dance floor, out of the club, and into the street toward the taxi stand. I get into the first taxi and close the door, locking myself into a safe space—all classical music and car freshener. A few seconds later, he is there, pounding on the door, swearing and beating the boot of the car as we drive away.

When my taxi finally stops in front of my apartment, I am so tired and so relieved. The driver turns around to take my payment and I notice that he has the same demonic look in his eyes. Is there, perhaps, a dark alignment in the stars tonight?

I go into my apartment block as quickly as possible. I feel someone sneak in behind me before the door clicks closed. It is probably my neighbour getting home. I should stop being so paranoid. To be safe, I start running up the staircase toward my apartment. I can hear the person behind me running up the stairs, following me. I try to go faster, but I am exhausted, drunk, and tired. He catches up with me a few steps from my door as I trip and stumble. He grabs me from behind, flips me around and pushes me down onto the stairs with a powerful grip. I am not strong enough to fight back.

"No," I whisper, "no, please, no."

As women, we often speak the most profound words in only whispers. I know that it is not only me. I am not alone. I am all the women who had to go through this before.

"Oh, God," I say a little bit louder.

I have been speaking softly all my life—and no one, ever really listens.

"God, please, please God, help me!" I start blabbering straight from my core. The volume of it is impossible for me to gage. I pray with all my power, but I do not even know for sure if any sound comes out at all. This is my final option, my last call for help—and I am even messing this up.

There is nothing more I can do, but to surrender to the moment where I will be raped. Yet it still shocks me when he pulls down his tracksuit pants and takes out his big, fat, blue-veined, pulsing pink thing.

This is really happening. Is it?

It is my fault for drinking so much. I do not have the strength to fight. Perhaps I deserve it after all.

I leave myself there on the stairs with him, rise up from my body and disappear into the light.

When I return to open my eyes, I see an angel with grey hair, dressed in red running shoes and shorts. He stands there at the top of the steps, looking at me with so much sad tenderness, almost as though I could be his own daughter. We stay in this moment for a while. I do not move and he does not look away. It is almost as though his gentle presence slowly lifts me up from the stairs. The strength to stand up again certainly does not come from within me. I take the two steps upwards toward him and my front door. He stands facing me, looking into my eyes as though he is passing a little bit of his own strength to me. I know that he knows. He must have seen the guy in the hoodie running away. Perhaps the guy even ran away because he heard my neighbour coming out for his morning jog.

We do not speak. The truth so often goes unspoken, unsaid, unheard. The most life-wrenching experiences of our lives simply hang there in the blank spaces between things and between people. The greatest human deeds are confined to quiet moments without grandiose words or actions. Sometimes, there are no words. There is no definition. No meaning. No happy resolution.

I am grateful that I am not alone. At this point in my life, I learn that the smallest kindness can give someone the strength to carry on. His kind presence makes all the difference. Yet I can not hold his gaze. I am not able to be as loving to myself as he is to me in this moment. In fact, I am entirely ashamed of myself. I look down and notice that my left breast is hanging out of my silver spaghetti dress, completely exposed. I do not even bother to tuck it back in as I quickly turn around and rush to my apartment door a mere two steps away. I do not realise that I am shaking until I open my handbag and start to fumble with the keys. It takes me a while to get it into the keyhole and then get inside as fast as I can. Without looking back, I step inside and double lock the door behind me. I do not want anyone to see me. Ever again. I am disgusting.

I drop my shoes and handbag on the floor, pour myself a tall gin and tonic and escape into the refreshing blankness, garnished with a slice of cool cucumber. It feels as though I am falling into my couch, falling and falling and falling. I wish to escape into hallucinations or fantasy, but for a change, my mind is completely clear.

I guess I asked for it, being so desperate for sex. It has been two years since I dated anyone. My body has been calling for it. So why wouldn't anyone respond? What happened to love? Am I too old now and all that is left is abuse and aggression? Why can I not be loved? Is thirty-five the expiration date for a woman?

My heart is beating me up. If I am creating my own world, then I must really hate myself. I hate that I hate myself. I can not bear to be seen because I do not want to see myself. I do not even want to be myself. Whoever I am. Whatever that means. When sleep eventually comes, it is like a blank page, the refreshing nothingness of it is so good that I no longer want to wake up. Nevertheless, when I do wake up, it is as though my empty dreams have swallowed all my memories and I struggle to recall the details of the night before. It may as well never have happened. Did it happen?

The Flower Fairy

December 2016, Munich, Germany

INSTEAD OF TAKING DELIGHT IN THE TWINKLE OF LIGHT on ice and catching snowflakes on my way to work, I have intense morning anxiety. I wake up exhausted and worn out. It feels as though something is pushing me down onto my bed and I can not move, or breathe. I fight with myself to get up—and then decide to wait until the bad feeling passes. I lie still and pull the duvet over my head. My alarm goes off again and I cringe. Morning is the worst time of the day. Today is extreme: I can not gather myself together. It feels as though I am trying to peel imaginary spider webs off my face, as if nets are holding me down on my bed. I have to battle whatever force is preventing me from starting my day punctually.

Gathering all the superwoman powers I can muster, I push through it and have a quick shower. Still trembling, I face an impossible dilemma: an entire wardrobe full of clothing and nothing to wear. I am already running late and yet I put on outfit after outfit, looking at myself in the mirror and thinking I can not go out into the world looking like that, or like this. People will laugh at me no matter what I wear. I can not even look myself in the eye in the mirror anymore. I am afraid of the monster peeking at me through my eyes. I want to hide away from everything and everyone I know so that I can grieve or switch to a new persona without anyone noticing. This time, however, I am too tired.

"Come on Poppie, get yourself together! You need to go to work" I say to myself.

"I can't," I whimper. "Look at the rings under my eyes. I look terrible."

"You look fine," I try to encourage myself, "it's a film agency, you know. Rings under the eyes is the cool look."

I start to panic. "I don't have the right clothes today. It's too cold. I'm too tired to find something to wear."

"Here," I say as I scratch through my wardrobe another time, "wear this cashmere jersey, it's soft and warm."

I am so grateful for the gentle feeling of the jersey that my eyes fill up with tears when I put it on. It almost feels like being held. A cashmere jersey is the most loving item of clothing that exists in this world. I put my arms around myself and cry.

"I can't go to work. I'm scared." I start to hear a rattling sound in my head.

"I'll call in sick for us," I comfort myself, "Don't worry, Poppie. We're going to be okay."

"You don't have to go to the office today." I convince myself. Then I call work and tell my boss that I have a migraine. It does feel as though there is something wrong with my head. As though I am trying to see through a gas mask. Or breathe through an invisible film blocking my airways. The lack of oxygen makes me feel slightly high, as though I am not completely in my body, but floating somewhere in the realm of the subconscious. My anxiety escalates. I struggle to do small things, such as making a cup of morning tea. I am not able to express my emotions to myself, or Audrey, or anyone. I would rather be asleep. I am living in my dreams and no longer want to face the day.

"Stay in bed, Poppie," says my boss and then, no surprise, he can not resist a little inappropriate flirting, "dream nice wet dreams of me when the migraine lifts. I look forward to seeing your hot ass back in the office tomorrow!" I do not say anything. If he fires me, then I have to leave the country; find another place to be. Go back to live with mall shootings and other daily criminal disasters in Cape Town. Or worse, face my father.

How much will I sacrifice to find peace, to be free from these nightmares? I cannot sleep. There is another me in the mirror. One who wants to die. Counting sheep. Counting dolls in the mirror. How many of us are we? We are going to be okay, aren't we, Poppie?

Yes, we are.

No, we are not.

I am tired. I can't anymore.

Let's go to sleep.

Sleep.

I can't sleep.

Counting sheep.

Counting dolls in the mirror.

How many of us are there?

Audrey, there is a point where it all becomes too much. Too much change. Too much lightness. Too much movement. Too much emptiness. Too much trouble. Too many versions of me. As soon as I get to that point where it feels as though life ends, a new one begins and I can move on. Again. But I do not want to move anymore. I do not want to have to remember. I do not want to have to run. I try to escape, but I can never get away from the trouble that follows me everywhere I go. It is hard to explain what it does to a person to live in so many different places over the span of 35 years. That alone is an exceptional challenge. I have been moving so fast and experiencing so much that it feels as though I have lived multiple lives—and maybe I have. Not everyone changes their job, their country of residence, their day-to-day habits, as often as they change their mind.

It is as though I have crashed into Munich and I am trying to rise from the ashes. My worthiness as a human being is challenged. I do not have a problem with myself, but I have a problem with fitting into my environment. It has nothing to do with Munich as a place. I do not fit anywhere in this world. I try to find my way, but it is exhausting to adjust to new sets of cultures, social expectations and pace of life.

"Inge!" An elderly man approaches me from amongst the skeleton trees along my walk. "Inge!" He opens his arms and the smell of cherry tobacco makes me choke. Snowflakes are making flimsy patterns on his grey wool overcoat.

I take a step back to escape his embrace. "I'm not Inge."

"Of course you are," he tuts as though I made a joke. "After that two hour talk the other day, on that bench next to the river down the road here. I'd never forget this face."

"I'm sorry. You must be mistaken." I continue walking past his puzzled presence without looking back. Either he is a weirdo, or I simply do not remember. The second option would be even weirder.

I thought Bavaria would be the safe choice, where swans grace the rivers even in winter—and the snow falls so quietly that I can, perhaps, finally focus on who I am. Who am I? Today, I am barely a cavity in the smile of a loony old man.

By the time I get home, I can no longer think of anything other than dying. Audrey's voice hums my name like a melody. "If you're feeling a bit strange, lie down on your bed and wait for the feeling to pass. You're just ill. It will pass once you get better."

I stay in bed all weekend. I do not have dinner. I do not do anything but lie in bed and shiver, trying to still the feeling that there is no place for me—but death. I dream that I am dead. I wake up wondering if I am dreaming that I am alive. It is as though I am trapped in my own body, never alone, but surrounded by several other internal people who have demands on my time. I am not getting enough sleep. When I wake up in the morning, I smell someone smoking, even though I am technically alone at home. The windows are closed, but I clearly hear the deep sucking in of smoke and the slow release that comes with a slight wheeze. Not even one of my neighbours smokes, so I brush it off to my dreamy state. Perhaps there are a few ghosts around me. Maybe my guardian angels smoke. Or I am being followed by evil witches from a childhood tale.

Same as the fairy princess who ate a golden apple, I need a prince to wake me from this deep sleep with a kiss of true love. Despite everything, I still believe in fairy tales. Just not the one with Michi. Instead, I am a prisoner of his eyes. My heart is chained by his lies. Michi keeps his focus on me, stealing my love without intending to return it. Getting closer and hesitating in a steady rhythm until he wears out my soul.

I TRY TO REINVENT MYSELF ONCE MORE, like the new iteration of this season's lingerie collection. I am so tired of my life, but I do not know for how much longer I will still have the energy to keep creating new lives for myself. I just want the past to be gone. The more I sleep, the more I can start over when I wake up. Refresh. Rethink. Colour my hair pink. Move to a new city. Get another job. Create a new self-perception. Move myself around until I can fit somewhere. At least blend into the scenery like a fashionable extra on a glamorous film set. Until I can find a place to be beautiful.

I have never been true to myself. I do not dance to my own beat. I do not even dance to the kind of music I like. I do not want to be different. I just want to be loved.

What if I loved myself? Would I then be able to forgive myself for what happened and honour my own needs? Would I allow myself to be vulnerable again? To believe again? To be open to the truth about my body? Would I dare to break everyone else's expectations of what it means to be enough? Instead of pretending to be fine. Putting on a well-trained stewardess' smile and sparkly stilettos. Hiding the damage behind layers of designer make-up and high-tech, doll-eye mascara. Would I allow myself to have the bank account of a man, instead of the debt of a woman? Would I step into my own beauty and claim my space on this earth? Would I look beyond being different and simply be; a dancing, breathing human being—made of the same water and dust as everyone else?

I am beaten by the images of beauty that I keep using against myself. Defeated by an impossible ideal that remains forever out of reach.

What if I loved myself?

What if?

Instead, I put on more stage make-up and glitter and false

eyelashes. It is more acceptable to see myself in the mirror wearing a lace-up corset and stilettos. If I am going to be perverted, then I will decide how. I want to control how I reveal my body, instead of having it stolen or forced from me. I will put on a make-up mask and hide my true self carefully away. This is what I do anyway—disappear behind myself, remove myself from the moment. I feel disconnected from others and am only able to live on the surface, pretending I am fine with being treated like this, or that. I am not. I want the right to be sexy without feeling shame. If I am going to be sexualised and objectified, then let me do it my way.

This is all I have left; to make light of myself. I throw myself into vintage pinup-style striptease as though it is the only thing I ever want to do. As if it is the only chance I will ever have to fight for my own sense of self-worth. To actively take control of my female sexual power. To connect with the wonder of being a woman who owns herself. To finally, be free of any physical and mental constraints.

It is as if my life is broken, as though I am a shattered trinket. It is not okay to be broken in this way, but I do not know how to change it. There is nothing solid about me, but when I keep moving the pieces take on new shapes. I can rearrange it.

I want to avoid any further destructive tendencies in men who come close to me. Therefore I either need to find myself a very good man, or stay far enough away.

A STAGE IS THE PERFECT DISTANCE, to feel the eyes of the audience, the adoration, the emotion—and be far away enough to be untouchable. On stage, I can seduce the audience and be out of range of predators. The stage is a place where it is safe to be myself, where I can be vulnerable and still own my beauty, instead of giving my power away.

I have internalised being treated as a pin-up so much that burlesque dancing seems to be the most natural thing to me. I try out a few classes and the girls believe I have a flair for it. Either way, I enjoy the power when I look in the mirror and see myself in high heels, fishnet stockings, and a corset that flaunts my full bust. If I can not fight the monster in the mirror, I will hide behind jewels and glitter. Look at me. See the dancer. I am not the creature. There is something more behind my eyes. I am a knockout.

My door bell rings as I am on the way to my big show. It must be a mistake. No one ever visits me. Then I hear a short knock. I look through the peep hole to make sure it is safe before opening the door. Since the attack, I just panic more often. My neighbour is standing there in his red running shoes, looking at me in tender awe. He is the only one who will ever know the truth of how I was raped on the stairs outside my apartment door.

"Hi, my daughter made some cake. I thought I would bring you some and see how you're doing." He holds out a porcelain plate with a chocolate cupcake, decorated with butter icing, and silver balls. At first I am suspicious, but the little girl in me jumps up in my heart. I am genuinely moved by the loving gesture, but I cannot cry because my stage make-up will run and there will not be enough time to redo it.

"Come inside," I say, as I quickly disappear into the bathroom to blot my tears.

From the corner of my eye, I see him stepping into my tiny apartment and looking back toward the door. I respond to his hesitation before he speaks. "Yes, you can close the door. I'm just making sure my make-up stays. I'm on my way to a show."

He puts the cake down on to my only table. "I don't want to keep you."

"Thank you so much," I say as I dab at my face. "I'll have it when I get back from the theatre. It will be the perfect midnight snack."

He offers me his hand. "I'm John. If you need anything, please don't hesitate to ask."

His skin is warm and he squeezes my hand gently. It is hard to let go. "You've already done enough. I'm sorry for what you've seen the other night."

"Don't apologise. I just hope you're fine." He looks at me without any sign of revulsion and it helps me to relax.

"My bruises are all healed by now. I'm even dancing again." I get flashes of the red, purple, and blue bruises on my back where the stairs cut into my flesh. My mind is drawn right back into the moment and I feel my body losing muscle tension. John catches me by the shoulders and that is enough to bring me back into the present.

"Poppie, are you sure you're well enough to go out?"

Sometimes I feel like I am imagining it. I have no more visible scars. I do not want to be judged for something that is not my fault. Or is it? "I'm sorry. I have to go now."

WHEN I RUSH DOWN THE STAIRS soon after on my way to my first burlesque show, I realise that a smile really does mean that much. The smile from my neighbour in his red trainers is almost holy as he passes me on the stairs again, hand-in-hand with his eight-year old daughter. She smiles at me too. This moment reminds me that we should all do for others what we can. It is not about making an effort to hold each other up, but simply about being kind. We must be kind. It is not possible to see what goes on behind the façade of a person. Behind my doll face, there is a lot of pain, but people do not know it.

Our show venue is a small theatre, complete with dark wood fittings and velvet curtains. I have a quick look at the posters in the foyer. They offer comedy shows and plays, jazz and flamenco. There is an atmosphere of anticipation. An elderly lady with thick round glasses is sitting at the reception desk, staring at me blandly. I explain that I am with the dance group that will be performing this evening and she shows me to the backstage area with listless, wide eyes.

Backstage, I feel the excitement all over my skin, as I start pulsing with energy. I take a breath of pure pleasure. The girls are already half in character. Mandy is wearing full body glitter and the white Brazilian slip that we decorated together, with golden tassels and clear crystal beads. Her sparkly stilettos catch the light at the studded ankle strap. I notice that the line at the back of her beige fishnet stockings is not straight and I make a mental note to adjust it from her thin ankles all the way to her juicy bum. She is concentrating on sticking on her nipple pasties and hardly notices me standing in the doorway.

Tiffany is sitting on the floor at Mandy's feet, still in her jeans, but wearing full stage make-up and a blonde wig with a long fringe and a short bob. She is putting on false eyelashes with a hairpin, her red lips pursing flat and wide.

"Poppie!" Katrin shrieks from the other side of the room and tripples toward me excitedly with open arms and cheek kisses. There is a clothing rail with coats and costumes and a table laden with make-up, glitter, safety pins, water, and Prosecco, not in any specific order.

I feel right at home and quickly find a corner for my small dance bag. Here I am allowed, even expected, to be a misfit. I do not have to pretend to be normal, whatever that means. I change into my fishnets and heels and frilled lace slip with gold and crystal details. For now, I keep my cropped T-shirt on as I still have to fix the top—some of the beads came loose and spilled into my bag. I came prepared with a needle and thread to fix it. First, however, I kneel down elegantly, knees together, next to Tiffany to do my make-up. She blinks at me with her long lashes, now perfectly in place.

This is still one of my favourite things, getting ready with the girls and seeing how a little make-up can transform me. I learned a lot while watching the make-up artists at Paris Fashion Week and I know what is easy and what works for me. First, I hide the blemishes on my face with a little extra concealer. I already put on foundation before I left home, so it only needs a little touching up. Then I start with my eyes, patting a few layers of light beige pigment all over and then some gold pigment on my eyelids. My skin has enough oil to hold quite a bit of this. Stage make-up needs to be exaggerated and I add as much as I can. Next, I add a few generous lines with a liquid eyeliner, a heavy hand of rose pink blush, and layers of red, red, lipstick, painted on thick. I add a quick layer of mascara before attaching my false lashes and then add another layer to comb the lashes together and add an extra bit of length. I am done.

I decide to take a little break and fix my top before putting on my wig. As I sit down at the table, Mandy pours me a glass of Prosecco. She flops down on the chair and her sparkly nipple tassels swish sideways as her breasts do a perky little bounce.

"Cheers, Poppie," says Mandy, "it's so much fun dancing with you!"

We are not really friends beyond the dance group, but when we are together, I feel loved. It is intimate to spend so much time together half-naked, doing sexy things with our bodies and helping each other put on full body glitter and nipple glue. I feel pure joy as I sit here with Mandy, sipping sparkling wine and sewing the missing beads back onto my bra top. These costumes are so much fun. Taking them off is even more satisfying than putting them on. It is about celebrating and honouring my beauty—with an extra helping of glitter.

Slowly, I get all the bits and pieces together. Then I slip on my wig and pin it back with a few sliding pins—and it is time to go. "Oh, yeah," says Mandy.

The rest of us smile and wink, take our places and wait for the curtain to rise. Our performance is first up for the evening. The stage lights are blinding. From the clapping and cheering, I can tell it is a large audience. The music starts and my body takes on a life of its own. I show off in a way I have never done before, taking the opportunity to claim my own erotic power. I thought I would be shy to take off my clothes in public, but I am not. I want to tease the audience, I want to turn them on, to make them look at what I have got, to take in how beautiful I am, and say "Don't you dare treat me as anything less". I am swept away by the buzz of the audience, by the energy of the dancers next to me and an inner power that drives me to survive, to claim my own body in all its glory.

When it is over, I am surprised that it is over so fast. I can not remember every single detail of the show. I space out in spots, as I often do. All I know is that I feel an unbelievable thrill. I did it. I stripped on stage.

IT IS ADDICTIVE, THIS FEELING OF UTTER LIBERATION. I want more. Not more stripping, but more power. For once in my life, I would like to know what it feels like to hold my power as a woman. To make a guy fall for me and get him to do anything for me. Instead of the other way around. Burlesque gives me confidence. More so than belly dance. The difference is that I no longer take myself seriously. I learn how to pose and how to pause, for effect. I feel nothing while creating the most erotic moments for others and then making fun of it. The secret of playing with sexual power is not in doing, but in not doing.

I decide to harness the power of the vixen and see what I can attract. Tonight, this definitely involves doing something. I put on a short red dress, matt silver kitten heels and some hoop earrings from South Africa. There is a gallery opening around the corner from my Munich apartment. As I enter, I make sure to look around. I settle on a buff guy with a bright tattoo sitting in the corner with his friends. I make eye contact and hold it for a few seconds.

A student is serving bubbly and canapés and he comes up to me with a silver tray. I take a glass of orange juice and pretend to be interested in the paintings. In the room at the very back, I find a high stool and wait for the guy with the tattoo to come and find me. Then I cross my legs and lean down to fiddle with my sandal. I nonchalantly let my fingers trace the shape of my leg. It is supposed to look cool and casual, but it is carefully rehearsed. I practiced preening with my burlesque teacher. I am committed to taking my power back. Once I have rolled myself back up straight like a cat, I shake out my hair with my left hand. I look to the right and smile. Sure enough, I have the full attention of the man with the colourful tattoos.

He walks right up to me. "What do you think of the exhibition?"

I look down at my glass. I have not even had my first sip. "I'm … uh, I'm more interested in your tattoo actually."

"Oh," he feigns surprise, "what's your name?"

I drag out the silence a little longer than I need to.

"Poppie," I introduce myself.

He takes a step closer to me. "Can I sit down?"

I pretend to look bored. "If you must."

"I'll fill you in on the artist," he says, not making it clear whether he refers to the Vernissage or the tattoo artist.

"Okay, then," I say without smiling and turn to him for the first time.

He looks into my eyes, enchanted. His sensual, bright stare flows right through me and fills me with a warm glow. His eyes are unusually iridescent. We do not talk much. I let him hold my hand. He secretly traces the outline of my wrist with his fingers while everyone else in the room has their attention firmly focused on the art. His skin is rough and bronze, as though he had just spent a summer in Greece. He tells me the story of his colourful tattoo. It is the tale of a tiger that goes all the way up his hard bicep and disappears into a magical forest under his shirt.

"I want to see more of that later," I say, even though I do not care much for tattoos. I do not wear my pain on my body. Rather, it is an inner pressure. A scar that is destroying me from the inside.

I do not get around to asking him his name. I do not really care. I am only interested in seducing him, just to see if I can. We leave the bar and go to my apartment. There is a package in front of my door. It is a notebook with an inscription from John.

The future is yours.

I put the gift to the side and focus on my future for the evening. I never thought it could be this easy. I keep my heart tightly closed, but take his body freely.

I feel myself switching, getting closer to this stranger; turning into a flirt. It is easier to handle transitions during the nighttime. It takes the edge off. There is not so much of an expectation to be consistent. It gives me the legitimacy to go mad without too many uncomfortable questions. I can shrug it off and whatever I say or do will be forgiven.

He takes advantage of my mood, right in the kitchen nook. As we enter my room, he approaches me from behind, pressing his body against me and then lifting my dress to run his rough hands along the outside of my thigh. Our physical attraction is intense. As I turn toward him, he immediately starts unbuttoning his jeans. When I run my hands under his T-shirt, it makes him bulge with an urgency that makes me feel so desired. He peels off his shirt. This guy is ripped like in the movies. I have never seen a man who looks like that in real life. There is no resisting it. I am drunk on awe, complying completely as he slips my panties off and moves in closer.

"Kiss me," I say.

I do not want to be used.

He presses his lips onto mine and I feel his tongue at the same time as he enters me. He picks me up and sets me on the kitchen counter. I open my legs wider and pull him closer to me with my feet. He lifts me again and swivels me around, holding me up with his strong arms, before putting me gently back onto the counter, all the while pushing deeper inside me.

"I am the goddess." I hear a voice inside my head. I wonder if it is the fairies, Audrey, or a message from God.

"Look at me," I say, trying hard to be present in the moment, but I am no longer in control. I watch as the goddess takes over my body and does what she wants.

He caresses my face before he lets his eyes drop to my cleavage. He slips the sleeve of my dress off my right shoulder and rolls down my dress to reveal my plump breast. For a moment, he leaves my lips to kiss my nipple gently. I start having many little tiny orgasms, expressing my pleasure in breath only. We try to keep it quiet; our little secret. My orgasms build up to a big and wholly satisfying release as we come together. I insist on holding eye contact and keep him inside me for a few moments longer than necessary.

I do not want to be used.

Afterwards, I want him to leave right away, but I am too tired to argue. In the morning, he wants to go for breakfast.

"No, I have plans." It is a lie.

He leaves me flowers in front of my door. Red roses. The kind that smells nice.

I do not respond.

He comes over spontaneously with a bottle of Champagne.

I say, "I'm tired. It's been busy at work."

He calls. He wants to pick me up in his luxury car and take me out for a five-course dinner.

I say I am not hungry.

He says he thinks he might be in love. "You're the most incredible woman I ever had and I do not want to spend another night of my life without you."

"I'm so sorry," I say, "I'm so sorry."

I see something in him break. Whether it is his heart, or his ego, I cannot be sure—either way, it is excruciatingly visible. I never thought that this could happen. I thought I would feel better, but I feel so much worse.

The power is all in me. In fact, there is so much power that I need to be careful what I do with it. It can be dangerous. Just as I can be destroyed, I have the power to destroy others. Sometimes, real power lies in simply not doing anything.

This is my first-ever snowy winter. It reminds me of fairy tale illustrations of ice-capped mountains. When I look around, it is almost impossible not to believe in magic. If I could wave a wand, I would just want to get away from myself.

"Be careful what you wish for," the words of my school ballet teacher, Miss Blom, echo in my mind. Some of my fantasies are, indeed, regrettable.

I DECIDE TO LEAVE MEN ON THE MARGIN of my life and return to my burlesque practice. I train hard. I want to dance in a burlesque show again and, before I know it, I find myself on stage again and again, wearing pasties and throwing my glittering bra into the air.

Glitter though, as with many of the shiniest things in life, can also be very dangerous.

The audience is sweating and screaming as we strip down to our sparkly G-string slips at a luxury establishment at a Bavarian palace in the middle of the old city. I never dance alone. Always in a group. Always making sure that I do not outshine anyone, escaping behind the other girls and not fully claiming my space or owning what I am doing in the moment. I am physically on stage, but hovering slightly outside of my body. A fluttering fairy, giddy with going rogue.

There are blinks as I leave the show with the girls. I laugh and talk, but I am only a husk of myself. The real me is drifting, dreading going home alone. I stay with them for as long as possible.

"Oh, look, Poppie has a boyfriend now," they cackle as they round up their boyfriends and husbands. I follow the direction of their giggles.

When I see him, I feel my already flimsy being diluting into the air. My back tingles and my knees wobble. It is Ehad. He throws his arms around me and pushes my face into his neck so that no one can see my expression. I feel my lipstick smearing under his pungent sweat. The jovial sound of the dancers disappear into the night. I can barely stand.

Ehad carries me to a bench on the sidewalk. He lays me onto

the bench and pushes me down, the fingers of his right hand interlaced with my left. "Aren't you happy to see me, my darling?"

I try to wrestle myself away, but my body has no inherent power to lift itself. He is clenching my hand like a squid. The muscle strength in his hand combined with his chunky ring hurts my flesh. There are still people coming out of the venue. High heels are clicking across the pavement close by, but it is dark outside. I want to scream for help, but then I feel a cloth being placed over my mouth. My head slowly winds down until the world switches off completely.

I WAKE UP FEELING REJUVENATED and ready to jump out of bed. It is an unusually energised feeling and I take a deep breath of gratitude as I linger a little while longer in my beautiful dream. I am dancing through a garden full of crystals and colours and flowers in a wide circle skirt that swirls and twirls in ripples of white silk. I am filled with so much light that it spills over in laughter and joy and illuminates everything around me. I can feel the vibration of every stone, leaf and butterfly around me. I am love. I start to move my arms up over my head as I stretch out in bed, relishing this morning—when suddenly I get stuck. My movement is restricted. There is something attached to my arm.

Oh, come on. I try to go back to sleep, but something does not feel right. I open my eyes, slightly annoyed at being disturbed. For a while, I see only a bright light. I have no idea where I am. It is a complete blank for quite some time before I realise that everything around me actually is, in fact, completely blank.

Am I in heaven? Audrey?

Nothing.

Slowly, I start making out more details. I am fascinated by the little white case attached to my hand and I stare at it for a while before I realise that it extends into a tube. I look at it for a long time. Nothing really registers. Though my mind feels clearer than it has ever been, it is empty.

"Good morning, Poppie!" I hear the kindest male voice.

I look up and see a curious, unfamiliar face showing signs of concern. "How do you know my name?"

He looks entertained. "You told me. Last night when I picked you up. Can you remember what happened?"

It takes me a few moments "I was performing at a party. I am a dancer. After the show I … I think I fainted."

The memories of the evening drop back into my mind with a thud. I look at the tubes attached to my arm. I am in the hospital and the kind man next to me is a doctor.

"Don't worry, I'm going to take that out right away." He holds my arm gently, as though I am a precious vase. I wish I could wake up with someone being this nice to me every day. "The guy you were with last night? He's your friend?"

I shake my head.

"He's not a very nice person," he says, "you can be lucky some bystanders called an ambulance when they saw you lying unconscious. I don't know your story, Poppie, but you might want to consider a restraining order."

His face changes and I can see tears behind his eyes. "Poppie, you know, it's a miracle that you're alive. You had two point six percent of alcohol in your blood. Your heart stopped last night and I didn't think you were going to make it."

"Can I go?" The kindness in his eyes is so intense, I feel myself veering away from it. It is so unfamiliar to me that I cannot bear it.

The doctor is holding back the tears with all his power. "You can go. You're so lucky to be alive, Poppie. Ask the nurses to call someone to come and pick you up."

He leaves the room very quickly.

I slowly get out of the hospital bed, still wearing my cherry-coloured bustier dance dress. There are two puncture wounds on my left wrist and blue marks on my fingers. My shoes are neatly lined next to the bed, ready for me to slip into. As I step outside the room, two nurses are smiling at me.

"Where are my things?" I ask.

"You had nothing with you." The one with the short, permed hair, glances hesitatingly at the other.

"Oh, no, oh, no," I whisper, "my house keys, my phone. I have to find my handbag."

We all stare at each other for a few moments.

"Why don't you call someone to pick you up?" The other nurse beckons me over. "You can use my phone."

I think about it and speak the realisation. "I have no one."

Then louder. "I have no one."

The nurses look like goldfish with their mouths wide open. The last thing I feel like doing now is explaining why a pretty thirty something like me has no one. Of course, I know some people in Munich, but the dance girls are not my friends and I do not really know John well enough either. I would not dare to call my boss or any of my colleagues. While I may have almost lost my life, I am still firmly in possession of my pride.

I quickly scan the room for the door. Wasting not a single second, I lift my chin and my chest, relaxing my shoulders. That is my power.

"Thank you very much for everything," I say and then take fast, determined steps toward the emergency room exit as they stare at me in complete disbelief.

As the sliding doors open, I splash into the freshness of the early summer morning. The air is filled with the smell of summer roses. My skin tingles at the vibration of birdsong. I feel a strange detachment as I walk all the way back to the dance venue. My body is pulsing with life, but inside I feel like a porcelain doll that has been badly packed and is being thrown around in transit, rattling and chipping away.

The Lenbach Palace is a grand old building with beautiful intricate details and large windows. I am grateful to see that there are still some people cleaning up after the party. I do not know if I could have made it any further. I am so completely drained that I simply flop onto the nearest couch, close to the bar. The natural leather is cool and welcoming.

"*Servus*," I hear the typical Bavarian greeting before I see a stout, bearded frame approaching me. "Sam, right? How can I forget?"

When I look up, the guy hesitates. It is unclear if he is taking a breath because of my good looks or if he gets the vibe that something is not quite right. "No, I'm not Sam. I'm Poppie."

He stops to take me in and then takes a few steps closer, lifting his eyebrows as he tries out my name. "Poppie. Listen, Poppie, or Sam, or whatever your name is, we're not open today."

I do my best to leave out any drama. "Last night, I left my handbag. Did you find anything while cleaning up?"

"*Nein*," he says with a straight face and a single raised eyebrow. "No, we didn't find anything like that." As charmingly as possible, he points me to the exit.

My eyes brim up. I am trying so hard to be strong, but cannot help it. I lift my head and shake my hair until I successfully gather enough pieces of myself. It takes everything I have not to let the tears roll, but I manage to keep my face dry.

"*Was ist deine Name?*" I try to make a human connection by asking for his name in German. My spirit is raw and I am simply trying to reach out and ask for help, from one human being to another. Without too much emotion that will mark me as unstable.

He looks irritated and I realise that I must have offended him by not using a formal form of address. I correct myself humbly. "I mean, *Ihre Name*, sorry for the mistake. I'm not German."

"*Ich bin Ralf.*" He checks me out before giving in and offering me a seat. "Wait while I double check about your bag."

The cool air coming in through the open windows caresses my face. The long wooden bar is already polished to a shine. There are hushed whispers in the background.

Ralf comes back with a cappuccino, decorated with a little cocoa heart. I add two sugars, stir and relish the first sip. All the while Ralf stands there watching me, his fascination turning into a kind concern.

"Yes, someone picked up a handbag. I can give you a phone number," says Ralf in a heavy German accent, "but I don't know if you should call. You might better just forget about the bag."

In the background, his colleagues pack bottles at the bar. Ralf writes down a name and a number in big letters on a small piece of paper.

"Can you call?" I ask. "I don't have a phone."

He looks annoyed, but then notices my eyes welling up again. I have used up all the sugar in my saucer, but I could do with some more.

"I'm sorry," I say, brimful of fragile feelings, "I stayed in hospital last night."

Ralf walks away with an uncertain look. Half of him wants to flirt with me and the other half anticipates the worst. He is awkwardly rugged, being asked for help by a damsel in distress, who has no one, who might be crazy—and, yes, I probably still am high on hospital drugs. The complete dependency makes him spin, but, at the same time, there is a sense of humanity and an authenticity in the moment that cannot be denied.

I sit quietly on my own for quite a while, considering my options. The only way I can see getting through the day without my house keys is to walk a bit further to the office and ring the bell, hoping there will be someone there. That would be taking a chance, but sometimes the producers work on weekends. There may also be some food in the office kitchen. I do not have a cent on me and I am getting hungry.

After a long time, I give up on Ralf ever getting back to me and slowly start making my way. Deep breath.

Ralph's voice interrupts my first step toward the door. "They're not answering," he says across the floor. "It's still too early. They only left the party a few hours ago. Try calling again in the afternoon."

He grabs a bunch of Fairy Thimbles, otherwise known as Bavarian Blue Bellflowers, from a vase on the counter. The purple flowers are tied up with silver tinsel, left over from the party decorations. He brings it over to me and says, "You know what, I'm sure I saw you last night with that guy. I thought you were just another gold-digger. You said your name was Sam. Your voice sounded strange, like a man's voice. Not at all like the sweet voice you are talking in today."

I push my chair back and hang on to the purple flowers as though my life depends on it. As though I can hide behind it when I walk out the door. "Thanks for these."

He scoots me away. "We were just going to throw them away."

I walk the city from one end to the other. When I get too hot, I jump on a bus without paying, drawing attention in my cherry red dress and with my purple flowers. No one checks for my ticket. People simply turn their heads to look at me and smile. I have never seen everyone smiling on a bus in Munich. Is everyone on those feel-good hospital drugs today, or is it only me?

"You look so beautiful today," says the bus driver in an unusual outburst of joviality as I get off.

I smile in gratitude and grasp the odd bouquet tighter.

Hopefully, it masks my body odour, I think, as I stand there in the dripping morning heat. Smiling like an idiot, I let him talk, without being able to take in any of it. He may as well be speaking Russian as I do not understand his heavy Bavarian accent at all. I gently excuse myself and move along, as graciously as possible, very much aware that I have not even yet brushed my teeth for the day.

When I get to the beautiful old office building next to the Isar River, I ring the bell. No answer. I try again. Nothing. It is a lovely Spring day. The Isar is paradise, glowing a bright, clear turquoise.

I walk further to Marienplatz and mindlessly enter a crowded department store. People are too busy shopping to notice my state and I am relieved. I do not want to stand out. Perhaps I should find a mirror and check what I need to fix to look acceptable. I move to the hair accessory area, which is emptier than the make-up counters.

At first sight, everything seems to be in place. My flawless stage make-up cover is still surprisingly perfect. The waterproof mascara really holds well and the fixing spray is a wonder. One would never say that I spent the night in hospital. I look deeper at myself in the luxury store mirror, beyond the obvious cover and then, for the very first time, I notice the cracks in my face. They are not wrinkles, but ugly, hard lines that map the betrayal of my own soul. The knowing feeling fills my upper torso. The truth.

My whole life has been a distraction from the grief of losing my original self. I am tired of being a puppet. The mad rush of trying to create images of myself that would please others. That would make me feel validated and accepted. Even give me the illusion of love. A love from outside to compensate for the lack of love in my own heart.

It is hard to be true to myself. That is not what the world

wants. I am too soft and delicate to exist. I face the pain of being alive without protection and I am not sure if I am brave enough to survive. Yet pretending to be rough and tough gives me an edge in the mirror that I can no longer face. The false lashes and the glitter have been my mask and my salvation. Until now. This is the part where I claim the superheroine inside me.

The further away I am from myself, the safer I am from the wounds in my soul—but that means that I am cheating myself, letting my life go by without really being in it. Leaning in to myself hurts, yet it is the only option I have left. I search for true beauty out there in the big wide world, but fail to look for it inside. I am going to have to be strong enough to face what I find, or stop being alive in this world. I can only be free as a woman if I find myself first. Find the strength in my weakness. The beauty in my own soul.

I have always believed that there would be someone out there who would treat me in the way that I deserve to be treated. I realise now that that person is myself. I am what I am searching for.

A little girl in the store twirls around like a dancer in a music box and then ducks under the tulle skirt of a mannequin. She is playing hide and seek. "You can't see me, but I am here."

"You can see me, but I'm not here," I say under my breath.

My senses call me back into my body as I hear the little girl squealing with laughter and I feel her smack into me before running back to her mom.

I become aware of the perfumes inside the store. Patchouli. Orange blossom. Magnolia. The taste of sweet cappuccino is still lingering at the corners of my mouth. I look back into the mirror.

For the first time, I see myself. I see the abalone and the floozy and the goddess. Yoh, Audrey, you're here too. I look deeper into my own eyes. Is there anyone else? Ehad. Inge. Sam. I can no longer escape from myself. This is my solar system. Everything

I am. Everything I experience. Everything I create. Everything starts within me. I do not need the world to love me. I choose myself. All of me.

When I release the barriers of my heart, I feel an excruciating pain shoot through my body. My eyes start tearing up as I let a shower of pure love flow through me. I stand fully in my pain and let it all be. The shame. The shivering. I am ready. I am enough. I have everything I have ever wanted. My own love.

"Can I offer you a makeover?" I snap out of my thoughts as the lady from the cosmetics counter approaches me. Her face is smooth and without expression. "We've got a special on our latest range. Come on, let me show you a new look. A new you."

"No." The word slips out of my gut. "No, thank you." The core of me speaks before I can think or filter. "I don't need another new me."

A stillness collects inside myself. Confidence gushes into my hollow spaces as if from an infinite source that has always been there, that will always be there. I let it flow through and through me, feeling all my body parts becoming fully animated.

"I already have everything I need."

Note from the author

THANK YOU FOR READING *Full Body Shaking*. Do let me know your feedback by leaving a review on amazon or goodreads and tagging me on twitter and instagram @lize_de_kock #fullbodyshaking

A special thanks to everyone who supported me with this novel, especially Katherine, Iain, Hanli, Arijana, Firoza, Prasanti, Melané, Erma, Heike, Golda, Diane, Silvia, Isabelle, Ina, Caroline, Kim, Dawn, Anne, Michelle, Lorna, Richard, Elisabeth and the stars below.

- To Allison and the Women Wellness Retreats,
  who gave me the courage to begin

- To Amalia and Aegean Arts Circle,
  who gave me the confidence to continue

- To my editor Nerine and beta readers
  Elspeth, Alexa, Gina, Yvonne, you are gold

- To my designer Carla, for cheering me on
  and helping me to wrap it up so beautifully

- To my friends and family for loving and accepting me
  even as I got lost in this world

CPSIA information can be obtained
at www.ICGtesting.com
Printed in the USA
LVHW020008270721
693705LV00013B/1915

9 783000 680861